FIRE
ON THE
WATER

WA

J. Michael Stewart

1

"You ever seen water burn?" he asks, his words dripping off his tongue in a cutting southern drawl that, despite the warmth of the bath water, sends an ice-cold shiver up her spine. Goose bumps form over her exposed arms and breasts. He stands above her, his short brown hair and thick mustache visible even in the dimly lit bathroom. Two large candles flicker on top of a small wooden stand behind him. The left side of his mouth turns upward in an evil grin, spreading across his face as his gray eyes inspect her nude body.

She sinks below the waterline to hide her nakedness, the water now up to her chin. Her long auburn hair floats around her. "No . . . no, I haven't," she says so softly it's almost inaudible.

"Well, I have," he responds. "My dad used to work on old cars in our garage. He always had a few cans of oil lying around. One day, I took one of the cans down to the small pond behind our house. My buddy from school, Willy was his name, but I guess that's not important to you right now." He smiles at her again, that same lopsided, chilling grin. "Anyway, Willy was with *me, and he didn't believe me when I told him that I could make water burn, so I proceeded to pour the full can of oil into the pond." His smile widens at the memory as he reaches down to the floor and picks up a large, red gasoline container. He swishes it in front of her; she can hear that it's almost full.*

Her hands tremble beneath the water, and her legs begin to quake. Her breaths come in short, fearful gasps.

The fear, the torment, the confinement she's lived with for the past six months boils up inside her. She tries to hide her emotion, tries to deny him the satisfaction of seeing his power over her again, but it's no use. A single tear trickles down her right cheek.

He removes the cap from the container and tosses it next to the marble bathtub. He laughs softly as he sees the terror consume her. "Then I pulled a book of matches out of my pocket and lit the oil as I backed away from the pond. Willy and I watched as the fire spread over the surface of the water, like some invisible dragon was breathing across the pond . . . our eyes must've been as big as silver dollars." He chuckles and tilts the nozzle of the can down until a large stream of thick, dark oil flows into the bathwater.

"Please . . . please don't," she cries, but watches helplessly as the black goop enters the tub.

"Dad beat my ass for that one, but as I stood there, watching the water burn, watching the black smoke roll into the air, I felt absolutely invigorated . . . I was hypnotized by it. It was worth the whipping I took."

He pours the oil faster now, causing it to splash wildly as it makes contact with the surface of the water. She feels several drops land on her forehead and cheeks. Soon, the entire surface of the water is covered with a coal-black sheen. "You ever had something like that happen to you? Where you couldn't look away, even if you wanted to?" he asks.

"Paul, please don't hurt me. I'm sorry . . . for whatever I've done . . . I'm so sorry."

"Shut up!" he yells, his voice suddenly filled with rage. He pours the last of the oil into the bathtub and throws the container behind him. She watches it skid across the tile floor and slam into the opposite wall. He pulls a wadded ball of newspaper from the left pocket of his jeans, and then from the right, a gold-plated cigar lighter. He flips the top open, and a long flame dances back and forth. He moves the newspaper near the fire.

"No . . . stop! Please! Stop!" She begins to sob uncontrollably.

"You should've never betrayed me. I warned you, but you wouldn't listen, would you? Don't you remember what happened the last time you disobeyed me?"

"I'm sorry. I really am. I'll do better next time, I promise I will. Just don't hurt me, Paul. Please, I'm begging." She tries to silence her cries, to hold on to what little dignity she has left—the little that hasn't been slowly stripped from her during the past six months—but she can't.

She screams as he lights the newspaper and drops it . . .

She watches the glowing ball float toward the oil-laden water. Everything is in slow motion now, and even though she feels herself continuing to scream, she can no longer hear her own pleas.

The room is enveloped in silence.

Her eyes wide with panic.

Tears running down her cheeks and into the contaminated water.

She tries to lift her arms out of the tub to catch the orange orb of fire before it touches the water, but her arms won't move. She's paralyzed by fear.

The flaming ball of newspaper reaches the surface, and the water begins to burn . . .

Tiffany Colson gasped as she sat up in bed. She felt as if she were smothering, not able to draw a single breath. Her heart was racing so fast she thought for sure it would explode and she would die right there in her own bed.

Calm down, she told herself, *it was only another dream.*

She struggled to pull oxygen into her lungs, to calm her runaway heartbeat. Her blue silk pajamas were soaked with sweat, and she ran her hand through her hair, clearing the matted clumps away from her forehead. At last, she felt her pulse slow and her breathing return to normal, but she was burning up, her flesh hot and clammy.

She threw the covers back and rolled out of bed, then walked to the small window on the outside wall of the cabin. She turned the latch and raised the window, letting the cool October air flow into the room. A stiff breeze whipped her auburn hair away from her face. She just stood there, staring up at the bright stars and drawing deep breaths of the mountain air into her lungs. Her hands were still trembling, her stomach roiling with anxiety.

When would it ever stop?

Would it ever stop?

It had been almost ten years since she had escaped the demon she had been foolish enough to fall for. November 10th had been her independence day, and she always marked the anniversary with a combination of joy and trepidation.

Afraid that, somehow, he would come back.

Come back to finish what he started.

With the ten-year anniversary less than a month away, it seemed her nerves had been more on edge than usual. The nightmare that had just awakened her was only the latest in a series of terrifying memories that haunted her nights, and sometimes even her days.

They played over and over in her mind like a movie reel. Just as if it had happened yesterday.

Her body still bore the scars from that night. The night he had tried to burn her alive.

The night she had barely escaped with her life.

And the night Paul had lost his.

Her hand slipped under her pajama top, as though it had a mind of its own, just as it had done countless times before. The silk gently caressed the back of her hand as her fingertips found the smooth, silvery skin. She traced each mark—each reminder—carefully, slowly. One ran from underneath her left breast all the way to her belly button, another from the inside of her right breast to the back of her ribcage.

The outside air chilled her sweat-covered body, and she slid the windowpane back down, locking it in place with the metal tab on top. She looked back across her bed, toward her alarm clock. It was 4:30 a.m. She did not have to be at work until 7:30. She should lie down and try to go back to sleep. But she knew sleep would not come, no matter how hard she tried.

It never did.

She sighed and looked out the window once more, the beams of soft light cast by the full moon streaking through the giant oak tree in her front yard and creating elongated shadows outside the cabin. She again thought about crawling back into bed, but instead turned and walked from her room toward the bathroom that lay just a short distance down the narrow hallway.

She let her damp pajamas fall to the floor and climbed into the shower. As the hot water streamed over her body, she tried to push all the horrible memories that seemed to have been dogging her lately out of her mind. But, once again, she failed.

She still didn't understand how she could have been so blind. How she hadn't seen the evil lurking behind the handsome face. She guessed that's what made psychopaths so dangerous, though—they looked completely normal on the outside.

She remembered the first time she had met Paul. She had been walking toward her car late one afternoon. It had been a long day, and she was still pissed she had gotten a C on her last English Comp paper. She only had a few more months until graduation. Then she would be finished with college and could find a real job and leave the late-night waitressing at the local truck stop behind for good.

If she made it a few more months.

Between work and classes, she felt like she was barely hanging on, the daily grind of her schedule exhausting her. To make matters worse, six months prior, she had been forced to bury her parents after a late-night car crash. They had been returning from a dinner party at their friends' house. The police said her father had fallen asleep at the wheel and drifted off the road before crashing head-on into a large pine tree. She had spent the last several months organizing her parents' financial affairs. Much to her surprise, her family had been deeply in debt, and by the time all the bills were paid with the money from the meager life insurance policy her father had carried, she was left with only a few inexpensive mementos to remember them by. So she had been forced to not only deal with the stress of school, work, and a rapidly shrinking bank account, but also the grief of losing the two people who meant the most to her in life. She was emotionally drained.

As she approached her car, she noticed that her rear driver's side tire was flat. "Damn," she whispered. *A perfect end to an already bad day,* she thought.

As she stared down at the deflated tire, she considered calling a service to fix it for her, but money was tight, and she just wanted to get back to her small one-bedroom apartment, have a glass of Merlot, and go to bed. Besides, her dad had taught her how to change a tire before she had even gotten her driver's license. It had been several years since she had actually changed one, but she was pretty sure she remembered how.

She opened the driver's door, threw her backpack inside, and popped the trunk open. She walked to the back of the car and stared into the trunk at the mound of items covering the carpeted bottom where the spare tire was stored. Frustrated, she huffed and began clearing the area. She removed her gym bag and set it down on the asphalt, then a pair of jumper cables, a large blanket, and a few other items that were in her way. When she had cleared out the trunk, she removed the panel that covered the spare tire and jack. *"You can do this, Tiff,"* she told herself as she looked down into the compartment.

"Excuse me, Miss?" she heard someone say behind her. Startled, she spun and found a young man approaching her. He was tall, maybe six feet, with brown hair and gray eyes that had just a hint of blue in them. "Looks like you have a flat tire there," he said.

"Yeah, I just finished my last class and was on my way home when I found it. It's been one of those days, you know?" Tiffany replied.

The stranger laughed softly. "Yeah, I know what you mean." He stuck out his hand. "My name's Paul."

Tiffany shook his hand and said, "I'm Tiffany. Nice to meet you, Paul."

He smiled. "Are you a student here?"

His warm demeanor put Tiffany at ease. "Yes, dental hygiene. Only a few more months and I'm finished. I can't wait, either. It's been a rough semester. How 'bout you?" she asked.

"Business administration, which, by the way, I have found to be incredibly boring. But my dad insists that if I want to take over the family business, I have to get an education first. I wish I had only a few months to go. I've got two more years of this shit." He laughed.

Tiffany found herself laughing along with him. She welcomed a little levity on what had otherwise been a pretty crappy day.

Paul pointed at the flat. "I can give you a hand with the tire if you like."

"No, no," she replied, waving her hand dismissively. "I think I can handle it."

"Don't be ridiculous." He paused and grinned. "I insist," he said as he began to roll up his sleeves.

Tiffany considered the stranger's offer. She didn't really want him to have to change her tire, but she was so tired, and a hot shower and that glass of Merlot were calling her name. With only a few second's hesitation, she motioned with her hand toward the trunk. "Okay. Thank you, Paul. That's very nice of you."

He didn't say anything in response; he just got right to it. She watched as he removed his backpack and went to work, lifting the tire and jack from the trunk. She offered to help, but he assured her he could handle it.

Fifteen minutes later, Paul was loading the jack and old tire into the back of her car. He slammed the trunk lid and smiled. "There you go. Should be fine now."

"Thank you. Thank you, so much." She ran her hand through her hair and smiled.

"No problem." He picked up his backpack, turned, and started to walk away, then stopped and spun around. "Would you like to have dinner with me sometime?" he asked, the inflection in his voice indicating he had just come up with the idea on the spur of the moment.

Tiffany smiled again, flattered by the invitation. Paul looked nervous, and that made her even more attracted to him. She had definitely noticed his good looks and athletic body while he was changing the tire, and dinner with a handsome man seemed like the perfect thing to take her mind off of school and her miserable waitressing job. After several seconds of contemplation, she replied, "I'd like that. Just a minute, let me give you my number." She leaned into the car and retrieved her purse. She pulled a pen and piece of paper from it, quickly wrote down her phone number, and handed it to him. "Give me a call. I'm free this Friday."

"Thanks," Paul said with his warm smile again on display. He folded the torn piece of notebook paper and stuck it into the front pocket of his blue jeans. "I'll be looking forward to it," he said as he turned and walked away.

That's how it had all started: as a simple, seemingly coincidental, meeting after a bad day at school. If Tiffany could have seen the future, she would have called a tire repair service, locked herself in her car, and refused the stranger's help.

If only . . .

But she hadn't.

Everything was good at the beginning. Paul was funny, polite, and treated her like a woman should be treated. But only a month into the relationship, he began to change. He became controlling, constantly calling, demanding to know exactly where she was and what she was doing every minute of the day. She had tried to break it off after only six weeks of dating, but Paul refused to even consider the possibility of losing her. He apologized profusely and promised to do better. Maybe if she could be patient, he would change, she had told herself.

But he didn't change.

Instead, things just kept getting worse. He became even more controlling, wrapping his tentacles around her like a boa constrictor smothers its prey—slow, but steady. After one argument, he backhanded her across the cheek, and she picked up the phone to call the police. He grabbed the phone and threw it to the floor, smashing it to pieces. Then he had whispered in her ear that if she ever tried to leave him again, she would be sorry.

He made sure she understood that he and his family were among the powerful elite in Georgia and could make her and everyone she cared about simply disappear—and no one would ever find them.

She knew he was telling the truth.

Tiffany turned the water off and stepped out of the shower. She wrapped herself in a towel, the feel of the soft cotton against her skin comforting, and she pulled it extra tight, wishing it were a pair of reassuring arms holding her.

She walked into the kitchen and grabbed her favorite mug and a coffee filter from the wooden cabinet above the corner countertop. The kitchen was a no-frills version, but it served its purpose. The counters were a baby blue laminate, and the white cabinets that hung above gave the place a clean feeling, which was good since she was a bit of a germaphobe.

Paul had always used fresh-ground French roast. She had hated it, but drank it anyway, afraid any minor disagreement would lead to him becoming uncontrollably angry. Right after she escaped, she had sworn to herself she would never drink French roast again. She picked up the canister of Folgers from the countertop and added three heaping spoonfuls of the pre-ground coffee to the paper filter. She filled the coffeemaker with tap water—Paul had always insisted on bottled water—and turned it on, then returned to the bathroom to dry her hair.

A few minutes later, the smell of fresh-brewed coffee wafted through the house, helping to drive the need for sleep from her body. Tiffany inhaled the smooth aroma deeply into her lungs as she walked back to the counter and filled her mug with her favorite morning drink. She added a splash of cream, then went into the open living area adjacent to the kitchen and curled up on the couch, wrapping herself in the heavy terrycloth bathrobe she now wore. She picked up the remote control and started to turn on the TV to check the weather, but then threw it next to her on the sofa, deciding instead to enjoy the early morning silence.

She stared into the cup of caramel-colored coffee and blew across the top as she lifted the mug to her lips and took the first sip. It went down smoothly and warmed her inside. As she drank, she wondered if she would ever get over the memories Paul had left her with.

Wondered if she would ever get a peaceful night's sleep again.

After Paul died, she had somehow managed to move on with her life, although it wasn't easy. She had taken a job as a dental hygienist in an Atlanta suburb and worked there for years, yet she never seemed quite at peace. She always felt on edge, often looking over her shoulder. Afraid that, somehow, he would come back. He always said that if he couldn't have her, no one would. She wondered if his reach stopped at the six feet of dirt that now rested on top of him.

That was ridiculous; of course it did. He was gone. Forever.

All that was behind her now. She had made a clean start, and things were going well. In fact, things were going great. She took another sip of coffee, the mug warming her chilly hands, then looked out the small window to her right and stared at the moon-drenched landscape that lay just beyond the front porch of her small cabin.

It was still hard for her to believe she was now working at a small mountain resort in Western North Carolina. The cabin she now called home was a world apart from the brick and marble mansion Paul had promised her all those years ago.

The cabin was provided to her as part of her employment contract with the resort. It was small, with only one bedroom, one bathroom, a tiny kitchen, and a small living room. It was nothing fancy at all: the walls were drafty, the pipes made noises when she turned on the water, and the old wooden floors in the living room and hallway creaked when she walked on them. But she loved it, and she was happy.

Finally.

As she stared at the giant oak outside her cabin, she remembered the first time she came to Mountain View Resort. It had been almost two and a half years ago, when she had traveled to the heart of the Smoky Mountains to help her best friend, Katie, search for her boyfriend, Cody, who had gone missing during a back-country fly fishing trip. They had found him several days later, almost at the point of death. He had been attacked by a large black bear, and Tiffany still found it hard to believe that he had found the courage to survive. But he had somehow pulled through, and he and Katie were now married with a young daughter. They, too, had moved from the Atlanta area and were now living their dream of owning a fly fishing shop and guiding clients on the many trout streams that flowed through the surrounding mountains.

Tiffany didn't understand their obsession with fishing, but she admired them, both of them, for leaving their old lives behind and following their dreams. And if Cody could survive a bear attack and find the will to keep going when all hope seemed to be lost, surely she could put the haunting memories of Paul behind her.

Tiffany would never have guessed that leaving the suburbs of Atlanta in a mad rush to find a missing fisherman would end up changing her life as drastically as it had. She had come along with the intention of helping her best friend during a difficult time, and then returning to Georgia and resuming her life. But something happened on that trip that she hadn't expected at all.

She met Jackson.

Jackson Hart had been the park ranger in charge of Cody's search and rescue operation, and, at first, Tiffany reacted to him the same way she reacted to most men she met—with suspicion and fear. She had been cold, even rude. She was still surprised he hadn't sent her and Katie back to Atlanta at his first opportunity. Tiffany smiled to herself. It couldn't have been easy for Jackson, putting up with her temper and Katie's sad face every day, especially in the midst of a stressful search and rescue operation—but thankfully, he had.

At one point in her life, she had been an outgoing, friendly person. But Paul had changed all that, and the old carefree Tiffany seemed to have been lost. She now thought of her life in two distinct parts—before Paul and after.

After Paul, she found social interactions challenging, if not downright impossible, especially with men. So she had treated Jackson the same way at first; he got the same cold, distant Tiffany every other man did.

But as the search for Cody continued, she had found herself falling for Jackson. He was kind, and his dogged determination to find Cody made her love him even more. She could see that he really cared about finding a man he had never even met. He could have called the search off after the first couple of days, but he didn't. He persevered until Cody was back with Katie.

After the search was over, they kept in touch, and their relationship slowly grew. He traveled to Georgia to visit her several times, and she had made the trip to the Smokies. After several months of long-distance dating, she had decided to move to North Carolina and take the job at the resort. There had been no pressure from Jackson to move; otherwise, she would have bolted like a scared rabbit. But she had been ready to leave the

Atlanta area for some time anyway, and the job offer at the resort seemed like an opportunity for a fresh start. She had hoped leaving Georgia and moving to the solace of the mountains would help her forget Paul, but, so far, that had failed.

She had worked for the resort for almost two years now, and her relationship with Jackson had continued to blossom over that time. It was not the white-hot fire of a new twenty-something romance, but rather the slow sizzle of more mature adults.

Still, she was in her thirties now and couldn't help wondering what the future held for her. She hoped to someday get married and have a family, but every time she had that particular longing, flashes of her past always intruded.

But maybe Ranger Jackson Hart was the one she had been waiting for. The one who would be able to open her soul and love her despite all the emotional baggage that was still tied around her neck like a millstone.

Much to her relief, Jackson had been understanding and supportive when she had finally opened up to him about her past. Just summoning the courage to mention Paul's name to him had seemed an impossible task. She was afraid Jackson wouldn't want someone with so much damage, so many hang-ups.

But the first time they had made love, when Tiffany had revealed the scars on her body that she had never shown anyone, other than Katie and her doctors, Jackson had proved her wrong. He had just kissed her and held her tight, even as she trembled with fear and uncertainty in his arms. She could still hear him whisper, "It's going to be all right, Tiffany. I promise. I'm here, now."

She took her last sip of coffee, tilting the cup upward to make sure the last drops flowed into her mouth, then got up from the couch and walked into the kitchen. She washed and dried the mug, then placed it back in the cabinet. She hated coming home to dirty dishes, so she always made sure everything was cleaned and put away before leaving for the day. Paul had always left a dirty plate, bowl, or glass in the kitchen sink for her to wash, and she had resented it.

The caffeine had failed to give her the jump-start she was hoping for, and she yawned deeply, stretching her arms over her head. Now, she wished she had gone back to bed after the nightmare had awakened her. Today was Wednesday, which meant she would be leading a hike on one of the many trails that surrounded the resort. It was rather short, only a three-mile out-and-back, but she was already tired, partly from the lack of sleep, but primarily, from the energy-draining dream.

She sighed and walked into her bedroom, where she dressed in a comfortable pair of jeans, a long-sleeved cotton shirt, and a fleece jacket. She pulled her hair into a ponytail and did her makeup, applying just enough to highlight her natural beauty. She hated the caked-on look some women wore. She grabbed her backpack and headed toward the front door.

As she bent over to put on her hiking boots, she glanced at her watch. It was only 6:45 a.m., which meant she was running way early this morning. That was all right, though. She would rather go in early than sit in the cabin thinking about Paul.

She opened the door and stepped into the new day.

2

That's it," Jackson said. He held the ring between his thumb and index finger, rolling it slightly. The solitaire diamond sparkled under the white lights of the jewelry store. The stone cast multi-colored rays that danced on the surface of the glass counter where he leaned. "How much?" he asked, looking up and holding his breath.

"$3,400," Charlie Hetherington replied.

Jackson whistled sharply. "Whew, Charlie. You trying to break me or something?"

"Hey, you already told me that was the *one*. Seems to me like I've got you by the short hairs now," Charlie said, his large belly shaking with laughter.

A crooked smile appeared on Jackson's face. "Yeah, I guess that's about right." He glanced back down at the diamond. There was no doubt about it; the ring he now held in his hand was *perfect*. "I'm not a very good poker player, Charlie, in case you couldn't tell," Jackson added, laughing softly.

Charlie ran a hand down his short white beard. "Tell you what, if you buy it today, you can have it for $3,200. Sorry, but that's the best I can do, Jackson."

Jackson hesitated for a moment, trying to make it seem as though he were in serious debate with himself, considering whether or not he would accept Charlie's price. He was hoping the old jeweler would knock another couple hundred bucks off in order to seal the deal, but after several seconds of silence between the two men, Jackson finally relented. "Deal," he said as he offered his hand across the counter.

Charlie grasped his hand with a firm grip. "Deal," he repeated. "You want it wrapped?"

"No, just the box is fine."

"Okay, I'll get it ready. Be right back." Charlie took the ring from Jackson and disappeared into the back room.

Charlie had operated the jewelry store on Main Street in Sylva for years. Jackson wasn't exactly sure how long he had been in business, but he had been here since Jackson was first stationed at the Twentymile Ranger Station five years ago.

Jackson had liked Charlie from their first meeting. He always enjoyed haggling with the genial old man whenever he was in the shop picking out a gift for Tiffany, even though Jackson seldom ended up on the better end of their haggling.

He relished trying to get the best deal possible, whether buying a new car or an engagement ring. He saw it as a challenge, and it was just part of who he was. He loved Tiffany and would have paid full price for the ring if it had come down to it, but he didn't see any harm in trying to save a few bucks.

A couple of minutes later, Charlie reappeared and handed Jackson a small, gray paper bag with U-shaped nylon handles. "Thanks," Jackson said as he handed his credit card across the counter.

Charlie ran the card, and once the receipt printed, he tore it off and pushed the slip of paper and a pen across the counter toward Jackson. "So who's the lucky lady, if I might ask?"

"Her name's Tiffany. I met her a while back. I might bring her in sometime . . . but then I'd probably leave here owing you another three grand." Jackson chuckled, then added, "She's one hell of a woman, Charlie."

"Must be to put up with your cheap ass," Charlie said, his deep laugh once again echoing off the walls of the small store.

"You know that's right," Jackson replied, grinning. He shook Charlie's hand again. "Thanks for the ring."

"Thank you, Jackson. Come back anytime," Charlie replied, genuine gratitude evident in his eyes now.

"You know I will." Jackson turned and walked out of the store, then stepped onto the concrete sidewalk that ran the length of Main Street.

As he stepped from beneath the jewelry store's awning, he paused and took notice of his surroundings. He loved fall. It was his favorite time of the entire year. He was thankful that the long, tiresome dog days of summer, filled with their oftentimes oppressive heat and humidity, were long gone.

Now, the trees were changing colors, painting the mountainsides surrounding the small town in hues of flaming orange, burnished gold, and the deepest, brightest red he had ever seen. A cold front had pushed through the area the day prior, ushering in clean, crisp air and deep blue skies. The sun was bright, warming Jackson's face, and a breeze was blowing out of the north, tossing his thick black hair around his forehead. He took a deep, invigorating breath of the fresh air, then continued walking toward his pickup truck.

He stopped at his vehicle momentarily to lock the ring inside the glove compartment, then continued west on Main Street. He had some extra time today, so he had decided to stop in and see Cody and Katie at their fly shop. But he didn't want his friends asking any questions about his recent purchase at Charlie's. For now, he wanted to keep that little piece of news all to himself.

As Jackson strode toward the fly shop, he felt the urge for an autumn fishing trip coming on.

3

They are in the yard, the main house directly in front of them. The antebellum mansion is the centerpiece of a palatial Georgia estate that covers almost ten acres. Its brick exterior and large white columns combine with a perfectly manicured lawn and flower garden that scream wealth and power to anyone gracing its presence.

The sunlight of the spring day warms her skin, and a gentle breeze ruffles the pink cotton dress against her legs. The giant southern magnolia on her right fills the air with a sweet citronella scent. The large branches of the ancient wooden sentinel weave across the sky above her head, the dark green leaves contrasting with the ivory blossoms. She glances over at the tree and extends her hand, the rough bark scratching at her palm like coarse sandpaper. She pulls closer and steadies herself.

She shouldn't have come here. He's angry, and she doesn't like being around him when he's out of control.

"You stupid bitch!" he screams from behind her.

She feels his hands grab her cotton dress, one between her shoulder blades, the other near the small of her back. Suddenly, she's thrust forward and slammed hard against the tree trunk. The rough bark bites into the tender flesh of her face, scraping painfully as he puts his full weight against her, pinning her to the tree. Her chest rests against a large knot that extends a few inches from the main trunk, and as he presses still harder against her body, she's sure that her breastbone will shatter into a thousand tiny pieces.

"I'm sorry, Paul! Please stop. You're hurting me," she cries out.

"Shut up!" he screams. "Why were you talking to that guy today at lunch? I saw you outside the dining hall at school!"

"He's just a friend, Paul! I promise. I didn't do anything wrong." She struggles against his grasp, but cannot move. "Let me go!"

He doesn't let her go; instead, he pulls her back from the tree, then slams her into it for a second time. This blow is harder than the first, and, for a moment, her vision blurs. She needs to hang on. If she loses consciousness, she'll be completely at his mercy.

"I don't believe you!" he yells, his words dripping with venomous accusation.

"I promise, I'm telling you the truth," she says through gritted teeth, the pain so intense that tears stream down her cheeks and onto her dress. She gasps for breath, her badly bruised ribs making each inhalation a painful experience.

"You're a liar!" He releases his right hand from between her shoulders, grabs a fistful of her hair, and snaps her head back. Then, grinding his knee into her back, he grabs her chin with his left hand and twists her face toward his. He leans in, his lips almost touching her warm cheeks. She can smell his stale breath. "If you ever do that again . . . I'll kill you."

"Miss? Miss, are you okay?"

The rough bark of the magnolia transformed into the smooth, light gray skin of a beech tree. She stared at the wood, transfixed. Her eyes wouldn't move. Her pulse raced, just as it had after the nightmare hours earlier.

"What's wrong with her?" she heard someone say.

"Ma'am? Are you okay?" the first voice repeated.

Someone placed a hand on her shoulder, and she screamed, jolting herself from the dreamlike state. An older gentleman with soft gray hair and a wrinkled face stood in front of her, with several other people behind him. There was a young mother with a baby sitting in one of those backpack carriers. The man beside her had a diaper bag over his shoulder, his face a mixture of shock and concern. There were several others standing nearby, about fifteen in total, a mixture of adults and children, all peering at her with confusion and worry.

The old man withdrew his arm from her shoulder. "It's okay. What's going on? Are you all right?" he asked again.

Tiffany didn't know what to say; she just stared blankly into the man's kind blue eyes. He smiled at her, and, after a few seconds, she finally managed to force her lips to turn upward just slightly, returning the gesture. Her mind was clouded. *What the hell just happened?*

"Yes, yes . . . I'm fine," she said, her voice trembling.

"You sure?" a blonde lady behind the old man asked. "You kind of zoned out on us there for a minute."

"What?" Tiffany shook her head slightly, feigning disbelief. "Really?"

"Yeah," a middle-aged man next to the blonde replied. "You were talking about this beech tree here," the man paused and motioned with his hand toward the tree in front of Tiffany, "then you just spaced out. Went into some sort of trance or something. Stayed out for a minute at least. We were about to go get help."

"Oh . . . I'm so sorry about that." Tiffany paused and ran a hand through her hair, trying to regain her composure. Her head was spinning, and she could feel the embarrassment washing over her face, but there was nothing she could do to stop it. "It's okay . . . everything's okay. I didn't sleep well last night, and I just got a little lightheaded. I'm fine now," she added.

Tiffany wasn't about to tell the group of strangers in front of her what had really happened—that she had been transported back to the occasion where she had first realized the frightening extent of Paul's jealous temper. She had seen him angry before that, even physical, but on that spring day in front of the McMillan mansion, she had finally seen the true monster behind the mask. After that, she couldn't lie to herself anymore—she knew he would never change.

She pulled the water bottle from her backpack and took a drink. "Must have been dehydrated, too," she lied. She knew it wasn't lack of sleep or dehydration that had caused the vision, or whatever it was, but she certainly didn't have an answer as to what had caused it, either.

What was happening to her? Why were the memories more vivid now, after ten long years? And why were they becoming more frequent?

She had no idea. But she knew one thing: she had to get a handle on herself before the wheels came off her life completely. She had worked so hard to move on, worked so hard to start a new life with Jackson, and she would be damned if she was going to let Paul screw up her life any longer.

"You sure you're okay?" the old man asked.

"Yes," Tiffany said with conviction in her voice and a smile on her face. "I'm fine; I really am."

She turned back to the beech tree and, at last, managed to clear the remaining cobwebs from her mind. She took a deep breath, then patted the large trunk and said, "This is a *Fagus grandifolia*, better known as the American beech tree. In the spring the canopy is dark green, but as you can see, it is most beautiful in the fall." She tilted her head back and stared up at the plethora of golden leaves, splotched with varying shades of crimson, making the tree appear as if it were ablaze. It was stunning.

Tiffany looked back at the group of people and was glad to see that most of their faces were now void of concern. Apparently, they had bought her story that she had just become lightheaded. Everyone in the group was now staring up at the tree. The baby in the backpack carrier pointed his little finger skyward and giggled.

Tiffany smiled, then added, "The beech nut is a favorite food of many of the animals who live in the Smokies, including squirrels, turkeys, bears, and deer, among others. They're slow to mature; some trees like this one take up to forty years to produce their first seeds. But they make up for their slow start with a long life expectancy. This particular tree is over two hundred years old." Tiffany heard a few gasps as the group took in the beauty of a tree that had been standing since well before the Civil War.

"Okay, let's keep moving. We've got a lot more to see." She turned and continued up the trail, the gaggle of tourists following close behind.

4

"I'll see you Saturday, Jeremy," Tiffany said as she put her backpack on and smiled at the lanky, acne-faced teenager who was working behind the front counter.

"Okay, enjoy your time off." Jeremy returned her smile with his usual awkward expression. The look on his face suggested a strange mixture of constipation and fear. Tiffany grinned and bit her lip to keep from laughing out loud. She had become very fond of Jeremy while working with him at the resort's recreation center. She thought he had a crush on her and didn't want to do anything to damage the young man's ego.

She turned and walked toward the door. "I plan on it. Have a good one." The teenager lifted his hand in a shy wave and gave her the constipated-looking smile again. She waved back and walked out the door, pulling it closed behind her.

Her cabin was a half mile from the recreation center and sat on the side of one of the numerous steep hills that surrounded Mountain View Resort. Although she owned a car, she rarely drove to work. Only when the weather was terrible did she allow herself the convenience. She preferred to walk anyway. She loved the grand beauty of this place, tucked deep in the heart of the Smokies.

She breathed in a healthy dose of the cool autumn air and quickened her pace up the street. Wednesday was her Friday, and she was looking forward to a couple of days off before the busy weekend ahead. This time of year the mountains were inundated with thousands of tourists, all coming to soak up the vivid fall colors.

She paused and looked up at the surrounding mountains; shades of orange, red, green, and yellow painted the landscape in an intense palette of color. The azure sky was void of even a single cloud, rays of the sinking sun adding golden highlights to the regal mountain peaks. She didn't blame the tourists for coming to visit this place—it was spectacular.

The mountain vista lifted her spirits, and she smiled to herself. After the week she had been having, she truly appreciated the moment of tranquility.

As she continued to walk on the asphalt, her muscles reminded her of the long week she had just finished. Her legs and back were sore, and her feet ached after the many hikes she had guided over the past five days. All she wanted to do was go home, take a long, hot shower— she no longer took baths—and pour herself a large glass of Merlot. Then she would curl up in her half-broken-down recliner and finish the cheesy romance novel she had been reading.

And hopefully forget the visions of Paul she had experienced in her sleep and again on the hiking trail. *But what if she couldn't?* That was what she was truly afraid of—that she would never be able to move on.

And even though Paul was gone forever, for some reason, he kept resurfacing in her life. Squeezing himself under the door of her soul. Escaping the prison she had put him in after that terrible night at his parents' mansion, constantly tormenting her with the memories.

Moving on was no longer an option—it was a necessity. Somehow, she had to find a way to relegate Paul to the ash heap of her past, once and for all. Katie had tried to make her see a counselor or join a support group after Paul, but she had refused. The idea of talking to strangers about what she had been through had been terrifying—still was.

Tiffany had hoped the wonderful memories she was making with Jackson would erase the ones Paul had given birth to, but, so far, that hadn't happened. Maybe if she opened up more to Jackson, told him more about what had happened between her and Paul, it would help. She had given Jackson enough details to make him understand why she was so distant at times, but she hadn't told him everything.

Definitely not everything.

She hadn't told him about the time Paul had locked her in a small closet inside his family's home for two days because she had made the mistake of calling a guy she knew from college to ask for his help with a difficult school assignment. During the forty-eight hours she had been held captive, Paul gave her only water to drink, no food at all. She couldn't sleep, and on the few occasions she had started to doze, Paul's heavy footfalls on the other side of the closet door would jar her awake. She was forced to urinate and defecate in the corner of the small room, the stench eventually causing her to vomit.

He came to the other side of the locked door every few hours and berated her for being such a cheating whore. She pleaded with him to let her out, told him he was wrong, that she hadn't cheated, but he wouldn't listen.

After what had seemed like an eternity to Tiffany, Paul finally released her. She wasn't sure why he decided to let her go; his parents were out of town and, even if he had been caught, she knew his family would have covered everything up for him. After listening to more of his threats that he would do something worse to her the next time she stepped out on him, she ran out of the mansion as fast as she could and drove back to her apartment, too ashamed to call the police or go straight to the hospital.

After a few days, she reconsidered, and had almost reported him to the police.

Almost.

She had gone so far as to drive down to the station, but she couldn't make herself step out of the car and walk inside. She ultimately decided against it, afraid that Paul would get word of her betrayal through his powerful family connections. If that happened, which was almost a certainty, the two days she had spent in the closet would seem like Disneyland in comparison.

He apologized, of course. He brought her roses, just like he always did after one of his "episodes."

He tried to explain to her that when he became violent, it was only because something inside him took over, and he couldn't stop himself. It really wasn't his fault, and he hated himself for losing control, he said. Tiffany didn't care who or what was to blame for his outbursts; she just knew she had to get away.

She finally summoned the courage to tell him it was over and that she never wanted to see him again. Ever.

When she refused to take him back, despite his tearful pleading, Paul disappeared for a few weeks. Stopped calling. Stopped following her any time she ventured away from her apartment. Tiffany began to breathe easier, convinced the nightmare was over.

But she could not have been more wrong.

Because Paul would not take no for an answer.

Maybe one day she would tell Jackson everything, but it was hard enough to keep her sanity as it was. Every time she vocalized what had happened to her, it all came back again in vivid detail, so she avoided talking about it whenever possible.

Tiffany started up the hill that led to her cabin, the steep incline straining her already worn-out legs. The hot shower and glass of red wine were beckoning her. The small restaurant at the resort made a pretty mean pizza; maybe she would splurge and order a large pepperoni with extra cheese, her favorite. She needed to relax and get some sleep. And she prayed she wouldn't be awakened by another dream.

She would go to bed early tonight, because she was meeting Katie for their monthly shopping trip in Asheville the next day. The drive to the only large city in this part of North Carolina was over an hour and a half from the resort, but she made the trip faithfully once a month. She loved spending time with Katie, and the thought of seeing the chubby-cheeked smile of Missy, Katie's daughter, made Tiffany even more anxious for the trip.

She spotted her cabin just ahead, tucked back into the woods off the right side of the road. Despite its modest simplicity, it had an elegant beauty all its own. The wooden siding was stained a honey color, giving the house a fresh and inviting exterior. The hunter green shingles blended well with the surrounding hardwoods, and she loved the small covered porch and the two dormers that looked like big, happy eyes staring back at her.

The small cabin was her home now, and the only place she wanted to be at the moment. It was her symbol of freedom and independence, a constant reminder that she had left her old life behind in Georgia and was starting over in North Carolina. Staring at her simple dwelling, she hoped that her past wouldn't steal away her future. She wanted to be happy again—with Jackson.

She passed her blue Toyota Corolla that was parked on the narrow gravel driveway in front of the cabin. As she reached the three steps leading to her front porch, she grabbed the damp wooden railing and let her hand glide over the small patches of lichen growing on the two-by-four. Her cabin was heavily shaded by the surrounding trees, which, coupled with the penetrating humidity of the region, made everything feel like it was in the middle of a rain forest.

She paused and stared up at the giant oak just off the front of the porch. Its scarlet leaves were moving gently in the breeze, and she noticed a few had already fallen onto the small patch of green grass that lay between the cabin and the gravel driveway.

She unlocked the front door, walked inside, and let her backpack drop to the floor. She removed her hiking boots, then strode across the hardwood floor toward the bathroom. The wood creaked as it bent, then reflexed under her feet, the familiar sound welcoming her home again.

The place she felt most at peace.

As she walked, she began to strip off her clothes, turning down the short hallway. She wadded the garments into a giant ball and shoved them into the plastic hamper next to the bathroom sink.

She groaned as she stretched her sore muscles, arching her back and stretching her hands toward the ceiling. It had been a long, hard week, and she was ready to finally relax for a couple of days.

She adjusted the water temperature until it was hot and steam had started to rise inside the cramped bathroom. She stepped inside and let the almost scalding water flow over her body. She pushed away a fleeting memory of Paul, as she applied a generous amount of shampoo to her hair. She was determined to enjoy her two days off. She promised herself she would not give the past another thought.

She stayed in the shower for almost thirty minutes, enjoying the feel of the moist heat over her aching body and taking deep breaths of the warm, humid air. When she was done, she dried off with a towel and walked to her bedroom, where she dressed in a pair of black cotton pajama bottoms covered with sunflower prints and an oversized red T-shirt. She grabbed a pair of thick wool socks from her dresser drawer and pulled them on her already chilling feet. The soft, warm clothes felt good against her skin, and drove away the autumn chill that had penetrated the drafty cabin. Part of her wanted to just crawl into bed right then and there and succumb to sleep. Instead, she turned the bedroom light off and headed back down the hallway toward the kitchen.

Tiffany reached up and retrieved a large wine glass from the cupboard over the sink. She pulled a three-quarters-full bottle of Merlot from the door of the refrigerator and poured a generous amount into the bowled glass. She walked into the living room, then plopped down into the faux-leather recliner that was catty-cornered to the sofa. She pulled the handle and let her feet swing out in front of her. She set the wine bottle down on the floor next to her and breathed a deep sigh of relief. It felt nice just to be off her feet, and she let her body sink fully into the cushioned chair.

She took a lengthy sip of the wine, then grabbed the paperback romance from the lampstand next to the recliner and opened it to the dog-eared page where she had left off the previous night. The protagonist, Suzanne, was just about to tell her husband, Gary, that their son wasn't really his. Tiffany knew how the story would end, or at least had a good idea. These types of books always had happy endings. And that's exactly what she needed right now—a happy ending.

Just as she was about to turn the page and read the husband's reaction to the stunning, albeit predictable, news, her cellphone rang.

She had forgotten to take her phone out of her backpack. She could hear the annoying chime ringing over and over, even though the backpack was across the room next to the front door. She thought about staying right where she was and just letting the call go to voicemail, but after a couple of seconds of hesitation, she grumbled under her breath and reluctantly pulled herself from the recliner, the broken spring in the cushion popping as she got up.

She walked to the backpack, picked it up, and retrieved the phone from the front pocket. She was afraid it was work calling to see if she would be willing to put in some overtime tomorrow. She really needed rest, and she wanted to enjoy a day out shopping with Katie, but she always had a hard time saying no. She knew if her boss called and asked, she would be forsaking the shopping trip and working instead. She breathed a sigh of relief when the caller ID indicated it was Jackson. She swiped her hand across the screen and put the phone to her ear as she walked back to the recliner. "Hey, babe," she said as she sank back into the chair.

"Hey, Tiff. How's it going?"

Just the question about her well-being prompted an almost overwhelming urge in Tiffany to just tell Jackson everything that had been going on. To finally be honest with him and admit that things hadn't been going the best for her lately. To open up to him and reveal all the details of her past she had kept hidden. But she couldn't bring herself to do it. As much as she wanted to, it proved impossible. Instead, she took a deep breath, pushed the urge for full disclosure away, and simply said, "I'm fine. How are you?"

"I'm good. Been pretty slow at work this week, nothing much going on," he replied.

Tiffany thought Jackson sounded different. Perhaps a hint of nervousness intermingled with his normally confident voice. She pulled a wool blanket that had been draped over the back of the chair into her lap, then extended the recliner for a second time. She spread the blanket over herself, drawing it all the way up to the bottom of her chin. "I wish I could say it had been slow here. It's been really busy. I just got home a few minutes ago, and I'm looking forward to a couple days off."

"You have any plans?" Jackson asked.

"Not really. Katie and I are going to Asheville tomorrow to do some shopping, but other than that, I'm just going to try to take it easy and get some rest." The wind picked up outside, and Tiffany watched a few more red leaves fall from the branches of the big oak through the large window in front of her.

"Well, how about you and I go out for dinner Friday night?"

Now Tiffany definitely detected some hesitation in his voice. "Are you all right, Jackson? You sound . . . different."

"Yeah . . . yeah, I'm okay. Just a little tired, I guess," he replied in a more upbeat tone.

"Dinner, huh?" Tiffany paused for several seconds, playing with Jackson, as if she had to weigh whether or not she wanted to accept his invitation. "I guess I could do that," she finally said. "Where are we going?"

"I thought we could go to DeVito's in Sylva."

They had eaten at the expensive Italian restaurant only once previously, on their first date. Tiffany smiled when she remembered Jackson's awkward discomfort when he first walked into the elegant dining room. He was more accustomed to eating microwave meals in his small house at Twentymile than to dining in a fine restaurant. "DeVito's? Wow, what's the special occasion?" she asked.

"Oh, nothing. I just thought it would be nice to take you there again and enjoy a nice meal together since we usually eat in. Maybe we could catch a movie or something afterward."

Tiffany grinned to herself. "Wow! Dinner and a movie, huh? I feel like I'm back in high school."

Jackson sighed. "I know it's hard to believe, Tiff, but I'm not the most romantic man that ever lived. Sorry about that."

Tiffany laughed softly. "You do an excellent job, babe. I was just teasing you. And you know I love our meals on the couch together. But . . . if you're going to spring for dinner at DeVito's, count me in."

"Great," Jackson said.

Tiffany could hear him exhale deeply over the phone, as though he had been unsure she would accept his invitation. This puzzled her; he should know she wouldn't turn him down.

"Pick you up around six?" he asked.

"Sounds good. I can't wait to see you."

"Me, too. I hope you get some rest tonight and have a good time with Katie tomorrow. Love you, Tiff."

"I love you, too." Tiffany set the phone down on the arm of the recliner and smiled softly to herself, happy that Jackson had called and invited her to dinner. She picked up the novel and began to read again.

Just before 9:00 p.m., Tiffany finished the last page and closed the book. She had guessed right. After some rough patches, Gary had forgiven Suzanne for her infidelity and agreed to raise Carl as his own. They moved from busy L.A. to the quiet mountains of Colorado and lived happily ever after.

Tiffany sighed as she set the book down on the small wooden stand to the left of the recliner. *I really have to start reading something with a little more substance,* she told herself. She reached up and turned the lamp off, then picked up the pizza box from the coffee table in front of the sofa. She had eaten two-thirds of the large pizza she had ordered from the resort restaurant and felt a twinge of guilt at her overindulgence. She gathered the wine glass and bottle, which was almost empty now, and walked into the kitchen. She opened the refrigerator door and placed the pizza box and wine bottle inside. Her head swam as she bent over, and she giggled at the woozy feeling. Maybe she should've left a little more wine inside the bottle. She walked across the room and placed the glass carefully in the aluminum sink.

Then she saw it.

A single coffee mug stared back at her.

She recognized it as the one she had used this morning. But that couldn't be, because she distinctly remembered washing the mug and returning it to the cabinet before she left for work.

Hadn't she?

Of course she had. She never left dishes in the sink in the morning because it reminded her of Paul. That was what he used to do. But if she had washed it and put it away as she remembered—as she always did—how was it in the sink now?

This isn't happening.

It couldn't be real.

She backed away slowly from the sink, her hands waving blindly behind her, searching for the refrigerator. When her fingertips touched the metal handle, she grasped it and steadied her wobbly legs.

You've just had too much to drink, Tiffany. You're imagining things.

Her palms were sweating, and her heart pounded against her sternum. Her mouth felt like cotton. She again scolded herself for drinking too much, knowing that was the reason she was seeing things. She turned and rested her forehead, wet with perspiration, against the cool metal door and exhaled slowly. A bead of sweat ran down her face and rested on her upper lip. She tasted the salty liquid as her tongue reflexively captured the drop, snapping her back to reality. It was all in her head. Paul had been dead for years. She was simply allowing her imagination to run away with her. That was all. Nothing more.

She rested for another moment against the refrigerator, taking deep breaths to calm her runaway heartbeat, her chin resting on her chest. At last, she raised her head and looked back at the sink, still holding tightly to the refrigerator handle. For some reason, she couldn't make herself turn loose and take another step closer, to walk far enough to see inside the sink. She fully expected the mug to be gone, to be back in the cupboard where she had placed it after her morning coffee. It had to be. Otherwise, she would be forced to face only one horrible conclusion, and she didn't think she could bear that truth.

But what if it was still in the sink?

What would she do? Call the police? What would she tell them? That her ex-boyfriend—her *dead* ex-boyfriend—had come back to torment her again? That he inhabited not only her dreams but now her home, too? And she could prove everything because a coffee mug was left in the sink?

Not unless she wanted to be sent straight to a padded cell.

But that wasn't going to happen. Because when she looked again, the mug would be gone.

She summoned the courage to ease away from the refrigerator, praying that it had simply been an illusion, the result of an alcohol-clouded mind. She took a small step toward the sink, her left arm still grasping the door handle. Then another step. She let her hand slide from the handle, down to her side. She paused, then took another hesitant step. Her breathing was heavy and rapid. Sweat formed on her forehead for a second time. She had to know. Struggling to make her body take the last two steps toward the sink, she took a deep breath, and said a silent prayer.

Please, God, no.

She held the breath inside, unable to exhale, and closed her eyes. She finally managed to force her stiffening legs to move the final few feet. She grasped the edge of the counter with both hands.

Look, Tiffany. Look, now!

She opened her eyes.

From the bottom of the sink, the coffee mug stared back at her. Taunting her. Laughing at her.

She gasped. Streams of salty liquid ran down her face again, but this time it wasn't perspiration.

It was tears.

The man watched the pretty redhead through the binoculars he had pulled from his backpack. He had a clear view into the kitchen, through the window centered over the sink. He could see her flowing auburn hair, her bright green eyes. She was more than just pretty.

She was stunning.

He watched as she first spotted the mug in the sink, and he smiled as the shock moved across her exquisite face. When she backed away from the sink and propped herself against the refrigerator, he lowered the binoculars.

He took another pull from the Marlboro Red he held between his index and middle fingers, staring at the bright cherry burning at the end. He had bought four packs at a gas station somewhere in North Georgia and had already smoked a pack and a half. He'd been denied the privilege of a good smoke for so long that he indulged the old vice with abandon. When the cigarette was almost down to the filter, he took one last drag, then rubbed it out on the sole of his boot.

He picked up the binoculars again and pressed them against his eyes just as the girl moved away from the refrigerator. He watched as she tentatively made her way back to the sink. He knew she was forcing herself to look again, unable to believe what she had seen the first time. Then she began to cry. He could see her lower lip start to quiver.

The man chuckled.

As the girl turned and ran down the hallway, he picked up his backpack, shoved the binoculars inside, and retreated into the forest.

This was going to be fun.

5

Tiffany woke with the cold steel of the Smith & Wesson .38 revolver resting in the palm of her hand. She traced the smooth lines of the metal with her fingertips under the pillow. After hours of sleeplessness, she must have finally dozed off. She felt a stream of drool at the corner of her mouth and wiped it away with her left hand, her right still firmly grasping the gun.

She had tossed and turned most of the night, unable to get the coffee mug out of her mind. Finally, around 3:00 a.m., she had braved going back to the kitchen once more—gun in hand—to check and see if the mug was still there, hoping again that the whole thing had just been a hallucination.

But as much as she wanted it to be, needed it to be, it hadn't been a hallucination at all. The mug remained at the bottom of the sink.

She readjusted in the bed. The lack of any restful sleep, coupled with the excessive wine intake, had left her with a horrible headache. That was probably what had caused her to freak out about the mug, too. That had to be it. It was the only thing that made sense.

She felt nauseated and wanted to just stay in bed all day. She looked down at her watch: 8:21. She let out a deep sigh and let her head collapse back into the thick pillow. She lay there for the next several minutes, seriously considering calling Katie to cancel their shopping date.

But she couldn't do that.

If she did, Katie would know something was wrong. They had been best friends since the seventh grade, and the two of them shared an unbreakable bond. They often finished each other's sentences and could read the other's emotions like a book. If she canceled, Katie would want to know why. And it wouldn't take her long to figure it out.

Tiffany didn't want to talk about Paul McMillan ever again.

She rolled onto her back and pulled the revolver from beneath the pillow. She stared up at the cottage-cheese ceiling; a few small areas were stained a dirty brown, evidence of minor roof leaks through the years. And although the cabin had been well cared for, it was more than fifty years old, so there was no denying that it had some scars. Tiffany moved her arm to her side, still gripping the wooden handle of the gun that now rested next to her thigh.

She continued staring at the discolored ceiling, mentally running through all the possible scenarios. After several minutes, she decided only one made sense: she hadn't washed the coffee mug before leaving for work the day prior. Even though it was a habit she followed with religious fervor, one she had developed in an attempt to rid her surroundings of any semblance of Paul, for some reason, she had simply forgotten to wash the mug. She had no idea why she had neglected a chore that had become such a part of her daily ritual, but she had—plain and simple. Perhaps she had just been so tired from the lack of sleep. That was the only logical explanation. It had to be.

Then, last night the alcohol had clouded her reasoning and thrown her into a panic when she saw the mug. Otherwise, she would have realized the truth then, saving herself a fitful night wrestling with the sheets.

She turned her head away from the ceiling, sat up in bed, and looked to her left. She scowled at the mirror above the dresser. She looked like hell. Her eyes were red and puffy; her hair was matted with dried sweat, pressed firmly against her forehead; and her complexion would present a challenge to even the most skilled undertaker.

At least she had come to her senses about the stupid coffee mug.

That in itself made her feel better, gave her a little shot of energy. She looked at her watch again: 8:45. It was at least an hour's drive to Katie's place, which meant she was running late. They were supposed to meet up at 10:00, and she still had to get herself ready. She swung her feet to the floor, allowing the lingering lightheadedness the wine had left her with to pass before standing up. Once she steadied herself, she walked to the closet and picked out a nice navy blouse and a comfortable pair of jeans, then laid them out on the bed. She spotted the revolver lying in the folds of the rumpled indigo comforter. She picked it up and put it in the bottom of her underwear drawer, where she always kept it, then went to the bathroom to shower.

Thirty minutes later, Tiffany walked into the living room, dressed and ready to go. The hot shower, along with two extra-strength Tylenol, had made her headache disappear, and she was feeling a thousand times better.

Her washed and blow-dried hair was perfect, and she had expertly applied makeup to erase any signs of stress on her face. Her eyes had been a little red, but drops had taken care of that. She put on a pair of her favorite tennis shoes, knowing they would provide all-day comfort while she and Katie wandered through who knows how many stores looking for the best deals. She dropped her cellphone into her purse and headed for the door.

Then she stopped. She had one more thing to do.

She walked straight to the kitchen, reached into the sink, and grabbed the coffee mug. She washed and dried it before placing it back into the cabinet where it belonged.

Then she turned and walked out the front door.

6

The water cascaded over three large boulders and danced down the mossy rocks into the deep pool ahead. A breeze, cooled by the mountain stream, drifted across Jackson's face. The cold water rushed by his lower legs, chilling and, at the same time, invigorating him.

He lifted the fly rod and began his false casts, letting out more fly line with each bend of the graphite. He aimed for the pocket of whitewater at the head of the pool and, with one final push, propelled the fly forward. It landed right on target. He watched the Yellow Palmer dry fly ride atop the swift, churning water, then gradually slow as it was ejected downstream into calmer currents. He stripped line with his left hand as the fly moved closer to him, eliminating any unnatural drag.

His heart rate increased, his breathing quickened, and he felt his right palm begin to sweat against the rod's cork handle. *Just a few more seconds,* he told himself. A large, dark shadow emerged from the depths of the pool of water, just in front of the floating fly. Jackson watched, waiting patiently. He saw the trout flare its gills as the dry fly moved directly toward its mouth.

Jackson jerked back on the rod, expecting to feel the weight of the large rainbow on the end of his line as the mighty fish began to fight. Instead, the bright green fly line zoomed over his head, and he watched as the fly landed in a large maple tree downstream, the monofilament leader wrapping around a small branch several times. "Dammit," he said under his breath.

He heard raucous laughter from the shoreline. He looked over and saw Cody sitting on a large, moss-covered boulder, newly fallen scarlet and golden leaves dotting the green mat under his legs. His sandy blond hair jutted from beneath the baseball cap he was wearing. Cody wiped his hand across his mouth and goatee, trying to make the mile-wide smile on his face disappear, but the effort proved fruitless. "Sorry, man, I can't help it. You jerked too soon," he said, still grinning.

"Thanks for the encouragement," Jackson said with a slight smile as he moved downstream toward the maple limb where the dry fly had gotten stuck.

"Don't worry, you'll get it. It just takes practice," Cody said.

Jackson let out a sigh of defeat. "I don't know about that. I just can't seem to get the hang of it." This was his third fishing trip with Cody, and Jackson was becoming frustrated at his inability to master the skill of fly fishing. Normally, he excelled at everything: his job, sports, and life in general.

He had only experienced problems in two areas—women and fishing.

But things had turned around for him in the female department after he met Tiffany, so now he had only fly fishing to conquer. He pulled on his fly line, bringing the low-hanging limb within reach. After an annoying few minutes, working to untangle the mess of line from the narrow branch, he finally freed the dry fly and made his way to shore. He stepped out of the creek and took a seat next to Cody.

Jackson let out an exasperated sigh, partly from the physical exertion of fighting the strong currents of Eagle Creek, but mainly from the irritation of missing another big fish on a day that had been less than stellar for honing his skills. They had received few looks from the wary trout and even fewer takes, so another lost opportunity wasn't sitting well with him. "Sorry about that," he said, "guess I just got overanxious."

Cody laughed softly. "It's all right. Trout are funny, Jackson. They can deliver a rush of adrenaline or a sinking feeling in the pit of your stomach. Men have chased them for centuries. If every one of them were easy to catch, I suspect the sport would have died out long ago."

Jackson took his hat off and placed it on his knee. The breeze stiffened and whipped his thick crop of black hair against his forehead. He ran a hand down his chiseled face, trying to wipe away any sign of the disappointment and embarrassment he was feeling inside. "Yeah, I guess you're right."

"I've been doing this for years, man. Becoming a good fisherman doesn't happen overnight." Cody pulled a couple of fat cigars from one of the many pockets on his fishing vest and offered one to Jackson. "Care for a smoke?" he asked.

Jackson reached out and took the cigar. "Sure."

Cody reached into another pocket and handed him a lighter and a cigar cutter. Jackson snipped off the end cap, struck the lighter, and touched the flame to the end of the large roll of tobacco. He took several pulls, exhaling between each one, until the end was glowing bright red. "Thanks," he said as he handed the lighter back to Cody.

"No problem. I don't smoke unless I'm fishing, but there's nothing like enjoying a fine cigar next to a mountain stream." After lighting his own cigar, Cody leaned back, stretching out on the boulder. The movement caused his pants to shift upward, exposing the bottom of his prosthetic left leg. The shaft of titanium glistened in the autumn sunlight and caught Jackson's eye.

Jackson quickly looked away and took another pull from his cigar, savoring the sweet tobacco aroma that wafted into his face. After a few seconds, he spoke. "How do you do it, Cody?"

"How do I do what?"

"How do you just move on after you experience something like you did? I mean, it's like it never happened. Doesn't it bother you to come back to the very creek where you almost died less than three years ago?" Jackson said in an even tone, hoping he wasn't offending his friend.

Cody didn't say anything. He just took a long drag from the cigar and blew the smoke above his head.

Jackson, still sitting, looked down at Cody and watched as the breeze scattered the tobacco smoke into the hardwood forest behind them. "Sorry, Cody, I didn't mean to—"

Cody laughed. "No, it's fine. And to answer your question, I guess I just decided that I wasn't going to live in the past. If I were afraid to come back to Eagle Creek or ever go into the mountains alone again, my life wouldn't be very fulfilling, now would it?" He paused. "I can't imagine living in fear the rest of my life. I just accept what happened as something that was out of my control. I've learned from it, and I'm moving on with my life. Simple as that."

Jackson pondered Cody's answer as he exhaled a mouthful of smoke. "I guess that's a good way to look at it," he finally replied. He turned his head back toward Eagle Creek. He watched as the wind plucked several leaves from their branches, then followed them as they floated down to the water, where the current quickly carried them downstream.

"Besides . . . to tell you the truth, what happened up here in these mountains was one of the best parts of my life."

"What?" Jackson asked, dumbfounded. He could understand Cody's positive outlook, but he couldn't imagine how it was possible to be grateful for losing a leg to a bear attack. He turned his gaze back to Cody, who was smiling again.

"Yep. It sure was." Cody grasped the cigar between his index and middle fingers, then moved it away from his mouth while he spoke. "It got me out of that mind-numbing law firm I hated so much in Atlanta and made me reprioritize my life. Helped me to see what was really important . . . what I had been missing out on for all those years." Cody took another puff from the cigar and then rested his hand on his left thigh.

"So you don't miss being in the courtroom, battling it out with some other attorney with millions of dollars on the line? You must've been knocking out some serious coin with that job. You don't miss any of that? The money? The acclaim? None of it?"

Cody exhaled, letting the smoke slowly rise from his mouth. "Nope, I don't miss it one damn bit. Not any of it. I may have lost a leg up here, Jackson, but the way I look at it, it was worth it. That might sound crazy to some people, but at least I'm happy now. I was dying on the inside in Atlanta. Yes, it sucks that I lost a leg, but at least I'm alive on the inside. I'm finally living life like I want to, and the part of me that's most important, the inner part, is thankful that I went through what I did, because the end result was what I really needed."

"Hmm . . . never thought of it like that," Jackson said.

"Well, it's the truth. And the best part is, not only did I leave the big city behind and move up here to the mountains, but I ended up with Katie, too." Cody paused, and a smile spread across his face. "And she's worth two legs, all by herself."

"Well, I'm really glad it worked out for you. I've got to say, when I first found you, I thought you were a goner. And if I hadn't had to look at Katie's sad eyes every day, I may have never found your sorry ass."

They both laughed. "Well, I'm glad you did."

"Me too, Cody. Me too," Jackson said as he stared across Eagle Creek, enjoying the view and the sound of the rushing water just feet away.

Both men remained quiet for a few minutes, enjoying the tranquility of the wilderness. Finally, Jackson broke the silence. "Yeah, a good woman is hard to find these days, but I believe I've found one in Tiffany." He paused and took a deep breath. "I'm going to ask her to marry me."

Cody shot up from his relaxed position and stared at Jackson. "Really?" he asked, a look of half-doubt, half-excitement on his face. "Are you joking?"

"Nope, picked up the ring at Charlie Hetherington's place right before I came into your shop yesterday. I didn't say anything then because I was worried Katie would spill the beans to Tiffany, and I want this to be a surprise."

Cody slapped Jackson on the back. "All right! That's great news, man. I'm happy for you two."

"So you think she'll say yes?" Jackson asked.

"I wouldn't," Cody said, stone-faced, looking Jackson straight in the eyes. Several seconds later, he burst into laughter and said, "Of course she'll say yes."

Jackson smiled. "I sure hope so. I can't imagine losing her." He paused and took another drag off the cigar. "But I've got to tell you, I haven't been this nervous about *anything*, ever."

"I know how you feel. When I asked Katie to marry me, I was a sweating, bumbling mess."

"But it went all right?"

"I'm married to her, aren't I?"

Jackson laughed softly. "Point taken," he replied.

"You sure I can't tell Katie tonight? She's been hoping this would happen ever since you and Tiffany started dating."

"No. Absolutely not. Not a peep about this, Cody. I mean it. You know how women are; they get so excited about shit they can't help themselves. The secret will be out before I even get a chance to prepare my speech," he said seriously.

"Okay, okay," Cody replied, smiling. "I won't say anything. Your secret's safe with me."

"Thanks, I appreciate that. Yeah, I've got a nice romantic dinner planned tomorrow night at DeVito's."

"Wow, DeVito's. You're going all out, huh?" Cody said. "What's that gonna set you back, a couple hundred bucks?"

"Something like that, I'm sure. But I want Tiffany to have the best; the whole night has to be perfect."

"I'm sure everything will go fine," Cody said, giving Jackson a reassuring pat on the shoulder. "And I promise, not a peep from me."

"Thanks, man. I hope so."

Cody looked down at his watch. "Well, it's almost one o'clock now. What do you say we hike up the trail a little farther and try it there, before we head back to the lakeshore?"

"Sounds good to me," Jackson replied. He ground his cigar into the side of the boulder, extinguishing the ashes, and shoved the remnants in his pocket. He stood up and made his way to the trail that ran only several yards behind them. Cody followed a few seconds later, and the two of them made their way upstream.

7

The oil slick is ablaze on the water's surface. The flames surround her, the heat licking at her flesh. He stands over her with his evil half-grin and laughs softly. "I told you, Tiffany, you'll never leave me," he says. The jealousy and rage burning in his eyes cut deep into her soul.

She screams, tries to duck under the water to escape the flames, but there's not enough room in the tub. The thick, black oil coats her face and hair. You have to get out, Tiffany, she tells herself. NOW!

He's still standing over her, blocking her escape. But she has to do something, anything, or she will be burned alive. She lunges, grabs his shirt, and pulls herself up and over the side of the tub in a split second, falling to the cold tile floor below. Small streams of the burning water are scattered haphazardly across her naked flesh. She panics. Desperately tries to smother the small infernos with her bare hand, but she can't get to all of them before she feels her skin start to burn. She pushes her oil-soaked hair away from her eyes and looks around the room. She sees a bath towel hanging next to the tub, *and with a single, forceful thrust, flings herself toward it. Her legs, slick with oil, slide across the floor as she reaches and latches on to the large cotton towel. She grips it firmly in her hand and then allows her weight to fall back to the floor. She hears the wooden rod snap as the towel is pulled free, the pieces falling next to her on the floor. She quickly wipes the cloth down her flesh, patting out the small flames as she goes.*

He laughs at her. "You stupid little bitch," he says through gritted, perfectly white teeth.

She is crying freely now. "Please, Paul, don't hurt me. I'm sorry. I won't leave you. I promise, I won't. Just don't hurt me. I won't tell anyone. Please," she sobs through watery eyes and trembling lips.

"It's too late, Tiffany." He pulls a large hunting knife from behind his back, the blade glimmering in the soft candlelight of the room.

She screams and tries to stand up, but slips on the slick tile, sending her crashing to her knees with a sharp thud that sends a river of pain up her thighs. She gasps for breath, her heart racing even faster now. She half-stumbles, half-crawls toward the bathroom doorway that leads to the second-floor hallway. She can still hear him laughing behind her.

"Go, Tiffany! Get away! Fast!" he taunts between vicious, sickening chuckles.

Her eyes are still burning from the few drops of oil that splashed into them. She can hear his footsteps behind her as she reaches the doorway and grasps the jamb. She pulls herself into the carpeted hallway and crawls to her left, toward the staircase that leads to the massive great room on the first floor. She peers through the wooden banister, staring down at the mansion's front door. It's massive, solid oak, with etched glass inserts along the top. And though it's so close that she could throw a rock and hit it from her perch on the balcony, at this moment, it seems miles away.

If she can just make it out of the house, she can run for help, and pray that she makes it. The closest neighbor is at least a quarter-mile away, but that's her only hope of rescue. There's no other option.

Just as she is about to lift herself from the floor and make a run for it, she feels her head snap back as he grasps a handful of her thick, wet hair. She screams out in agony. "Stop! Please!" He only pulls more forcefully, causing her torso to rise from the floor. She feels as if her hair will be ripped from her scalp at any moment. Then, in an instant, she feels the cold steel of the knife against her flesh, just under her right breast. "Noooo!" she screams.

He bends over and places his head next to the left side of her face, the smell of his minty breath wafting into her nostrils and temporarily overpowering the smell of burnt oil. She can feel his breath against her cheek, and it sends a torrent of cold chills over her body. "I told you I'd teach you a lesson if you ever tried to leave me," he whispers into her ear.

"Please don't hurt me, Paul," she begs again through trembling lips.

The blade slices through her flesh in a flash of pain as Paul swipes the knife backward. He releases her hair, and she falls to the carpet once more. She hears him laughing again. Her vision begins to blur, and the room starts to swim in front of her. Her right side is burning, and she makes the mistake of moving her hand to the wound. When she pulls it away, it's covered in blood, her hand a crimson glove.

Although a part of her wants to turn and face him, she dares not look back. Instead, she stretches her bloodied hand out in front of her and pulls herself forward, still hoping to reach the staircase and eventually, the front door. Then she puts her left hand forward and repeats the process. Keep moving, Tiffany, she tells herself.

As she continues to crawl, she hears his relentless pursuit behind her. He's just toying with me, she thinks. But she keeps moving, keeps struggling to escape. Her sobs are broken only by intermittent screams of pain as she draws closer to the top of the stairs. She knows he will never let her out of the house alive.

But she moves another foot.

He kicks her in her left thigh with his heavy hiking boot. She cries out, her bone feeling as if it has been shattered. He laughs again. "Go, Tiffany, go!" he taunts her. "Hurry up! Keep trying!"

She ignores his ridicule and continues crawling, the carpet fibers scratching and stinging as they invade the wound on her right ribcage. She glances back and sees a red trail marking her slow progress on the beige carpet. She's losing a lot of blood.

And she sees Paul's big, black boots only feet behind her. He's waiting. Playing. Having fun. She snaps her head forward again and pulls herself another foot or so. She's almost at the staircase; just a few more feet. Maybe if she can slide down the stairs on her belly, she can make it out the front door before he catches her.

But she knows that's not true.

He's just amusing himself, dragging out her punishment for as long as he wants. Part of her wishes it would just end . . . but deep down, she still has hope.

Just a flicker, but it's there.

She turns right at the end of the hallway and pulls herself down the wooden staircase that leads to the great room below, the sharp edges of the steps digging into her sliced ribcage. She rolls over, an involuntary reaction to the pain, and tumbles. Her arms and legs bang against the wall, the railing, the stairs. Then her head smacks against something hard, and she sees stars. She rolls and rolls, flashes of the McMillan mansion's ornate furnishings whipping past her eyes. She finally manages to get her arms in front of her to stop the out-of-control descent. She slides the last few feet on her stomach and bounces violently against the steps. She feels the wound on her right side tear even further, blood streaming down the hardwood.

As soon as she hits the floor, she begins to crawl toward the door. She moves as quickly as her broken body allows, but she knows it's much too slow. She hazards a quick glance behind her and sees Paul standing halfway down the staircase. Staring and smiling at her. His eyes are cold, void of any compassion. His muscular arms glisten with sweat in the soft light of the crystal chandelier hanging from the vaulted ceiling. He takes another step down, then another. He's in no particular hurry, knowing she is helpless to escape.

The sight of him moving toward her sends a burst of adrenaline through her body, and she begins crawling again. The front door is still so far away, but she keeps moving nonetheless, inches at a time.

The pain is almost unbearable, her left leg deeply bruised, if not broken, from Paul's boot, and her right side bleeding freely now where his knife had done its work.

"You'd better hurry, Tiffany! I'm coming!"

She hears his menacing laugh behind her again. And it's closer than before. She moves forward in a flurry of kicking legs and grasping arms, but her blood makes the hardwood slick, and she loses traction. She's almost to the foyer when she hears Paul quickly descend the remaining stairs and cross the floor toward her, his footsteps pounding a death knell.

She whimpers, the tears still flowing down her cheeks, and surges again toward the door. But before she moves even a foot, he's on her once more, grabbing her hair and snapping her head back.

She screams as he rolls her over and straddles her body, still gripping the bloody knife in his right hand. He runs his fingers along the side of the blade, smiling. "You know, Tiffany, I thought you would be different. I really thought you would be. I imagined us living together forever, but you ruined everything, didn't you?" He moves the edge of the blade over her abdomen until the sharp point just pierces the outer layers of skin below her left breast. A small trickle of blood appears at the tip of the knife.

"Please, stop," she whimpers.

He ignores her pleas and drags the blade down her abdomen, sinking the knife deeper into her flesh as he moves it toward her navel.

She screams.

But he doesn't stop.

She writhes and squirms beneath him as the blade slices, but can't free herself from his weight across her hips and legs. He cuts her all the way to her belly button, then stops and withdraws the bloody knifepoint. He shows it to her and smiles. "I told you you'd never leave me, Tiffany," he says, the wicked grin on his face again. He tosses the knife away, and she watches as it skids across the floor, scattering traces of her blood on the polished hardwood.

She feels the heavy weight on her legs vanish, and she turns her gaze away from the knife and back to Paul. He's standing over her now, straddling her body and unzipping his khaki pants. Oh, God, no, she thinks to herself. Another whimper involuntarily escapes her lips.

But she's done begging.

He drops his pants and underwear and kicks them away. As he starts to lower himself onto her, she sees her chance, her last hope of getting out of the house alive.

She cocks her right leg back toward her bleeding stomach and kicks out as forcefully as she can, striking Paul right between the legs. He gasps, bending over in pain, then falls onto her lower legs. He gags, trying not to vomit. "Damn you, you little bitch," he whispers between ragged breaths.

She kicks her legs frantically, freeing them from his body, and scoots away from the doubled-up figure on the floor. The one she had once thought could be the perfect man. But she had been wrong. So wrong.

She spots the knife lying on the floor only a few feet away. She rolls onto her knees and crawls as fast as she can. The pain is worse, and she feels lightheaded. She can almost reach the knife's handle when Paul grasps her left arm. She can feel his rapid breathing on her skin as he rests his head on her back. "It's going to be much worse for you now," he whispers. "You shouldn't have done that, Tiffany."

She doesn't hesitate. She swings her right arm backward, twisting her body simultaneously, and her elbow connects with Paul's ear. He's stunned. She spins around and gouges him in the eyes with her fingers. He jerks back, howling in pain. Free of him once more, she turns back toward the knife and crawls the last two feet. She grips the cold, black handle in her right hand, then pivots to face her attacker. He's coming toward her again, his eyes red and watering profusely. "Stop!" she yells, but he keeps creeping toward her on his hands and knees. He slips in her blood and falls to the floor, but quickly rises again. "Don't come any closer, Paul!" she yells. He laughs softly, his face splotched with her blood. His brown hair and gray eyes—the same features she had once found attractive—now belong to a monster. He crawls another few inches toward her. "Stop!" she warns again, her hand holding the knife out in front of her and trembling.

But he keeps coming.

She strikes out with the blade.

The cold steel hits home and sinks deeply into his neck. He screams, his eyes wide with shock; then, a few seconds later, his screams are replaced by the low gurgling sound of a man choking on his own blood.

She kicks him in the chest, sending him backward onto the hardwood, and pulling the knife free of his neck. She hears his head crack against the floor, his lower legs pinned beneath his own body.

Her heart pounds, her breathing is rapid and shallow, and a mixture of sweat and blood runs down her palm, causing the knife blade to slip in her hand and fall to the floor. Paul lies in front of her, gurgling, spitting blood from his mouth. A large pool begins to form under his neck.

He begins to speak. "You'll . . ." He coughs, then spits another stream of blood from his mouth. He inhales deeply. "You'll never be free, Tiffany . . . never."

The pent-up fear she has dealt with the last six months boils over inside her, and she screams out in a moment of sheer rage, tears streaming down her face. She feels herself palm the knife handle once more, lunge toward Paul, and drive the blade deep into his heart. His eyes go wide, the evil smile frozen on his face. He gurgles three more times, then falls silent.

She glares down at him. She can't believe what has just happened. After a few seconds, she releases the knife and crawls away, but collapses after only a few feet, exhausted.

She lies on her back, the cool hardwood against her bare skin, staring vacantly at the cathedral ceiling above her. Gasping for air.

Then, as the adrenaline begins to leave her body, she sobs uncontrollably.

"Tiff . . . Tiff!"

Tiffany felt someone shaking her arm.

"Tiffany! Are you all right?" she heard Katie ask, although her voice seemed to emanate from a distant tunnel.

Tiffany opened her eyes and found herself staring at a case of large hunting knives. It took several seconds for her to regain her composure, to remember where she was. Finally, she replied, "Yeah . . . yes, I'm fine," turning her gaze from the knives, to her friend standing next to her.

Katie's brow was furrowed, worry in her normally happy blue eyes. She wiped her blonde hair away from her face. "Are you sure everything's okay?" she asked again.

Tiffany looked away from Katie and toward the young clerk behind the glass counter. His eyes were wide, a bewildered look on his face. "I'm fine. Sorry about that," she replied.

Katie placed her arm around Tiffany's shoulders. "Maybe we'll come back later," she said to the pale clerk. "Sorry."

The clerk didn't respond as Katie led Tiffany out of the store and into the mall, pushing Missy in a stroller. Once they were well away from the storefront, Katie grabbed Tiffany by the arm and said, "Tiffany, what in the world is going on?"

"Nothing, I'm fine," Tiffany replied.

"I don't believe you," Katie said bluntly. "Look, I've been your friend long enough to know when something is bothering you . . . and when you're lying."

Katie's piercing blue eyes might as well have been truth serum. Tiffany knew there was no use trying to hide what she had been going through from Katie any longer. "Can we go somewhere and talk?" she asked, her voice cracking.

Katie let out a sigh of relief. "Sure," she said. "You feel like grabbing lunch?"

Tiffany nodded her head slightly.

As they headed toward the food court, Tiffany was angry with herself. She had tried so hard to avoid another incident, but her lack of self-control had allowed it to happen again. She felt the numbness of humiliation flow through her body.

8

Tiffany stretched her legs out as she pulled back on the recliner handle. The day had been a disaster. What was supposed to have been a fun day of shopping with her best friend, and one she had been looking forward to all week, had been marred by another flashback of Paul.

They had been shopping for a birthday present for Cody, but at the sight of the shiny steel knife blades, she had once again been thrust into the past. Afterward, Katie had forced her to come clean about everything. Once she had explained what had been going on, Katie assured her that everything would be fine, told her that experiencing vivid memories was a normal reaction for someone who had been through such a traumatic experience, even years later.

It sure didn't feel normal, though.

Katie had even offered to go with her to counseling, but she had refused. The last thing she wanted to do was spend more time talking about Paul—to anyone.

Tiffany wondered if she would ever truly be free of Paul. Or would his last words haunt her forever? The

fear that she would never be normal again made her sick
to her stomach.

She picked up the glass of wine she had poured for
herself and took a long sip, her mind reeling. She set the
glass back down on the small wooden table next to the
chair, her gun staring back at her. Maybe Paul had been
right all along. Maybe she would never be able to escape
him or his powerful family.

The McMillan family owned the largest lumber
company in Georgia. Paul's great-great-grandfather had
started it in the late 1800s, and the family had amassed
a fortune through the years. Old money. Not the new
kind that might come with winning the lottery or selling
a start-up Internet business. No, this was the kind of
money that bought lots of power and influence. The Mc-
Millan family had important friends in virtually every
city in the state and more than a few in Washington, too.

After Paul's death, Tiffany was certain she would be
locked away for life—if not worse—and she probably
would've been if it hadn't been for Sheriff Lansing. He
had known Paul wasn't the squeaky clean young man
his family portrayed him to be. The sheriff shared with
Tiffany that Paul had been in and out of trouble constantly as a teenager for minor drug offenses, breaking
and entering, and assault. The sheriff had tried to lock
him up on several occasions, but the McMillan money
and influence had always triumphed. That was all news
to Tiffany, but she was relieved to know that someone
else knew the truth about Paul.

So when Paul had ended up dead on the floor of
the family mansion, Tiffany had found an unexpected
ally in Sheriff Lansing. He believed her story, and his investigation had determined the killing was self-defense.
Justifiable homicide was the legal term for it, Tiffany had

learned. The sheriff had somehow convinced the district attorney not to file charges against her, which couldn't have been an easy task, given the enormous pressure the family had placed on the county to bring Tiffany to justice. She still wasn't sure how he had managed to pull that off.

She took another sip of wine and leaned her head back, closing her eyes. She was tired—tired of thinking, tired of everything.

At least the coffee mug was still in its place in the cupboard when she returned home from her shopping trip. She was thankful for that. She had convinced herself earlier that she had simply forgotten to put the mug away the day before, but now, after experiencing another vivid memory of Paul, she wasn't so sure. It was as if her subconscious was trying to warn her of something. Of what, she wasn't sure, but just the thought chilled her to her core.

She pulled the wool blanket she always kept on the recliner up to her chin and took another sip from her glass. She looked at the revolver again. Sitting next to the lamp, the hunk of stainless steel looked so innocent. But Tiffany knew that, with one pull of the trigger, it would become a very effective killing machine.

And she was willing to pull the trigger, if it came down to it.

She stared out the front window toward the branches of the big oak in front of her cabin. The evening sky was laden with thick, billowing gray clouds, darkness fast approaching. The wind had picked up, whipping the limbs of the giant tree back and forth. A storm appeared to be brewing, and she wondered if that was an omen for her own life.

She sank back into the chair completely, letting her tensed muscles finally relax. She closed her eyes and took a deep, cleansing breath. She was just being paranoid, she told herself. Paul was gone, and his family's attempts to see her doing twenty-five to life in state prison had failed.

Everything will be fine, Tiffany.

As soon as the thought entered her mind, she knew she didn't believe a word of it. As much as she wanted to believe it, she couldn't. For some reason, everything didn't seem fine. Something was wrong—she just couldn't put her finger on what it was.

She had the urge to pick up the phone and call Jackson to come over, but what would he think? That she was just an over-imaginative female who needed him to protect her? She didn't want him to see her like that because that wasn't who she was. She had proved that ten years ago. Besides, she would see Jackson tomorrow for dinner, and she could talk to him about what had been going on then, if she still felt it was necessary.

Things would be better tomorrow. All she needed was a good night's sleep.

She was just about to doze off when she heard a loud bang from the hallway. It sounded like someone had dropped the toilet lid, letting it free-fall onto the commode. Tiffany gasped. Her heart pounded against her ribs. She grabbed the revolver on the table next to her. "Hello?" she yelled. "Is someone there?" Her mouth was dry, and she swallowed hard.

Maybe it was nothing.

Then she heard another noise but couldn't tell what it was this time. She eased out of the recliner and pushed the gun out in front of her. She pulled the hammer back, cocking it. "I've got a gun!" she yelled, her voice cracking under her mounting anxiety. Tension and fear coursed through her body, her hands shaking wildly as she struggled to hold the gun steady.

She began to walk slowly out of the small living room and toward the hallway that led to her bedroom and the bathroom. She peered across the open area into the kitchen and looked out the small window above the sink. She saw nothing unusual.

The wind picked up again, and she heard a loud thud outside, behind the cabin. *Just a falling tree limb, Tiffany.* She took another step closer to the hallway on her left. Her heart was racing, her breathing shallow and rapid. Her palms were sweating, making the wooden grip slick and difficult to hold steady.

She paused just shy of the dividing line between the living room and the kitchen, not quite able to see down the hallway on her left. She drew in a deep breath and held it, then swung around the corner, sighting her weapon down the length of the darkened passage.

It was empty.

She exhaled sharply, relieved to see there was no one in the hallway. But the sound had come from the bathroom, she was sure of it. She looked down the right side of the hall and could see the bathroom door standing ajar. She thought she had closed it when she finished her shower just a half hour ago, but wasn't certain.

She raised her left hand to the wall and flipped the light switch. Soft light from the single forty-watt bulb flooded the short hallway. She scanned the area once more, searching for anything suspicious or out of place, but saw nothing. Her bedroom door, halfway down the hall on the left, was still closed, as was normal.

She took a couple of hesitant steps forward, both hands now back on the revolver, though still shaking badly. She looked toward the bathroom door again, her heart rate increasing with each step. A gust of wind blew across the roof of the old cabin, sending an eerie, swooshing echo down the hallway.

She paused and tried to steady the gun in her hands. But when that proved futile, she steeled her nerves as best she could and traveled the few remaining feet to the bathroom door. She stopped and listened.

Nothing but the sound of the wind whipping through the trees outside.

The door was open only a few inches. She tried to peer inside, but the light was off, and all she could see was a blanket of darkness.

She spun, moving quickly to the far side of the door, adjacent to the hinges, and placed her back against the wall. She pulled the gun close to her body, holding it directly in front of her face with the barrel pointed toward the ceiling, just as she had seen in numerous movies and in overly dramatic television shows.

Part of her wanted to laugh, convinced she was just being paranoid, memories of Paul making her overly sensitive to every little noise, every strange bump in the night. But a greater part of her was scared and anxious about what could be waiting inside the bathroom.

She cut her eyes to the left, staring at the white wooden door, then down to the brass doorknob. She thought perhaps she should retreat to the living room and call for the resort security guard, but then decided against that. What would they think of her? That she was just a weak city girl who freaked out every time the wind blew?

She took another deep breath and hardened herself for what she had to do.

She kicked the door open with her left leg and simultaneously pivoted her body in front of the opening, extending the revolver the full length of her arms in one fluid motion. In the next instant, she toggled the light switch up with her right elbow, coating the small room in light.

It was empty.

She moved the gun from left to right, sweeping the room, waiting for someone to jump out at her. The combination tub and shower was to her left, but the blue nylon curtain was closed.

Is he in the tub, hiding behind the shower curtain?

Without hesitating, she shifted the gun to her right hand and flung the curtain back with her left. She gasped, expecting to have to fire the shaking weapon in her hand, but instead of finding herself face-to-face with an intruder, the sights of the revolver were aimed directly at the dripping faucet. The faucet had leaked ever since she had moved into the cabin, so there was nothing unusual about that. She immediately turned her gaze forward, where the toilet and sink sat opposite each other.

The small window on the far wall was open, the stiff breeze from the approaching storm blowing the blue cotton curtains in like a wind-rippled flag. She stepped forward and pushed them away. She stared outside, looking for anything out of the ordinary, but saw only the quiet forest that surrounded the back and sides of her cabin. She reached up and pulled hard on the window frame, the decades-old wood halting and rasping as it moved downward. She latched the single metal tab at the top and exhaled deeply.

She racked her brain, trying to remember if the window had been open when she showered. She thought it had been closed, but she did open it occasionally, to let fresh air into the bathroom, so she wasn't positive.

She looked down at the toilet seat. The lid was down. She couldn't recall if she had left it up or down. But her first thought when she had heard the sound earlier had been that the toilet lid had been dropped. Perhaps a gust of wind from outside had hit the already teetering lid and forced it closed. She wasn't convinced that was what had happened, but the only other explanation was that someone had been inside her cabin, and she could *not* let her mind go there.

It must've been the wind.

It had to have been. That was the only logical explanation.

She sighed. Her arms felt weak from the anxiety rush of the last few minutes, and she lowered the gun to her side. Was she going crazy? Was everything she had experienced the last couple of days just some kind of warped figment of an overactive imagination? Had there ever even *been* a noise from the bathroom, or had it just been another trick of her overwrought mind?

She walked out of the bathroom, turned off the light, and closed the door securely behind her. She walked into her bedroom and, once again, found nothing. She even checked the small closet and under her queen-size bed. Again, nothing.

She returned to the living room, picked up the wine glass, and headed for the kitchen sink. She was exhausted. All she wanted to do was crawl into bed and sleep.

She set the revolver down on the kitchen counter, then turned the faucet on and washed the glass. After drying it with a towel, she put it away in the cabinet.

She picked the gun up, then double-checked the sink. It was empty.

The sound of a branch breaking outside the window.

Tiffany snapped her head up and peered into the darkness, her heart racing.

Standing outside her window, just a few yards away, was a man, his hair whipping about in the stiffening breeze.

She couldn't make out his face, but she could tell he was staring at her.

And that he had a mustache.

It looked like . . .

No, it couldn't be.

The man stepped forward, into the circle of light spilling from the kitchen window.

She screamed.

It was.

His mouth turned up in an evil grin.

The Smith & Wesson slipped from her trembling hand and crashed onto the linoleum floor. But she didn't even hear it. She was frozen with fear.

She slammed her eyes closed and grasped the edge of the sink for support.

This isn't real, Tiffany. It's just a dream.

She didn't want to look again.

But she had to.

She slowly opened her eyes. She scanned to the left, then the right, her pupils darting back and forth.

Searching.

He was gone.

Had he ever really been there?

9

Tiffany stared out the windshield of the Ford pickup. The cloudy sky was gunmetal gray, but the autumn leaves were even more vibrant this afternoon than they had been the day before, providing a mosaic of color on an otherwise dreary day.

She rolled her window down as they drove onto Main Street in Sylva, the crisp air blowing in her face and lashing at her auburn hair. She looked at the quaint shops that lined both sides of the street: a hair salon on the right, a jewelry store on the left, and a small bookstore where a young man and an attractive blonde woman sat outside on a wooden bench, talking over cups of coffee. She took a deep breath and closed her eyes. Everything was going to be okay.

She glanced over toward the driver's seat and looked at Jackson. He turned his head and smiled at her. She smiled back, admiring his jet black hair and strong facial features. He was in excellent physical shape, his arms and legs toned by miles of hiking in the North Carolina and Tennessee backcountry. When she was growing up in Georgia, she would never have dreamed she would fall in love with a park ranger. She had envisioned marrying a doctor or a lawyer. And yet here she was, riding down the center of a small mountain town in a Ford pickup truck with Jackson beside her. But she wouldn't have traded him for the richest, most successful doctor in all of Georgia.

She turned her gaze back out the front window and watched as they traveled off Main Street and toward the outskirts of town. She wished she could be all that Jackson wanted in a woman. Wished she could let go of her past and just live in the moment. She wanted to spend the rest of her life with Jackson, she was sure of that, but how could she if Paul kept creeping back into her mind?

Jackson deserved better.

She turned her head to the right once more, letting the cool air from the open window blow against her face. She was so drained, and she hoped the fresh air would invigorate her before dinner. She allowed her eyelids to close again, and she felt as if she could drift off to sleep at any second, secure and protected with Jackson by her side.

She hadn't slept at all last night, afraid to go to sleep alone in the cabin. She had spent the whole night locked in her room, cuddled on her bed and grasping the revolver. She had managed to take a short nap during the afternoon, convinced that if someone was trying to harm her, they would be less likely to do it in broad daylight.

As she had lain on her bed, dark thoughts raced through her mind. She had even contemplated the fact that Paul was somehow still alive. Had she really seen him outside her window? Or, as she feared might be the case, was she going insane?

She hadn't seen Paul's body after the police arrived at the mansion. Nor had she talked to his family or attended the funeral, for obvious reasons. Had he somehow survived and was now returning, after ten years, to exact his revenge? She knew that was crazy, but inside, she felt as if her world was falling apart.

Tiffany felt the truck slow and looked up to see them pulling into the parking lot at DeVito's. It was full of vehicles, from Chevys to Beemers. Sylva was a mountain town, after all, and DeVito's was the closest thing the residents here had to five-star dining. The stucco building sat on a hill overlooking the town and the surrounding mountains. The restaurant faced west, and the setting sun had just peeked through a small break in the low cloud deck, the fire-orange sphere beaming as it sank below the mountaintops. Streetlights from the town below flickered in the twilight, and she smiled at the sight. It was beautiful. She was looking forward to a relaxing dinner with Jackson, away from the recent turmoil that had invaded her life.

Tiffany rolled the window up as Jackson turned off the engine.

He placed his hand gently on her thigh. "Wait just a second." He hopped out of the truck, jogged to her door, opened it, and offered her his hand. She took his hand and stepped out, letting her black cocktail dress fall to her knees. "Thank you, Jackson," she said.

"You look magnificent," he said.

Tiffany smiled and looked up at him, grasping her slim, black purse in her right hand. He was dressed in tan slacks, a white shirt, navy tie, and a gray sport coat. "You're not looking too bad yourself," she replied.

Jackson laughed softly. "Well, thank you." He extended his arm to Tiffany.

She stepped forward and wrapped her arm in his, then walked with him toward the restaurant. The outside of the building was highlighted with soft light from old kerosene lanterns that had been converted to electricity. Several large windows overlooked the mountain vista. A green tile roof and matching window shutters complemented the sandstone color of the stucco exterior.

The two followed the concrete path to the heavy, double oak doors. Jackson grasped the handle and pulled the door open. "After you," he said, smiling.

Tiffany released his arm and walked ahead of him. "Thank you." She looked toward the hostess station and smiled at the young lady standing behind the wooden lectern.

Jackson moved to Tiffany's side, placing his hand on the small of her back, and said to the young brunette, "We have a reservation for two under the name Jackson Hart."

The hostess tapped the computer screen in front of her a couple of times, then looked up and smiled. "Right this way, please."

Tiffany followed the young lady into the main dining room; she felt Jackson take her hand as he walked beside her. Just that simple act filled her with comfort and hope. Crystal chandeliers hung from the ceiling, casting yellow light on the white cotton cloths covering the round tables. They passed a young couple speaking softly, holding hands and laughing in the glow from the candle on their table; a man and woman who appeared to have their hands full keeping three boisterous children on their best behavior; and an elderly couple who were obviously still in love after decades together. Tiffany looked up at Jackson and smiled. He winked at her and put his arm around her shoulders.

"Here you are," the hostess said, motioning with her hand toward a small round table in the back corner of the restaurant. Tiffany looked out the large window just beyond the table. It afforded a panoramic view of the rapidly darkening Smoky Mountains. "That's gorgeous," she said softly.

"I thought you would like it," Jackson said as he let his hand glide down the center of her back. "These are for you, too." He motioned toward the center of the table, and Tiffany looked down. The white tablecloth perfectly framed the large crystal vase filled with red and white tulips. Two tall white candles sat on either side of the vase, flickering in the low light of the restaurant.

"Oh, Jackson, they're beautiful."

"Good, I'm glad you approve." He smiled at her and then pulled her chair away from the table.

"Thank you," Tiffany said as she removed her hand-woven pashmina jacket and hung it off the back of the chair.

While Jackson was taking his seat, Tiffany gazed out the window. The sky was almost black now, and she looked into the valley below. The distant lights of Sylva were even brighter than when they had first arrived, casting an amber glow onto the cloud-laden sky.

Unexpectedly, her thoughts turned back to Paul. Why would they intrude now? She pushed them out of her head, then sighed softly to herself.

"Is something wrong?" Jackson asked.

She snapped her head away from the window, disconcerted that Jackson had seen her angst. Tiffany cleared her expression. "No, nothing. Sorry, I was just enjoying the view."

"Breathtaking, isn't it?"

Tiffany smiled and looked out the window again. "Yes, it is," she whispered, afraid that Jackson sensed something was not quite right with her. She quickly turned her attention back to him. He had obviously gone to a lot of trouble to plan a special dinner for her, and the least she could do was be a pleasant companion. A waiter walked to the table, filled their tumblers with ice water, and placed two menus, a bottle of Pinot Grigio, and two wine glasses on the table.

"I hope you like the wine," Jackson said. "I ordered it when I made the reservation." He laughed softly as he poured them each a glass. "I'm not much of a wine drinker myself, but it comes highly recommended by the teenager who answered the phone."

Tiffany forced a friendly chuckle at his joke, then grasped the tumbler of ice water and took a small drink. As she set the glass back down, she noticed her hand was trembling. Her nerves were still on edge, and she hoped Jackson had not noticed. "Thank you for this, Jackson," she said with the best smile she could manage.

"I don't get to take you out to a nice restaurant very often, so I thought we could make a special evening of it." He smiled, picked up his menu, and began perusing the dinner options.

Tiffany opened her menu as well and looked down, feigning deep concentration but, in reality, she couldn't focus at all. Even the beautiful vase of tulips Jackson had arranged for her reminded her of Paul. It wasn't so much the tulips, but the absence of the customary romantic flower, the red rose.

Jackson had made the innocent mistake of bringing her red roses on their first date. He had been able to tell by her timid reaction that she didn't like them. Months later, after they had become intimate, she had explained to Jackson that Paul used to bring her red roses after he had roughed her up. And that, sometimes, he would even sneak into her apartment and leave a single red rose on her pillowcase as a sign of his repentance.

Now, she hated roses.

As she stared across the table at the bouquet of tulips, she realized that part of her, on this particular night at least, resented the fact that she didn't like roses anymore.

And that just made her think of Paul even more.

Jackson stared over the top of his menu at Tiffany. The soft candlelight on her face made her even more lovely, if that were even possible. She was the most beautiful woman he had ever seen, much less dated. She had arranged her thick auburn hair in a French twist, and the string of pearls he had given her for Christmas hung gracefully around her neck. The black cocktail dress she wore was sleeveless, exposing her perfectly-toned arms. The fabric hugged her slim figure, the neckline plunging to reveal her cleavage, and Jackson stared a little longer than he probably should have while Tiffany gazed out the window. But he just couldn't help himself. She was simply gorgeous.

He took his left hand from the table and moved it down to his thigh. He felt the lump in his pocket formed by the ring box. His hand was sweating like a teenager's on prom night, and he could feel his heart rate increase as he touched the box. He had rehearsed this over and over in his mind. He would ask her right after their meal arrived. He was fairly confident she would say yes, but he was still nervous.

He wiped his hand on his pant leg and returned it to the table. He took a deep breath and tried to calm himself, then looked down at his menu again. "So what're you going to have, Tiff?" he asked. He waited for a response, but when none came, he looked up from the menu toward Tiffany. She was peering out the window again. "Babe, what're you going to have?" he asked for a second time.

Still nothing.

Jackson studied her. She seemed to be staring into empty space, oblivious to her surroundings and his presence. He slid his hand across the table and placed it on top of hers. She still didn't move or acknowledge him. Instead, she just kept looking out the window. And he thought she looked . . . different. Almost dazed. He shook her hand gently and said, "Tiffany," this time a little louder than before.

She jumped at his voice, then quickly turned her face toward him. She looked frightened, her eyes distant.

"Is everything all right?" he whispered, not wanting to embarrass her by alerting any of the other patrons.

"What?" she asked, a puzzled look on her face.

"Is everything okay?" he repeated.

"Yes . . . yes, everything's fine. I'm really sorry. I didn't hear you." She smiled and picked up her water glass.

She didn't look fine to Jackson. She looked worried and scared. He watched as she took a sip of water, then placed the glass back on the table. Her hand was trembling. "You sure?" he asked, his hand still covering hers.

She smiled at him, but to Jackson, it looked forced, as if her life depended on executing a perfectly believable smile.

"Yes, I'm fine," she persisted.

Jackson removed his hand from hers. "Okay." He stared down at his menu, worried about Tiffany, not sure what was going on.

"I think I'll have the eggplant parmesan," he heard Tiffany say, a hint of cheerfulness in her voice again.

He looked up from his menu. She was smiling, and it didn't look forced this time. He smiled back. "Sounds good. I think I'll go with the spaghetti and meatballs." He folded the menu and placed it on the table. Tiffany was taking a sip of the wine. "How's the wine?" he asked.

"Good," she replied. "You're teenage sommelier did a great job." She laughed and set the wine glass back on the table. Her hands didn't shake this time.

Jackson breathed a sigh of relief. He had planned this night for months, and he wanted it to be perfect. He had the sudden urge to pull the ring out right then and propose, but forced himself to wait. He had planned the perfect speech, and he didn't want to screw it up by changing things mid-game.

After the waiter returned and took their orders, Jackson stared at Tiffany as they ate their salads. He just couldn't help looking at her; as enjoyable as her beauty was, though, it only served to increase his anxiety. His hands were sweating again, and he found himself having to stop eating and dry them on his pants every other minute or so. *What if she says no? But that's not going to happen. Think positive, Jackson,* he told himself as he attempted to mentally prepare for the big moment.

He tried to enjoy his salad and paused to take a small drink of wine occasionally, but now his mind was reeling, trying to remember the speech he had crafted so carefully. Suddenly, it seemed to have been wiped from his memory. He couldn't even remember the opening lines. He started to panic, almost choking on a piece of lettuce. He should have written it down. No, that would have been awkward. He imagined himself pulling out a folded piece of paper and reading to Tiffany while he dragged the ring out of his pocket. That wouldn't go well.

Dammit, Jackson! What is WRONG with you? What were you going to say?

He looked up when he saw the waiter approaching, carrying a large tray at shoulder height. This was it. His heart began to race, his palms sweating even worse than before. He still couldn't remember even the first word of his speech. He would just have to wing it and hope for the best. He took a deep breath, tried to smile at the waiter, but was sure his face was betraying the anxiety he was feeling in the pit of his stomach.

"Thank you," Jackson said as the waiter placed the two plates of food down on the table. After determining they needed nothing else, the waiter returned to the kitchen. He and Tiffany were alone now, staring at each other across two dishes of Italian food and a bouquet of tulips.

He suddenly felt sick to his stomach.

He hadn't expected to be this nervous, but he had also never proposed to a woman before. The thought that he would've known what to expect seemed a little absurd to him now. He took another deep breath, trying to calm his nerves, and said a silent prayer he wouldn't mess it up.

He picked up his fork from the linen napkin as though preparing to eat, while simultaneously slipping his left hand into his pocket and palming the velour-covered box. "Tiffany," he said, fighting to keep his voice from cracking.

She looked up from her eggplant parmesan. "Yes?"

He froze.

His tongue wouldn't move. It felt three times its normal size, refusing to function normally. He reached for the tumbler of ice water and took a long gulp, trying to think of something to say and praying his paralysis would end. Finally, he removed the glass from his lips and said, "Do you like the tulips?"

What a stupid, idiotic thing to say, Jackson!

The smile on Tiffany's face disappeared, and she lowered her eyes to her dinner plate. "Yes . . . yes, they're lovely, Jackson."

You idiot! He was going to do it. He had to make his move now. "Tiffany, I . . . I—"

A tear rolled down her cheek. Had he said something wrong? Did she know he was planning on proposing tonight? That, for whatever reason, she couldn't say yes? "Tiffany, is everything okay? Would you like to leave?" he asked, his voice shaking slightly.

She didn't answer. Instead, she picked up her napkin and dried her eyes. Then she began to sob into it. "I'm . . . I'm sorry, Jackson. I can't do this right now," she said through the linen cloth that now covered the lower part of her face. She slowly scooted her chair back from the table, stood up, and headed for the restroom.

Jackson's heart sank in his chest. He didn't need to hear anything else—her body language told him everything he needed to know.

Her answer was a resounding *NO*.

His fingers slipped off the small black box in his pocket.

10

Tiffany glanced back over her shoulder as she stepped inside her cabin. Jackson was backing his pickup truck out of the gravel driveway. She waved goodbye with a small motion of her hand, but she doubted he saw it. She eased the front door closed and leaned against it. She hung her head and sighed, still grasping the brass doorknob in her right palm.

She felt horrible.

The evening couldn't have gone worse. She had ruined the dinner that Jackson had obviously worked hard to plan. She had thought she would be able to forget everything that had been going on and just have a nice, relaxing meal with him; she'd hoped it would help clear her mind and get past the memories that had been torturing her.

But she had been wrong.

Another vivid memory of Paul had flooded her mind while she was staring out the window at the restaurant. She had tried to recover, to make everything appear normal, but failed miserably when Jackson commented on the tulips, bringing them to her attention for the second time.

She had apologized for her behavior several times during the quiet, awkward ride back to the cabin, assuring Jackson he hadn't done or said anything wrong. She had lied and told him that she was just stressed out, worried she would lose her job after the autumn tourists left the resort.

As much as she wanted to, she couldn't tell him the truth.

She certainly didn't want him to know she had been experiencing flashbacks of Paul and chasing down scary noises in her cabin while holding a trembling .38 revolver in front of her. Or that she had seen someone standing outside her window one second who vanished the next. Jackson would think she was losing her mind, or was possibly already past crazy and now on the brink of total insanity.

She wondered if he would be right.

Maybe she was never meant to be happy. Maybe that was the price she would have to pay for taking a man's life. Paul's final words rang inside her head once more.

Part of her wished she hadn't insisted she was fine when Jackson asked several times, that she had, instead, invited him to spend the night. At least she would've had someone to hold her and tell her everything was going to be okay. Even if she could no longer believe it herself.

She sighed, engaged the deadbolt, and pushed away from the front door. She dropped her purse, then pulled the pair of black heels off her sore feet and tossed them into the corner next to her backpack. Her muscles ached, and her eyelids felt like they were made of lead.

She hadn't had a solid night's sleep in days, and it was taking its toll on her, both physically and mentally.

She took her hair down and unzipped the back of her dress as she walked toward her bedroom. As she shimmied out of the dress and hung it in the closet, all she was thinking about was taking a hot shower, making herself a cup of warm chamomile tea, and hopefully getting some sleep. She was supposed to be at work in the morning, but she was so tired, she decided she wouldn't set an alarm. She hoped she would sleep until noon. If she overslept, she would apologize to her boss and beg his forgiveness, but right now, she just didn't care.

She opened the bottom drawer of her dresser and pulled out a pair of pink cotton pajamas. When she straightened up, she saw herself in the mirror that hung above the oak dresser. She looked half-dead. Bags hung under her eyes, the makeup no longer concealing the utter exhaustion that was dragging her down. And her face looked gaunt, the stress having wiped away the fresh countenance she was accustomed to seeing.

She turned from the mirror at once, not wanting to see the person she no longer knew. She had thought that her past was behind her, that she had left it all in Georgia when she moved to North Carolina and accepted the job at the resort. But the last few days had proven her wrong.

Very wrong.

She took a large blue towel and washcloth from the hall closet. She flipped the light on in the bathroom, then turned the water in the shower to almost scalding. Soon the tiny room was full of steam, the old cabin lacking an exhaust fan, but tonight, she was thankful for that. She took a deep breath of the warm, humid air and stepped inside the shower, letting the hot water flow over her body and the steam relax her tense muscles.

By the time she turned the water off, things seemed much better. Instead of feeling like a knot in the middle of a rope, being pulled taut at both ends, she was now relaxed. She dressed in the pajamas, the soft cotton comforting and smooth against her skin. She wrapped her hair in the towel, then walked to the kitchen to make a cup of tea. Chamomile always made her sleepy, and she hoped its sedative properties would overcome any impending nightmares.

She heated a large mug of tap water in the microwave, then dropped the tea bag into the steaming liquid. While she waited for it to steep, she walked into the living room and double-checked the deadbolt on the front door. It was secure, which she already knew was the case, as she remembered locking it after she waved goodbye to Jackson. But she also knew she wouldn't rest easy unless she checked it again, and the one thing she wanted to do on this night, more than anything, was to rest easy. Tomorrow, she would call Jackson and apologize again. Maybe she would even tell him what she had been going through. She should've been more open with him about her former life, but she had thought if she didn't talk about it, it would just stay where it belonged—in the past.

On her way back to the kitchen, she flipped the living room light off, enveloping the front of her cabin in darkness. She smiled to herself, still thinking about Jackson. He was a good man—a very good man—and she wished again that she had invited him to spend the night. But she had been so upset after dinner, had felt so horrible about ruining their evening, that she had doubted he would even say yes. As she removed the tea bag, she laughed softy. Of course he would have stayed . . . he was a man.

She selected a new paperback romance from the small bookcase that stood behind her unimpressive dining table—she found she needed yet another happy ending—and walked into her bedroom, taking a sip of the tea as she turned the light on.

The paperback fell from her hands first, then the cup of hot tea, splashing on her bare feet and spilling over the novel.

She gasped. Then screamed.

A single red rose lay on her pillow.

11

Jackson took a long swig of his Coors and stared at the popcorn ceiling above his bed. He could hear Twentymile Creek flowing down the mountain just past his backyard, the gurgling and splashing water creating a soft, persistent roar in his ears. The dull ceiling over his head was a perfect complement to the drab brown paint on the walls of the small room. It felt somewhat claustrophobic, but the depressing room matched his feelings exactly, so, for the moment at least, it was the perfect place to be.

The window next to his bed was open, and the cool night air blew into his bedroom as a stiff autumn breeze moved through the mountains. He was dressed only in his underwear, but wasn't cold at all, his body heated by frustration, worry, and more than a little anger.

He turned his head to the left and stared at the small black box that held Tiffany's ring, sitting atop the wooden dresser on the opposite side of the room. He took another drink, then gazed back at the ceiling, trying to figure out what in the hell had gone so wrong at dinner earlier.

He didn't have a clue.

Had he said or done something wrong? He didn't think so. But if it wasn't that, then there was only one other reasonable explanation, and he bristled at that thought. Despite his promise, Cody must have told Katie about the impending proposal, who then relayed the message to Tiffany.

And Tiffany simply did not want to marry him.

He took another drink of beer and looked out the window to his right. He would often stare up at the star-filled sky from his pillow, although on this night, all the stars were hidden behind a thick cover of clouds. He loved living here, away from city lights that would have drowned out the beauty of the night sky with a tawny haze of sodium lights and neon signs. He had hoped to share his modest home with Tiffany, but he now knew she didn't feel the same about him.

It was obvious by the awkward silence during the drive back from the restaurant that Tiffany wasn't telling the truth. She wasn't worried about losing her job. She was lying to protect his feelings, which didn't surprise Jackson at all. Tiffany was too nice a woman to hurt him.

At first, he had been furious at Cody for running his mouth, but after he cooled down a bit, Jackson realized it was probably better that things had worked out the way they had. It was embarrassing to leave the restaurant in the middle of the meal, but it would have been doubly so if he had gotten down on one knee in the middle of the crowded room, only to be rejected. At least this way, it had been easier for both of them. Tiffany hadn't been forced to tell him no to his face, and he had been spared total humiliation.

He sighed, turned his head, and stared at the ring again. It was over. His plans for the future, of having a family with Tiffany, had been crushed under the weight of whatever, or whoever, was competing with him in her mind.

How could he have been so stupid in the first place? What made him think a woman like Tiffany would want to spend the rest of her life with a park ranger? She deserved more.

Much more.

He would never be able to give her a fancy house or a healthy bank account, something that, with her looks and personality, she could have for the asking. But he hadn't thought she was that type of woman.

Maybe he had been wrong about her.

But as soon as the thought entered his mind, he dismissed it as ridiculous. If there was one thing being a park ranger had taught him, it was how to sniff out phonies and liars.

And Tiffany was no phony.

No, he hadn't been wrong about her, he decided. She was a good and decent person, not motivated by greed or ambition. And he thought that she really cared for him, which left him without a satisfactory explanation as to why she didn't want to marry him.

Maybe she just wasn't ready.

Tiffany was only the second woman that Jackson had ever been serious about. The first had been his high school sweetheart, Amanda. After high school, they had attended the University of Wisconsin in Madison together, and planned to marry after graduation. But at the beginning of their junior year at the university, Amanda had told Jackson she didn't love him anymore, dropped out of school, and ran away with another guy.

Amanda and her new boyfriend moved to Texas, and he never heard from her again.

Jackson had been devastated by the loss, certain he would never find another woman who fit him like Amanda had. After graduation, he completed the Ranger Training Program and began his career with the U.S. Park Service. He eventually began to date again, but just as he expected, never found anyone he loved like he had Amanda.

That is, not until he met Tiffany. And now, it was happening all over again. She had left him, too.

His thoughts turned to the first time he saw her. It was at the Mountain View Resort Marina. He had just finished an initial search for Cody and was surprised to see two attractive women waiting for him as he pulled his boat back to the dock.

Tiffany had confronted him right away, accused him of not doing enough to find Cody, and even though her accusations pissed him off, he had been immediately attracted to her. Their friendship grew during the search and then in the months following. After she moved to North Carolina, their romance intensified as they spent more and more time together.

He had finally found another woman he wanted to spend the rest of his life with. She was the perfect companion; she loved the outdoors and didn't need lots of money to make her happy. She was a woman who could take care of herself. She was fiery at times, but Jackson actually liked that she had a temper. To him, it made her more exciting, more interesting.

He had fallen in love with her. But now, after the way the dinner had gone, he wasn't so sure Tiffany felt the same way.

He didn't know what he would do if he lost her. Would he end up a bachelor for the rest of his life, spending his last few years in some stuffy nursing home with no one to visit him? He hoped not.

He looked at the ring box again and took another healthy swig of the Coors.

No, he wouldn't just curl into a ball of self-pity and let Tiffany walk out of his life. He knew deep down that she loved him. He didn't know why she didn't want to marry him, but he would wait for her if he had to. He would give her as much time and space as she needed. He wasn't about to let his own eagerness ruin their future together.

He would fight for her—fight like hell if he had to.

Because Tiffany Colson was worth fighting for.

He picked up his cellphone and started to dial her number, intending to apologize for moving things along too quickly with a marriage proposal. But at the last second, just before he hit the call button, he stopped and put the phone back down beside him on the bed.

He decided he should give her some space, a little time to work through her feelings. He certainly didn't want to smother her or appear overzealous, and he had noticed on the ride back home that she seemed tired, almost to the point of exhaustion. Perhaps she would feel more like talking after she had slept, and then they could figure things out together.

He would wait and call her in the morning.

12

Tiffany couldn't believe what lay in front of her. Her heart pounded against her chest, but not the slow rhythm of a bass drum, rather the breakneck pace of a snare, racing so fast she thought it would burst at any second. She began to hyperventilate. The single rose lying on her pillow catapulted her mind to the past. What she had hoped was only an overactive imagination was now a reality. How could it be? He. Was. Dead.

She had killed him.

So how was he here—in her cabin—alive? It made no sense. She struggled to find an answer, but none came.

The scream that had involuntarily escaped her lungs a second earlier echoed off the bedroom walls, piercing the silence of the isolated cabin. She had to get out. Had to escape before it was too late. She started to turn and run, but then froze in panic when the sound of his voice reached her ears.

"Hello, Tiffany," he said behind her. It was a cold, calm voice, void of any emotion, save for the slight twinge that only revenge can produce.

Tiffany had heard that voice from only one person—Paul.

She struggled to maintain control as the world she knew came crashing down around her. She felt light-headed and took a step toward the bed, ready to catch herself if she fell.

You have to get out of here, Tiffany. NOW!

She stopped at the edge of the bed and stared at the small window on the opposite side of the room. She would never be able to unlock it and climb outside before he caught her. She was trapped. She stood motionless for what seemed like an eternity, struggling to somehow devise a way out of this situation, hoping that this was all just another one of her vivid dreams. Praying it was just a nightmare.

But she knew it wasn't.

It was real.

Her only option was to somehow get past him, run to the living room, and then out the front door. She really had no other choice. If she stayed in the cabin with Paul, she knew she would never survive.

She spun, the initial shock of Paul's return now obliterated by the pure, unfiltered adrenaline screaming through her body. Her dizziness was gone, her vision laser-focused on the only viable exit from the room. She rushed the tall figure that stood in the doorway of her bedroom, throwing a forearm against his chin as she lunged toward the hallway.

Her quick movement caught him off guard, and as he flinched in response to Tiffany's assault, she simultaneously threw a knee into his breadbasket, causing him to turn to the left and allowing her a momentary opportunity to slip past him. She didn't hesitate. She barreled through the doorway and into the hall. He grabbed at her as she pushed past him but, still stunned by the blow to his midsection, his hands caught only empty air.

Tiffany ran down the hall toward the living room. She could hear Paul behind her, cursing and struggling to regain his footing. She turned right at the corner and darted into the living room. Her bare feet slipped on the hardwood floor as she made the turn, and her legs flew out from under her.

She crashed to the floor, the impact jarring the right side of her body and sending her skidding across the hardwood. She smacked into the side of the recliner, then, ignoring the pain in her hip, she frantically tried to get back on her feet. The living room was dark, but she could see Paul moving toward her, his large body backlit by the bedroom light that was spilling into the narrow hallway, his angry strides sending powerful reverberations through the cabin floor.

She screamed, hoping that someone outside might hear her, but she knew that wasn't likely. It was late, and the closest cabin was over a hundred yards away.

She screamed again.

She managed to make it onto her knees and elbows, scrambling quickly around the back of the couch and toward the front door. She heard footsteps behind her, moving closer. Everything seemed to happen in slow motion now. She tried to move faster, but felt like she was encased in Jell-O, her movements sluggish and clumsy.

She was almost to her salvation; she could see the doorknob clearly now, even in the darkness of the room. If she could just make it off the porch, she could lose him in the woods surrounding the cabin, then go for help. She reached for the brass doorknob, her hand trembling violently in front of her. She grunted and heaved herself toward it. She almost made it.

Almost.

She felt the weight of his body crash into her back, his massive arms encircling her waist. She kicked and squirmed, trying desperately to escape his grasp, but it was no use. She collapsed to the floor, her arms unable to support his weight any longer. "Help!" she cried.

She struggled once more against the hold he had on her, unwilling to cede her freedom just yet, but she couldn't move an inch, pinned against the floor by his body. His weight was crushing, and she struggled to breathe. Her heart was pounding, requiring more oxygen, and she fought to draw even a single breath into her lungs.

Tears rolled down her cheeks. But they weren't tears of fear anymore, but rather, tears of sorrow. Knowing the life she had dreamed of with Jackson would never happen saddened her. She wished she had done more with her life, wished she had lived for the present, and even the future, instead of being held prisoner by the past.

Then, as she lay on the floor, suffocating, a strange thing happened. All the fear she had experienced during the last ten years left her in a moment of clarity. She didn't need to be afraid any longer.

It was over.

13

Jackson picked up his cellphone and stared at the screen again. Still nothing. He must have checked it at least fifteen times since he had gotten home for lunch thirty minutes ago. He tossed it back onto the table and took another bite of his peanut butter and jelly sandwich. He wondered why Tiffany hadn't responded yet. He had tried to call her before he left to go on patrol earlier but got no answer. He sent a text message a few hours later when he found a spot in the trail that had good cell reception, but he hadn't heard a word from her.

He had spent all morning patrolling the trail that ran alongside Twentymile Creek, as was his custom on Saturday. This time of year, the area was busier than usual due to the influx of visitors who came annually to experience the autumn colors of the Smokies. But on this particular Saturday, it had been quiet. The most exciting thing he encountered was a young family whose two-year-old boy had fallen and skinned his knee on the rocky trail. Jackson had cleaned and bandaged the wound with supplies from the first aid kit he always carried in his backpack, then said goodbye and wished the family well as he continued up the trail.

He had run into a couple of fly fishermen a little later, spending several minutes talking and checking their fishing licenses, before turning around and heading back downstream toward the ranger station he called home. He arrived back just before noon and was now almost finished with his sandwich. He sighed and glanced at the phone's screen again. It was still blank.

Maybe she really didn't want to see him anymore.

He didn't know what to do with that thought. Maybe he should drive to her cabin and demand that she explain what was going on. Still, he didn't want to push her. If their relationship truly was over, he would be forced to deal with it, but until then, he would stay positive and hope for the best.

He pushed his chair away from the round wooden table in the small dining area just off the kitchen. He picked up his plate and walked to the sink. He had intended to drive out to the marina on Fontana Lake after lunch and take the Park Service boat over to Hazel Creek for patrol, but now he decided against it. He hadn't slept well last night, and was exhausted from the mental wrangling of trying to figure out where he stood with Tiffany.

Staring out the small window above the sink at the gravel road in front of his house, he decided to take the afternoon off and try to relax. Maybe he would even grab his fly rod and fish for a couple of hours. Besides, he needed some more practice before Cody took him fishing again. That was the great thing about being a park ranger, he got to live inside a national park, with miles of both fishing streams and hiking trails right out-side his front door. He couldn't imagine wanting any other job.

Jackson placed his dish in the sink and turned around. Today, even the kitchen made him think about Tiffany. When he first met her, the kitchen countertops had been a hideous pastel yellow and flower-patterned laminate, and the floor was covered with old, stained linoleum. After they started dating, Tiffany insisted that Jackson update the house. He had never really seen a need for it, but with her persistent prodding, he got ap-proval from the Park Service to make updates to the 1940s house. They had replaced the linoleum with gray tile, which complemented the hardwood floors that ran throughout the rest of the house—well, at least that's what Tiffany said. Jackson was clueless about interior design. The maroon-striped wallpaper had been replaced with a fresh coat of cream paint, and the countertops were now forest green granite, which always reminded Jackson of the large pines that grew along Twentymile Creek.

He stared across the countertops toward the open living room. They were going to spruce up that area next. He had gone along with all of Tiffany's de-sign plans without resistance, hoping that one day they would share this house as husband and wife. Now, that seemed like just a distant dream.

As he walked past the table, he grabbed his glass of sweet tea and then headed down the hallway on his right toward his bedroom. He took off his uniform and hung it in the cramped closet, then pulled out a pair of blue jeans and a tan Carhartt work shirt.

As he was buttoning the shirt, he heard his cell-phone ring in the kitchen. He spun and jogged down the hallway, hoping it was Tiffany finally calling him back. When he reached the table and picked up the phone, he was puzzled to see the caller ID read *Mountain View Resort*. He swiped his thumb across the screen and put the phone to his ear. "Hello?"

"Hi, is this Jackson?"

"Yes, this is Jackson. How can I help you?" he replied. The caller on the line sounded like a young man, and Jackson thought he recognized the voice, although he couldn't immediately put a face with it.

"Do you know Tiffany Colson?"

Jackson hesitated, surprised by the unexpected question. Finally, he spoke. "Yes . . . yes, I know her. What's going on?"

"Okay, good. I just wanted to make sure I had the right person. This is Jeremy at the recreation center. She was supposed to be at work at seven-thirty this morning, but never came in. We assumed she had just overslept, but when she didn't show up by ten, we sent someone over to her cabin. There was no answer at the door, and her car was gone. We thought maybe she had forgotten she was on the schedule for today and was with you. She had your number listed as an emergency contact on her employee form, and I—"

"Wait. What?" Jackson interrupted. "She didn't show up for work?"

"That's right," Jeremy replied. "We thought maybe she forgot—"

Jackson cut the young man off again. "No, she didn't forget. She told me yesterday she had to work today." Jackson's heart sank. Thoughts raced through his mind. Maybe she had been so upset by the impending proposal that she had packed up and gone back to Georgia in the middle of the night.

Maybe it was already too late.

"So you saw her yesterday?" Jeremy asked.

Jackson finally put a face with the young man's voice. Tiffany had introduced him to Jeremy one day when he picked her up from work. An awkward-looking fellow, if he remembered correctly. Jackson sighed heavily, then said, "Yeah, that's right. We went out to dinner last night, then I dropped her off at her cabin around ten."

"Hmmm, okay. Well, maybe she decided to take the day off and just forgot to call in. If you hear from her, would you mind asking her to give us a call?"

Jackson didn't know what to think, his mind confused by this new information. After a few seconds, he answered, "Sure . . . I'll let her know."

"Thanks," Jeremy said and hung up.

Jackson put the phone back on the table and walked to the kitchen window. He looked outside, hoping he would see Tiffany's Toyota Corolla pulling into the driveway—hoping she had changed her mind. He was disappointed, but not surprised, when all he saw was the green and white Park Service Suburban and his personal vehicle, a red Ford pickup.

He sighed again. He had screwed up. He had been presumptuous and pushed her away, and he silently cursed himself for being so stupid.

He walked back to the dining table and sat down, defeated. He should have known better, but things had been going so well between them that he was sure she would accept his proposal. He considered trying to call her again, but decided that would probably just make the situation worse. She was going to do whatever she wanted, and there was nothing he could do to stop her. Not that he would have tried anyway. If she really didn't want to be with him, he certainly would never try to force her.

He put his head in his hands, resting his elbows on the wooden table. He didn't know what to do. He had ruined everything, and now Tiffany was on her way back to Georgia, or maybe even somewhere else. He had no idea.

He had to be sure, though.

If there was one person in the world Tiffany would've told she was leaving, even in the middle of the night, it would be Katie. Those two were like sisters. Actually, they were closer than most sisters Jackson knew.

He picked up his phone again and dialed Katie's number. She picked up on the third ring.

"Hello?" she said in a rushed tone.

Jackson could hear Missy crying in the background and Katie trying to console her. He regretted calling already. "Hi, Katie, this is Jackson . . . I'm really sorry to bother you. Should I call back later?"

"No, it's fine. Missy just fell and bumped her head right before you called. Can you hold on a minute?"

"Sure," Jackson replied. He heard Katie put the phone down on the counter and then listened as she took ice from the freezer and made a compress for Missy's head. Her soothing, motherly voice seemed to come so naturally, though he knew she was tough as iron inside. She had proved that while Cody was missing and during the long months of his recovery. Jackson felt like an unwelcome eavesdropper listening in as Katie asked Missy if she wanted more juice, then heard Missy stop crying as she began to drink. He almost hung up but decided that since he had already disturbed Katie, the least he could do was be patient until she was ready to talk. He held another minute, then heard Katie pick up the phone again.

"Sorry, Jackson. What's up?" she asked.

He felt he needed to apologize again for his untimely call, but was unsure exactly what to say, so instead got straight to the point. "Have you heard from Tiffany?"

"Not since Thursday, when we went shopping. What's going on? Is something wrong?" Katie asked in a rapid cadence.

Jackson paused for a few seconds, then said, "Well, I think Tiffany left last night. I was hoping she had called you and told you where she was going. I assume she probably went back to Georgia—"

"Wait, what are you saying, Jackson?" Katie interrupted. "I don't understand. You're saying Tiffany's gone?"

Jackson could hear Katie's concern. "Yeah, I guess so. Jeremy, from the resort, called me a few minutes ago and said she didn't show up for work, asked if I knew where she was. I told him that we had dinner last night and that I dropped her off at her cabin afterward, but that I haven't seen her today. I thought if there's one person she would call to say she was leaving, it's you."

"Why would you think she would just take off in the middle of the night?" Katie asked, confusion in her voice.

Jackson sighed and paused for a few seconds. How could he explain to Katie, without getting into the details of the disastrous dinner the evening before, why he thought Tiffany had left? "She got pretty upset last night at dinner, started crying, and ran into the bathroom. She didn't talk much on the ride home. I assumed she knew that I—"

"Oh, no . . ." Katie whispered.

"Oh, no, what?" Jackson asked forcefully. There was a lengthy pause on the phone. "What's going on, Katie? Do you know something?" he persisted.

He heard Katie clear her throat on the other end of the line and then say in a panicked voice, "I'm ... I don't think Tiffany just ran away last night."

"What are you talking about? What else could've happened to her?" Jackson asked, a mixture of frustration and worry now in his voice.

Katie ignored his question. "Meet me at Tiffany's cabin in two hours."

"Katie! What's going on?" he yelled. He waited for an answer, but all he heard in response was her hanging up the phone.

14

Jackson glanced down at the digital clock on the truck's dashboard—2:08 p.m. He pulled his Ford pickup off the paved road and onto the short gravel driveway that led to Tiffany's cabin. The crushed stone made a grinding, popping sound as the truck's large tires rolled over them. He stopped just short of the covered front porch and moved the gear shifter into park. He stared at the rustic cabin through his windshield. The porch was littered with fallen leaves, and he watched as the wind added several more to the growing pile under the living room window. He didn't know what was going on, but he realized his feelings of rejection and sadness had morphed into anxiety and speculation. What if he'd been wrong? His conversation with Katie, coupled with Tiffany's strange behavior recently, only increased Jackson's unease.

He had hoped to find Tiffany's blue Corolla back in the driveway, sitting under the large white oak tree where she always parked it. But it was nowhere to be seen, just as Jeremy had said. Jackson had even stopped by the recreation center on his way to the cabin to speak to Jeremy in person and to make sure Tiffany hadn't shown up for work. She hadn't.

He opened the center console and grabbed the .45-caliber Glock he always kept inside, then opened the door and stepped outside. The breeze had stiffened over the past few hours, and he pulled at the bill of his baseball cap, snugging it against his forehead. He clipped the holstered gun to his belt, concealing it beneath his untucked Carhartt shirt.

Jackson walked toward Tiffany's front porch, his eyes scanning the ground as he went, searching for anything out of the ordinary. He realized he was instinctively looking for signs of a struggle, although he didn't want to seriously entertain that possibility just yet. He saw nothing. Next, he walked to the west side of the cabin and continued around the entire exterior. None of the windows were broken or even opened. He scanned the surrounding forest, and again, found nothing that raised his suspicions. Everything looked normal.

Just as he completed his exterior search, he saw Katie pull up and park her 4Runner right behind his truck. He walked over to meet her as she exited the vehicle. "Hi, Katie. I wasn't expecting you for another twenty minutes or so," he said as she closed the driver's door and looked up at him.

"I drove fast," she replied matter-of-factly. "I would have been here sooner, but I had to drop Missy off with Cody at the fly shop." She pushed past Jackson, brushing his shoulder as she walked toward the small cabin. "You just get here?" she asked over her shoulder.

"Yeah, I stopped by the recreation office on my way in. They still haven't heard from her. Checked the outside of the cabin, too."

"Find anything?"

"No . . . no, I didn't." Katie was still walking away from him, her purposeful gait frustrating Jackson. "Can you just hold on a minute, Katie, and tell me what the hell is going on?" he yelled.

"Not right now. You probably wouldn't understand anyway."

Jackson took two large strides forward, drawing within an arm's length of Katie. He reached out and grasped her shoulder, spinning her around to face him. As soon as he looked into her eyes, he sensed her anguish, their normal bright blue appearance duller, almost melancholy. Her skin was pale, and her long blonde hair whipped across a face lined with tension. Her appearance startled Jackson, and he stood there for several seconds just staring at her, his feelings of frustration suddenly replaced by a wave of apprehension.

He knew something was wrong.

"Dammit, Katie. Tell me what's going on. I care about her just as much as you do . . . and I deserve to know the truth," he finished in a calm, low voice.

"Look, Jackson, I'll tell you everything. I promise I will. But right now, let's just get inside the cabin and make sure everything's okay." Her voice was authoritative, letting him know her decision was not up for debate.

Jackson released his grip on her shoulder. "Okay." As the two of them walked onto the porch, he added, "I tried to call her several more times after I talked to you, but her cellphone just went straight to voicemail."

"Yeah, I tried too, and got the same thing," Katie replied.

Jackson opened the screen door, then pulled his key ring from his pocket. He fumbled with the mass of keys and finally found the spare that Tiffany had given him over a year ago. He had never had an opportunity to use it before because Tiffany had always been at the cabin herself whenever he visited. He inserted the key into the brass doorknob and turned. The door inched open, and he reflexively placed his hand on the Glock as he stepped inside.

The cabin was clothed in shadows and smelled of the lilac air freshener Tiffany kept on the small coffee table in front of the sofa. He scanned the living room and kitchen area quickly, looking for any signs of trouble—there were none. He reached to his right and flipped the light switch, then stepped a few more feet into the room. He noticed the shoes Tiffany had worn at dinner lying on the floor. The screeching of the screen door pierced the tense silence as it closed behind Katie.

"Tiffany! It's Jackson. Are you here?" he yelled. He waited for a response, but heard nothing. He stepped a few feet closer to the hallway ahead and to his left. He pulled the .45 from its holster and held it at the ready, pointed toward the floor. "Tiffany, it's Jackson and Katie. Are you here?" he repeated. He waited again for an answer, but heard only the wind blowing through the trees outside. He moved forward until he was at the corner of the hallway. He could feel his heart thumping against his breastbone, the intense throbbing of his pulse in his temples.

He could now see the entire kitchen area from his new vantage point, and nothing seemed amiss there, either. He raised the Glock in front of him and moved around the corner of the wall, where he had a clear view of the short hallway, the kitchen and living room now at his back. He found no immediate threat in front of him, so he took his left hand off the pistol and reached for the light switch. Soft yellow light flooded the narrow hall.

He quickly surveyed the area for any signs of a struggle: blood on the floor, a picture that had been ripped from the wall—anything. Everything looked normal. He turned his head back toward Katie and whispered, "Wait here."

"Okay," she responded.

He crept down the hall and searched the bedroom and bathroom, neither of which offered him a clue as to where Tiffany was. When he was satisfied the house was empty, he called back to Katie, who was still waiting at the end of the hallway. "Okay, it's clear."

"See anything?" Katie asked as she stepped into the doorway of the bathroom. Jackson was in front of the sink, examining the single, small window on the exterior wall of the room.

"No, I didn't." He turned from the window and looked at Katie. "But now that we know there's no one else here, let's take a closer look. You check her bedroom, and I'll take the kitchen and living room. Look for anything you think is out of the ordinary, anything out of place."

"Okay," Katie said as she turned and headed for Tiffany's bedroom.

Jackson searched for the next several minutes. He checked everything he could think of, scoured every cabinet and every corner, but found nothing unusual. He walked back down the hall and stopped at the bedroom. Katie was going through Tiffany's closet. "Find anything?" he asked.

Katie closed the accordion doors and stepped toward him. "Not really. How about you?"

"Her backpack is missing, and I can't find her cellphone. But if she left, she would have taken those with her, so that's not surprising."

Katie pointed to the floor in front of Jackson's feet. "I did notice a stain on the carpet that I don't remember being here."

Jackson looked down and saw an irregular-shaped stain on the carpet. He knelt and placed his hand on top of it. The beige carpet was dry and only slightly discolored. "Hmmm," he said, "looks like just a coffee or tea stain to me."

Katie was huddled over him, staring at the carpet as well. "Yeah, you're probably right." She sighed, then straightened up and walked out of the room.

Jackson flipped the light off as he followed Katie into the living room. She was standing next to the recliner, and she looked up at him as he entered. "I think we should call the police," she said.

"And tell them what, Katie? That our 32-year-old friend didn't show up for work today, and we found a coffee stain on her bedroom carpet? Not exactly an airtight case. I'm sure they'll put their top man on it right away," Jackson replied, his voice elevated and his words dripping sarcasm.

Katie rolled her eyes in response, then turned her head away from Jackson and stared at the wall. "I knew you wouldn't understand," she said, her voice barely audible.

"Understand what? You haven't told me anything, so how am I supposed to understand?" Jackson threw his arms up in exasperation. He was beyond frustrated that Katie had gotten him all worked up, made him believe something terrible had happened to Tiffany, when he had been right all along—she had simply run away. And there was nothing in the cabin that led him to believe otherwise. "Katie, this is exactly what it looks like."

"And what's that, Jackson? What does it look like?" Katie snapped her head away from the wall and back toward him.

"It looks like she was afraid to make a commitment, and instead of facing me and telling me the truth, that she doesn't love me, she just ran away!" Jackson yelled, the feelings of rejection he had been suppressing boiling over in a moment of anger.

"What are you talking about?" Katie asked, a baffled look on her face.

"Don't act like you don't know. It's embarrassing enough for me as it is. I sure don't need to drag the cops into it and have it end up on the six o'clock news. I already feel like a fool. Please, don't make it worse . . . just let her go."

"Jackson, you're wrong. I don't think Tiffany ran away." She slumped down into the recliner and looked up at him with worried eyes. "Sit down. You need to tell me everything that happened at dinner last night," she said.

Jackson obeyed, plopping down on the gray sofa. The way he immediately complied reminded him of being in Principal VanDreel's office as a seventh-grader back in Wisconsin, and he resented it.

"So what happened last night?" Katie persisted.

He looked at her, sure she knew exactly what had happened, but was going to make him say it out loud. Oddly, he found himself willing to tell her anyway. He took a deep breath and began to speak. "Last night, I had this nice, romantic dinner planned at DeVito's in Sylva. I'd been planning it for months." He paused and rubbed his hand down his face, grasping his square chin for a second before continuing.

"Anyway, I got here last night around six and picked her up. Everything seemed fine. I mean, I noticed she wasn't talking a lot on the ride up, but I didn't think much about it. So we got to the restaurant and ordered dinner. Everything was going well, but she seemed a little distracted, like maybe she was worried about something. Then she got this glazed look in her eyes while she was staring out the window. I shook her arm and spoke to her, and she finally snapped out of it. She seemed fine for a few minutes, just like her usual self. I remember she even made a joke about the wine I ordered." Jackson paused and stared at the ceiling.

"Okay, so then what happened?"

"Well, that's when things went south, I guess you could say." He paused again and took another breath. "Just when I was about to pull the ring out of my pocket and propose, she started crying and ran into the bathroom. I—"

"What?" Katie interrupted, shocked. "You were going to propose?"

"Don't act like you didn't know, Katie," he said, still staring at the ceiling.

"No! I had no idea," she insisted.

He turned his gaze back to Katie, who now had a pleased smile on her face. She looked genuinely surprised. "I thought you knew already."

"I promise, I didn't."

"Really? I just assumed Cody had told you after our fishing trip the other day and I—"

"I swear, Jackson, I had no idea. Cody didn't say a word about it."

Jackson looked at Katie. He knew she was telling the truth. Besides, she had never lied to him before, and he had no reason to doubt her now. "So you're telling me that Tiffany had no idea I was planning to propose to her Friday night?" he asked.

"Well, if she did, she didn't hear it from me. I swear."

"Then she didn't know," Jackson stated emphatically. "I told Cody about it during our fishing trip Thursday, but swore him to secrecy, and if he didn't tell you, then he kept his word. The only other person who knew was Charlie Hetherington. He owns the jewelry store where I bought the ring. But he doesn't even know Tiffany, so he couldn't have told her."

Jackson placed his hands on his knees and dropped his head, staring at the hardwood floor. He was trying to figure out what had upset Tiffany, since he now knew it hadn't been the impending proposal. His mind reeled. Now, Tiffany's behavior at dinner took on an entirely different meaning. He was relieved to find out that Tiffany hadn't run away from a life with him after all, but in an instant, the relief vanished as he realized her odd behavior could have a much more sinister explanation.

Katie spoke and disrupted his train of thought. "So she started to cry, then got up and ran to the bathroom. What happened after that?"

Jackson looked up at Katie again. Her smile of a moment ago, after hearing about the proposal, had been replaced with the same mask of anxiety she had worn since pulling into Tiffany's driveway. "Well, after several minutes, she returned to the table and apologized. I told her not to worry about it. She said she wasn't feeling well. I figured Cody had told you that I planned to propose, and that you leaked the news to Tiffany." He sighed. "And that she just didn't want to marry me."

"Well, I can promise you that's not what happened." Katie hesitated, then asked, "What happened next?"

"We left the restaurant, and I drove her home. She was quiet for most of the ride back to the resort, and she looked exhausted. Once we got back, she kissed me on the cheek, apologized again, and walked into her cabin. That was the last time I saw her. I spent all last night and this morning thinking she ran away because she didn't love me and knew she could never marry me."

"No, Jackson. That's not the case at all. I know Tiffany, and she really loves you." She paused and looked at him, empathy in her eyes. "And I know she would've said yes."

Jackson knew what Katie said was true. He was dumbfounded. He had been wrong all along. He sucked in a lungful of air and said, "Well, now that we know my theory about why she left is completely wrong, let me ask you a question." He could feel a knot forming in his stomach, not sure he really wanted to know the answer to the question he was about to ask. "Why are you so sure something has happened to her?"

Katie sighed and stared out the living room window.

"Katie, what do you know?" he persisted. "If Tiffany is in trouble, I don't care what kind of promise you made. You need to tell me everything. Now." As she slowly turned her head back toward him, he saw the tears. A single one escaped and ran down her right cheek.

"Have you ever heard of Paul McMillan?"

15

Katie jumped behind the wheel of her 4Runner as Jackson shut the passenger door. "Let's make a swing around the resort, then check some of the surrounding roads," he said.

"Okay," Katie replied as she drove away from Tiffany's cabin.

"So, what can you tell me about Paul McMillan?" Jackson asked.

"You sure you want to hear this?"

"Probably not, but I need to know. If her relationship with him has anything to do with her disappearance, I need to know the details."

Katie took a deep breath before continuing. "Paul McMillan was an evil man, Jackson. Truly evil. Didn't Tiffany ever say anything to you about him?" Katie asked, as she reached the end of the driveway and turned right onto the paved road.

Jackson scanned his memory, trying to remember what Tiffany had told him about Paul McMillan. After several seconds, he answered, "Yes, she mentioned some guy named Paul."

"Do you remember what she told you about him?"

"Well, it was after we had been dating for several months. We had been to dinner and a movie. We were having a glass of wine at her cabin, and she started to open up to me." Jackson paused and squirmed uncomfortably in the seat cushion.

Katie glanced over at him. "Go on," she persisted.

Jackson sighed. "We hadn't been . . . intimate, I guess you could say, prior to that night." He paused again. "Sorry, Katie, I'm just not used to talking about these things with another woman."

Katie smiled softly. "It's okay. But I need to know what she said about him. Maybe she told you something I don't know, something that will help us find her."

"Okay . . . I understand." Jackson shifted again in the seat and stared out the windshield. "So anyway, on that particular night—maybe it was the wine, I don't know—she seemed to let the wall down. We were talking, just chitchat really, when all of a sudden she said she needed to tell me something. She had been so happy the entire night, but then she got very quiet, solemn. I told her to go ahead, that she could tell me anything." He paused and rubbed his sweaty palms against his thighs.

"I could tell she was hesitant, but finally, she told me there had been a man in her past, that he hadn't treated her right, that, you know . . . he had beaten her, I guess. She said that one night, he was in a rage and attacked her with a knife. She said she somehow escaped, and that she hadn't seen him after that." Jackson paused again and swallowed hard before continuing.

"When she stood up, she took off her blouse. I saw the scars and . . . I didn't know what to say; I'd never dealt with anything like that before. She was crying, Katie. I couldn't say anything, so I just stood up and gave her a hug. She buried her head in my shoulder and sobbed. I just kept holding her . . . I didn't know what else to do. We just stood in the living room and held each other for a long time. Then, eventually, we went into the bedroom and . . . well, you know."

Jackson looked back at Katie, who now had tears streaming down her cheeks. She wiped them away with her palm and said, "Jackson, she must really love you, because you are the only other person in the world, besides me, she has ever shown the scars to. And I know you think you're not good with situations like that, but I just want you to know that I think you handled it perfectly." She paused, and Jackson saw another comforting smile come across her face. "Did she ever say anything else about Paul?" she asked.

Jackson stared at the floorboard, trying to remember if Tiffany had ever shared anything more. "The only other thing she mentioned was the reason she didn't like roses. But after that night, she seemed happier, like a weight had been lifted from her shoulders or something. And I never brought it up again; I couldn't see that it would accomplish anything."

Katie sighed. "And she never mentioned his last name to you?"

"No, I'm sure she didn't. I would have remembered that."

Katie looked at Jackson. "Well, there's a good reason she kept that to herself. She probably didn't want you to realize how serious the situation had actually been. Paul McMillan was the son of Fredrick McMillan, a very powerful man in Georgia. He wasn't just a bad boyfriend, Jackson, he was a truly evil man. And if there's anything worse than an evil man, it's an evil man with money and power . . . and unfortunately, Paul had both."

Jackson felt his heart rate increase. "What are you talking about?"

She sighed and ran her fingers through her long blonde hair. "The McMillan family owns the most lucrative lumber company in Georgia, and it's been in the family for generations, since the 1800s, I think. Their net worth is measured in hundreds of millions, if not billions. They're well-connected with politicians and other officials around the state, and they don't hesitate to use their influence when they need to. Heck, the county where Tiffany and I grew up is even named after one of them. Hayward County was named after Hayward McMillan, an influential entrepreneur and lawmaker before the Civil War, so we're talking about a *long* legacy of important McMillans in Georgia history. They're *powerful* people, Jackson, and they're ruthless to anyone who challenges them."

"So how did Tiffany get mixed up with people like that?" Jackson asked, his palms still sweating. He wiped them on his jeans again.

"When Tiffany was a senior in college, she met Paul one afternoon after class. She had a flat tire, and he just *happened* to be there to give her a hand. You'll never convince me he hadn't already spotted Tiffany, stalked her, and waited for the opportune moment to strike. Anyway, he helped her change the flat tire, which he probably caused in the first place, and then asked her out. She didn't find out he was a McMillan until after their first date." Katie paused and sighed.

Jackson could tell it was difficult for Katie to relay the details of what had happened to Tiffany, but he had to know. "Go on, Katie," he prodded.

Katie nodded her head and took a breath. "He was good to her at first. You have to understand, Jackson . . . Paul was a psychopath. Men like him pick an easy target, reel them in like a fish, and then pounce. And that's exactly what Paul did to Tiffany. He quickly became possessive and abusive. She kept all this from everyone, even me. She didn't want anyone to know she had been duped or to judge her for being so gullible. To everyone who knew her back then, Tiffany appeared happy, and she and Paul seemed to be the perfect couple—she was beautiful, and he was being groomed to take over the family business." Katie paused and wiped the tears from her cheeks. "But for Tiffany, it was a horrifying relationship. I can't imagine how scared she must've been. I wish she had told me so I could've helped her, but she didn't. Not then. I didn't find out the truth until after it was all over."

"So why did she stay with him?" Jackson asked.

"Mainly out of fear, I guess. But I think she also felt ashamed for not seeing Paul for who he truly was in the beginning. Felt stupid for being so naïve. Once she realized who she was dealing with, the type of power he held, she was afraid to tell anyone. She told me later that she hadn't sought help because she feared that Paul would harm me or someone else close to her. He was horrible to her, Jackson. One time, he even . . ."

Jackson couldn't believe what he was hearing. He'd had no idea Tiffany had been through so much trauma. He realized Katie had stopped talking, and he waited for her to continue, but when, after several seconds, she remained silent he asked, "What did he do to her, Katie?"

She took a deep breath before continuing. "One time he caught her calling a classmate, a male friend, for help with a school assignment. It was totally innocent, but Paul became enraged. He locked her in a closet at his parents' mansion for two days."

Jackson didn't say anything; he just sat there, stunned. His blood was boiling. Just knowing that someone had done that to Tiffany made him want to rip the guy's throat out with his bare hands.

"After that, I think Tiffany knew she had to find a way out. She finally left him, and for a few weeks, he left her alone. But then, one night, he reappeared. She had been shopping at the mall and was walking back to her car. It was dark, and the parking lot wasn't lit very well. I guess she probably thought he was gone since she hadn't heard from him in a while." Katie paused. "Anyway, as Tiffany approached her car, Paul drove up behind her and blocked her in. Then he grabbed her and threw her in the trunk of his car. She screamed for help, but there was no one around to hear her. The whole incident only lasted a few seconds." Katie stopped talking again, the strain of relating the story obviously taking a toll.

"Go on," Jackson said quietly.

"Look, I really don't want to tell you this . . . it's hard for me to even say the words, but I think you need to know what type of people we're dealing with here."

"I can take it, Katie. Just tell me the truth," he responded.

The tears began to flow from Katie's eyes once more, her voice trembling as she spoke. "He took her to the mansion, made her strip, and then tried to burn her alive in the bathtub."

Stone silence.

"My God," Jackson finally whispered. He buried his head in his hands, letting Katie's words sink in. It all made sense now. That was why Tiffany had been so distant, so cold, when they had first met at the marina. He hadn't understood at the time, but now he did. He loved her even more. Knowing that she had been through hell and had somehow managed to move on with her life, to allow him to become so close to her, made him admire her for the strong woman he had always known she was. Sitting there next to Katie in the 4Runner, he promised himself he would find Tiffany, and if anyone had hurt her— His thoughts were interrupted when he heard Katie begin to speak again.

"She somehow got out of the bathtub without being seriously burned. How she did that, I'll never know. Then she tried to make it to the front door and escape, but Paul caught her. And that's when he cut her with the knife." Katie paused, and Jackson, still staring blankly at the floorboard, heard her take another deep breath. "He was going to kill her, Jackson," she stated matter-of-factly.

Jackson remained silent for a few seconds, processing the information as best he could, then looked up and stared at Katie. "So how did she escape?" he asked, his voice rife with the growing hatred he felt inside for a man he had never met.

"She killed him."

16

Jackson and Katie walked through the front door of Tiffany's cabin after a fruitless search of the nearby roads. He began to pace between the living area and the kitchen, his hand to his forehead. "I can't believe she never told me all of this."

Katie shifted her body to face Jackson squarely. "You have to understand, Jackson, it's been a ten-year struggle for her. She's been forced to deal with all that happened and to try to move on with her life, all at the same time. It couldn't have been easy for her to even tell you about the scars, much less let you see them. That, in itself, was a huge step for her. I'm sure she would've told you everything when the time was right. Please don't hold it against her."

"No . . . no, of course not. I would never do that," he responded, still pacing across the floor. "I just wish she had told me."

"I'm sure she wanted to. She just didn't know how."

He stopped, stood behind the sofa, and looked at Katie, who was now standing next to the recliner. "Okay, so we know that Tiffany didn't run away because of my proposal. But why did she?"

"That's what I've been trying to get you to see, you idiot! It has nothing to do with you; it's all about Paul!" Katie paused, then lowered her voice and said, "I'm sorry, Jackson, I shouldn't have—"

Jackson waved his hand dismissively. "No, it's fine. I'm sorry. I guess it's just hard for me to believe that something that happened ten years ago has anything to do with her disappearance now."

"Well, I don't think Tiffany ran away. As upset as she's been, it's possible, I'll grant you that, but I believe we need to consider other possibilities. I think we should start by calling the authorities."

"Okay, okay." Jackson began to pace again, thinking. "But if she killed Paul almost ten years ago, and nothing has happened since then, why are you so convinced something has happened to her now?" he asked.

"To tell you the truth, I'm not sure. Like I said, it's possible she just left of her own freewill, but I know something has been going on with Tiffany lately. She seemed distracted . . . and, well, afraid. When you told me how she zoned out at dinner the other night, I became even more concerned. She should've been happy having dinner with you, not focused on the past, but I'm convinced that's what she was thinking about."

"Why?" Jackson asked.

Katie walked toward Jackson and looked directly into his eyes. "Because she did the same thing with me the day before when we were at the mall."

"What?" he asked, surprised.

"Yeah, it's the truth. Normally, when we go shopping together, we have a great time. We laugh and joke around with each other. Do a lot of talking about you and Cody, too." A slight smile spread across Katie's face for a moment, so quick it was almost imperceptible, then it was gone.

"But this Thursday was different. I could tell something was bothering her as soon as we got in the car. I thought maybe you and she had gotten into an argument or something, so I just let it slide. I didn't think much of it at the moment, I guess."

"So what changed that worried you so much?"

Katie turned away and walked to the large window in the living room, her back to Jackson. "I was stupid, that's what happened."

"I'm sorry, I'm confused. What do you mean, 'You were stupid'?"

Katie was still staring out the window at the oak tree. "I needed to find Cody a birthday present. I thought he might like a nice hunting knife, so we went into a sporting goods store. While we were standing at the counter, with the sales guy showing us some knives, Tiffany just zoned out on me . . . exactly the way you said she did at the restaurant." She paused, and Jackson saw her raise her hand to her cheek to wipe more tears away. "I realized something was terribly wrong with her, so we left the store right away. We've been friends so long that I could just tell . . . you know what I mean?"

"Yeah, I know what you're talking about," Jackson said, still staring at Katie's back.

"Over lunch, I *made* her tell me what was going on. She was convinced that, somehow, Paul had come back. She even made the statement that she never saw his body after the cops took her away. I think she thought he might not have been dead after all."

"That's ridiculous though, right?" he asked.

"Yes, it is. He was dead . . . there's no doubt about that. The story was all over the news, and the McMillan family came after Tiffany with a vengeance. They wanted her prosecuted for murder." She paused and rubbed her other cheek. "No, he was dead all right. But somehow, Tiffany had this crazy idea that he was after her again. She said she had been having vivid nightmares and visions where she was reliving the things he had done to her."

"I don't understand. Nightmares caused all of this to surface again?" Jackson asked.

"No, it was more than that. She told me something about a coffee mug that she was sure she'd washed and put away mysteriously ending up back in the sink. She said she felt like someone was watching her while she was here at the cabin. I'm telling you, Jackson, she was not doing well. It's my fault. I should've stayed with her, and I sure as hell shouldn't have taken her to a knife store, for heaven's sake."

Jackson walked between the sofa and the coffee table toward Katie. He put his hand on her shoulder. "It's not your fault, Katie. It's not. You were just trying to help."

"I wish I could believe that, Jackson. I really do." She turned around to face him, her eyes red and her cheeks stained with tears.

Jackson wanted to say something more that would console Katie, but he couldn't find the words. He knew she loved Tiffany as much as he did. "So do you believe someone was stalking her? Or do you think it was all in her mind?" he asked.

Katie wiped her face free of tears again. "I don't know, to tell you the truth. Part of me wants to believe that it was all in her head, but somehow, I know that's not the case. She's not a crazy person, Jackson. And though the last ten years have been a struggle, she hasn't experienced anything like this before. No, this is different."

"I know Tiffany's not crazy, Katie. But we don't have much to go on here. If you're so sure something has happened to her, why didn't you just call the cops as soon as I told you she hadn't made it to work?"

"Because I didn't want to overreact. I wanted to meet you here at the cabin and make sure she wasn't just curled up in bed, afraid to go outside. If I had called the cops and she had just been in here, scared to leave, it would've embarrassed her and made things worse. I know it sounds stupid, but that's what I was thinking."

"No, it's not stupid. I understand," Jackson replied, patting her on the shoulder. He wasn't sure if he had succeeded in comforting her or not.

"But now, I really think something must've happened to her. I can't explain it, but I just have a feeling, you know?"

"Well, we'll call the local police, ask them to file a missing person report, but I wouldn't get my hopes up. I know how law enforcement works. There's nothing illegal about an adult just deciding to disappear and start a new life. Even if you and I think something bad has happened, convincing the police to start an active search for her is another matter entirely." Jackson pulled his cellphone from his front pants pocket and swiped the screen, then put it to his ear. He nodded at Katie, then said, "But we'll sure give it a try."

17

Tiffany's head was pounding. It felt like someone was beating the inside of her skull with a sledgehammer, and it made her stomach roll with nausea. She opened her eyes slowly and found herself staring down at a wooden floor, similar to the one in her own cabin, but with wider boards that had been rough-cut to achieve an older, more rustic look. The place smelled of a mixture of pine and cigarette smoke. She coughed and her lungs burned.

She raised her head slightly, but stopped when she felt a sharp pain on the left side of her neck. She winced, letting out a grunt, which only made her body hurt worse.

She reflexively began to move her left arm to her neck, hoping to identify the source of the pain, but immediately, the natural motion of her arm was halted as thin cotton rope dug into her wrists. She tried to move her right arm but was met with the same result. The realization that her hands were tied behind her back brought a wave of fear over her. She looked down and saw that her feet were also bound to the small wooden chair where she sat. Another rope ran across her thighs and a final one across her chest. She wiggled and pulled against the restraints, but couldn't move more than an inch in any direction.

She was wearing the same pink cotton pajamas that she had put on the previous night. At least, she assumed it was just last night, but her head was swimming and she felt sluggish, like she had been drugged, so she couldn't be sure. At some point, she had urinated on herself, a dark stain expanding from her crotch on the pajama bottoms.

Her anxiety only increased when she finally raised her head enough to see the room she was in—she wasn't at all familiar with it. She struggled to remember what had happened to her, fighting through the pain of the pounding headache in her brow and the back of her skull. The last thing she remembered was being on the floor of her cabin back at the resort. And feeling the fear leave her body as she drew what she had known would be her last breath.

She should be dead.

Now the nightmare was starting all over again. And it scared the hell out of her.

She looked around the unfamiliar room, hoping to find some clue as to where she was, but she saw nothing that wasn't completely alien to her. The ceiling above her was vaulted high above her head, with large exposed logs serving as rafters. The walls appeared to be solid pine, on which hung several taxidermy mounts. There were two deer heads, each sporting a set of large antlers, two trout, a ring-necked pheasant, and a smallmouth bass, which hung above the wooden door.

The sight of the front door, so close, yet just out of reach, reminded her of being trapped inside the McMillan mansion with Paul. She shivered.

Tall, rectangular windows located on each side of the door gave Tiffany an unobstructed view of a spacious deck extending out from the house. There were olive curtains across the tops of the windows, but enough of the glass was exposed that she could see a beautiful mountain landscape outside.

To her right was a small, open kitchen area. A stainless steel refrigerator hummed quietly, and beside it, a microwave sat on a black and silver granite countertop. Three stools were pushed up to a large island in front of the refrigerator. She turned her head and could see a wing of the house extending all the way to the wood line through a window to her left. A small patch of grass was beginning to go dormant ahead of the coming winter, leaving the green surface speckled with areas of light brown.

A massive bearskin rug covered the hardwood floor between her and the front door. The fur of the black bear looked soft and comfortable, and Tiffany found herself longing to stretch out on it instead of being tied to the hard chair. Just to the left of the rug was a large leather sofa in front of a fireplace, the natural stone that formed the chimney extending through the vaulted roof of the house. She craned her head as far as she could to the left, over her shoulder, then to the right, trying to see behind her. She thought she could see a hall leading away to other rooms, but she wasn't sure, and it hurt too much to turn her neck any farther in that direction.

The house looked similar to a vacation cabin, although more spacious than most she had seen. It reminded her of the pictures she had seen advertising honeymoon packages just across the state line in Gatlinburg, Tennessee. Still, she thought it could be someone's primary residence, based on the larger-than-average size alone.

Even after looking over every square inch of the room, she still had no idea where she was. But it really didn't matter. What mattered was the fact that somehow, Paul had come back.

But how was that possible? Maybe he hadn't been wounded as badly as she thought when she stabbed him on the floor of his family's mansion. Had he somehow faked his own death? Had his powerful family helped him escape by bribing the coroner? The funeral home?

Everyone?

Then she realized the words Paul spoke on the floor of the mansion that night ten years ago had indeed been prophetic . . .

She would never be free of him.

She whimpered, then began to sob. She wanted to be strong, to find the courage to keep going, but found her reservoir empty.

And now she was going to die—alone and afraid. No one would be with her, to love her and hold her, as she breathed her last. She wondered if anyone was even looking for her. Jackson was probably still angry about everything that had happened at dinner, and Katie wasn't expecting to hear from her until next week, so she wouldn't be concerned. Only the people at work were expecting her to be somewhere specific. The thought of acne-faced teenagers holding her fate in their hands almost made her laugh.

Almost.

Another thought leapt into her mind—she wasn't blindfolded or gagged. She knew instantly that it wasn't a blessing. Paul didn't need to blindfold her, because he had no intention of letting her out of the house alive. And no gag? That just meant there was no one within earshot to hear her scream. She trembled at the thought. *No one to hear her scream.* A cold chill ran down her arms and legs, all the way to the tips of her fingers and toes.

She jumped when she heard footsteps on the front deck and the wooden legs of the chair screeched across the floor, shattering the silence of the room.

She jerked her head up and peered out the windows next to the front door. She caught a glimpse of blue jeans and a brown shirt as someone passed in front of the glass, but she couldn't see his face.

She didn't need to.

She was afraid to scream, afraid of what Paul might do to her for even attempting to get help. The terror she had struggled to hold at bay now stormed through her body.

No! Please, God, help me! Please!

Then she saw the doorknob begin to turn.

18

Dammit," Jackson whispered under his breath. He swiped his finger across the screen of his cellphone, ending what had been a less than productive discussion with a local sheriff's deputy. He heard Katie behind him as she walked back into the living room.

"Sorry, I had to use the restroom. What did the police say?" she asked.

"Exactly what I expected them to." Jackson paused and turned to face Katie. "Actually, it was the same thing I would've said if I were in their position."

"And what's that?"

"The deputy took an initial report, and they are going to be on the lookout for her, but he said that because Tiffany is an adult and there aren't any obvious signs of foul play, they won't start an active search for at least twenty-four to forty-eight hours. He said most cases like this resolve themselves within a day or two . . . you know, the person just returns of their own accord." Jackson sighed and turned his gaze away from Katie. He stared across the kitchen and out the small window above the sink. The wind had picked up outside, causing several crimson and gold leaves to fall from the oaks and poplars behind the cabin. He watched silently as they floated down to the ground, while, inside, he was struggling to come to terms with what was happening.

Jackson turned his eyes back toward Katie and added, "And I've been in law enforcement long enough to know that he is one hundred percent right. Most adults who disappear aren't really missing at all. They just decided to leave one day. Maybe they got overwhelmed with work or their family or a combination of things, and instead of sticking around and facing their problems, they just ran away. Hell, one time I spent five days looking for a husband and father of three small kids who disappeared from a park campground. When we finally found him, it turned out that he hadn't vanished into the wilderness at all, he just ran away with his mistress. So convincing the authorities to start a search for a woman who left in the middle of the night without any signs of trouble? Well, that's probably not gonna happen."

Katie placed her hands on her hips. "She didn't just run away, Jackson. You know that."

Jackson rubbed his face slowly with his large hand, elongating his chiseled facial features before answering. "I know. But what am I supposed to do? I have nothing to go on other than the fact she didn't show up for work, which is hardly evidence of a crime."

"What are you talking about?" Katie asked, her voice laced with anger. "Just a few minutes ago you listened as I told you what Tiffany had been going through! And now you doubt that something has happened to her?" Katie's flailing arms punctuated every word.

"It's not that I don't believe you, Katie; I just don't know what to do, okay!" Jackson was gesturing with his hands for emphasis. "I have nothing to go on. If someone took her, we don't know who it was. You said yourself that Paul was dead. And even if we had a suspect, we have *no* idea *where* he would've taken her." Jackson stopped talking and put his hand to his forehead. After a brief pause, he looked at Katie, then motioned toward the round dining table just behind her. "I'm sorry. Can we please have a seat and think logically about this for a minute?"

"No! We have to do something!"

Jackson took a deep breath, placed his hand on Katie's shoulder, then spoke in a low, calm voice. "We will, Katie. I promise. I'll do everything in my power to find her. But please, I just want to discuss all the possibilities and make sure we're making the best possible decisions under the circumstances. That's all."

After staring at him for several tense seconds, Katie finally sighed and said, "Okay," the exhaustion evident in her voice. She pulled her shoulder away from Jackson's hand, then slid one of the oak chairs away from the table and sat down, staring at the floor.

Jackson took a seat across from her. "Look," he said as calmly as he could manage, "what information do we have that indicates someone took Tiffany against her will?"

Katie snapped her head back to Jackson, her piercing blue eyes now glaring at him. "Dammit, Jackson, I don't know. Not much, I guess, but we have got to do something. Let's call the cops back and demand they start searching right now. I feel like we are just wasting time."

Jackson dropped his head and huffed. "Yeah, that's going to help the situation," he said sarcastically, "*demanding* they search now." When he looked up, he could see the stress and frustration on her face and immediately regretted his statement.

"Katie, I'm worried about her, too. Really, I am. But there are no signs of forced entry here at the cabin, no blood, no broken windows, nothing. Her car is gone, along with her backpack and cellphone, but that wouldn't indicate to the police anything bad had happened to her. Have you found anything else?"

"No, I haven't. But you're the park ranger, have *you* found anything?"

Jackson sighed and pushed away from the table. He was a law enforcement officer, trained to detach himself and look at situations logically, not emotionally. He wished there was something more to explain Tiffany's disappearance, but he couldn't just make evidence appear out of thin air.

"I'm sorry, Jackson. I shouldn't have—"

He waved his hand in the air, dismissing her apology. "Don't worry about it. We're both stressed out. I know you just want to make sure Tiffany's safe, and so do I. No apology necessary." He reached out and patted the top of her hand. "We're on the same side, Katie." He stood up and walked toward the front door. He needed to find some fresh air and breathing room so he could think clearly, but he stopped when he heard Katie begin to cry.

"You don't understand. You just don't," she said behind him. "When Cody was lost up on that mountain, Tiffany was the one who kept me going, kept me believing every single day . . . even when I was ready to give up . . . she kept me going."

He turned to face her and could see tears flowing from her blue eyes. She kept wiping them from her cheeks with the side of her thumb. He wanted to put his arm around her and cry right along with her, but he couldn't. Part of him was dying inside, knowing that Katie was probably right, that something awful had happened to Tiffany. But as much as he loved Tiffany—as much as he wanted to find her, safe and sound, and then spend the rest of his life with her—he couldn't let his emotions control him if he was going to have any real chance of making that dream a reality. "You're right, Katie. I probably don't understand. But you have to believe me, I want to find her as much as you do. I love her—I was going to ask her to marry me, for goodness sake. But if we're going to find her, we have to think logically and try not to let our emotions get the best of us."

She looked up at him. "Yeah, I know you're right; it's just so hard, you know?"

He sighed and walked back to the table. He sat down across from her again. "Of course, I know it's hard, but we'll get through it together. Okay? I need your help, Katie, because you know her better than any-one else in the world."

She nodded softly.

"All right." He reached over and squeezed her hand. "Is there anywhere you can think of that she would go, someone else she might call if she did just decide to leave? Maybe a family member, or another friend?"

"I told you, that's not what happened."

He removed his hand from hers and let it rest on the table. "I know you did, and I believe you, but just humor me, please? The quicker we can rule out that pos-sibility, the faster we can move on to something else."

Katie's silence told Jackson she was deep in thought. "She has no family in Georgia. After her parents died, it was just her, so I doubt she would go back there."

"What about her aunt in Virginia?" Jackson asked. "Tiffany talked about her a lot."

"Yes, I guess it's possible she might've heard from Tiffany."

"Okay, great," Jackson said, encouraged that Katie was opening up again. "Is there anyone else you can think of?"

Katie looked down at the table and shook her head. "No, no, there's not. That's the only person I can think of." The tears had stopped flowing now, and she reached up to wipe the last traces from her cheeks.

"Okay. Well, that's a good starting point. Since it doesn't look like we're going to get much help from the local authorities, at least for a while, let's go ahead and get started."

Katie raised her head and gave Jackson a soft smile. "Thanks, Jackson. I really mean it. Thank you."

He smiled back and patted her hand. "Do you have her aunt's phone number?" he asked.

"Yeah, I think I have it in my phone. Tiffany went up there for a visit several months ago, and she gave me her aunt's home number in case I couldn't reach her on her cell."

"Okay, great. Why don't you go outside, get some fresh air, and call Tiffany's aunt? Check with the local hospitals and the state patrol, too. I'll poke around in here some more and make sure we didn't miss anything."

She stood from the table and said, "Okay. Sounds good to me."

Jackson watched her cross the living room and then exit through the front door. Once she was outside and the door closed behind her, he threw his head back and stared at the ceiling. He wiped both his hands across his face and let out an exasperated sigh. The realization that he had no idea what to do next punched him in the gut, and he started to panic. What would he do if he lost her?

You have to find her, Jackson.

What had happened to her? Who had taken her? And more importantly, what were they *doing* to her? He said a silent prayer she was okay. The idea of someone harming Tiffany made him numb inside, but then he forced the negative thoughts out of his head. He had to focus.

He stood and pushed the chair back under the table, then walked down the hall to the bathroom. He would start his second search there and work his way back to the front door. Maybe he had missed something the first time, and he hoped that if he had, he wouldn't miss it a second. Tiffany and Katie were both counting on him.

Again.

19

Jackson was in the kitchen, almost finished with his second search of the house, when Katie opened the front door and came back inside. He looked up from the chalk-colored linoleum floor he had been staring at, searching for any clue that might have escaped him the first time. "Did you get in touch with Tiffany's aunt?" he asked as Katie closed the door behind her.

She stopped next to the sofa, pushed her cellphone into her front pocket, and sighed. "Yeah, I called her. She hasn't heard from Tiffany since last week. She said everything seemed perfectly normal the last time she talked to her, but that she would call me back if Tiffany contacts her."

Jackson allowed his eyes to fall back to the floor. He wished he could find something, anything, but so far, the only thing that was even slightly suspicious was the carpet stain in Tiffany's bedroom—and that hardly seemed like a smoking gun. He was bent over, his hands on his knees, scanning the area where the kitchen counters met the floor. "What about the state patrol and the hospitals?" he asked over his shoulder.

"Yep, I called them, too. There were no reports of Tiffany being in an accident, and the state patrol said her tag number had not been run through their system in the last forty-eight hours."

Jackson pushed against his knees and stood up. "Hmm, I was really hoping you had some luck, because so far, I've come up empty-handed, too. I'm almost finished in here," he motioned with his arm toward the living room. "Do you want to take another look in there while I finish up?"

"Sure," Katie replied. She walked around the sofa and began studying the corner nearest the recliner. Her cellphone rang, and she answered it. Jackson listened carefully, hopeful it was Tiffany calling. He soon realized it was Cody instead. He turned his attention back to his search.

He was disappointed Katie hadn't gleaned any information from her phone calls to Tiffany's aunt and the authorities, and the gnawing feeling in his stomach that she had been right all along was growing steadily.

He finished his search of the kitchen floor, then walked to the trashcan and flipped the lid up. The bag had been changed recently. He could see a few items resting at the bottom, but couldn't get a clear view of them. He removed the lid and set it down on the floor, then reached into the bag cautiously, not knowing what might be in there.

He fished with his fingers and withdrew three items. He laid them out on the floor in front of him, checked the trashcan a final time to ensure he hadn't missed anything, then set it back against the wall. As he knelt down and examined his find on the floor, the three items seemed inconsequential. There was a coffee mug, a stained paperback novel, and a used tea bag—that was it. Still, something seemed odd about the collection; he just couldn't put his finger on what it was. But he had that familiar feeling that always told him to slow down because he was about to miss something important.

"Hey, Katie," he called over his shoulder.

"Yes?"

"Come in here a minute, will you?" He heard her walking across the hardwood floor of the living room as she approached the kitchen. She was still talking to Cody.

"I've got to go, Cody. I promise I'll call you later. Thank you. I love you, too."

"Did you find something?" she asked as she tapped the screen of her cellphone and leaned over his shoulder.

"No, I don't think so . . . well, maybe . . . I don't know." He motioned with his right hand to the three items on the floor in front of him. "I found these in the bottom of the trashcan. They were the only things in there, and it just seemed kinda odd to me. That's Tiffany's favorite mug, isn't it?"

Katie moved to his left side and knelt beside him. She picked up the coffee mug and turned it in her hands, inspecting it. Once she spun it around, Jackson could see the same picture of Katie and Tiffany posing in front of a mountain landscape that he had watched Tiffany grasp in her hands numerous times before.

"She wouldn't have thrown this away," Katie said, her voice trembling slightly.

Jackson was afraid she was about to start crying again at the sight of the picture.

"We got two of these made during one of our shopping trips to Pigeon Forge. I have an identical one at my house." Katie turned the mug over in her hand again.

"She loved this mug. Every time I was over here, if she was drinking coffee or tea, she had this mug in her hand."

"I know. I saw her use it almost every time I was over here, too. Maybe it's cracked or something," Jackson said. "That would explain why she threw it away."

Katie lifted the mug by the handle, then put it close to Jackson's face so he could see. "No, it's not damaged at all. And besides, she would have glued it back together rather than throw it away. It meant that much to her."

Jackson took the mug from Katie's hand and examined it himself. It was in perfect condition.

"Tiffany didn't put the mug in the garbage, Jackson . . . someone else did."

Jackson set the mug down without saying anything, then picked up the paperback novel. The pages were discolored, obviously stained by something. He handed it to Katie and asked, "What is that, tea?"

She took the book and examined the pages. "Well, it's hard to say, but it looks a little too light to be a coffee stain. And not to state the obvious, but there was a tea bag in the trash." She picked up the bag by the cotton thread and let it swing in front of her face.

Jackson laughed softly. "True," he said, then picked the book up again and examined the stains a second time.

"The tea bag probably just fell on the book and stained the pages," Katie said.

Jackson shifted the novel in his hands again, then opened it. The stains penetrated well into the pages, almost to the spine. "No, I don't think so," he countered.

"Why not?"

"Well, for one thing, look at the pages." He shifted the open book toward Katie. "There's been quite a bit of liquid poured on this. Much more than you would get from just a used tea bag."

"Yeah, you're right. I didn't notice that."

He closed the book and tossed it on the floor next to the mug. "And for another, the tea bag was in the bottom of the can, then the mug, then the novel. No way could the tea bag have stained the book in that position."

Katie looked at him, her blonde bangs scattered haphazardly over her forehead, which was furrowed with worry. "So what are you thinking?"

Jackson didn't answer. He knew the common household items were trying to tell him something, but he couldn't make the connection. Then, several seconds later, it hit him. He picked up the mug and the novel, then said, "Follow me." He walked toward Tiffany's bedroom, Katie following behind. Just inside the door, he bent down and stared at the irregular-shaped stain on the carpet.

"What is it?" Katie asked as she entered the room.

"Here, look at this." He traced the outside of the stain with his index finger. "I thought there was something strange about the shape of this stain. I just didn't have enough information, until now, to figure out why it looked so odd."

"I don't understand," Katie said as she knelt beside him.

"If someone drops a cup of liquid on a carpet, it generally makes a pattern with smooth edges as the liquid flows and soaks into the fabric. There may be splatter here and there," he pointed at some smaller drops away from the main stain, "but it's generally one continuous stain, right?"

"I guess so," she responded, a quizzical look on her face.

"Well, this stain is smooth on the right side," he again pointed with his index finger, "but look at the left. It isn't smooth at all, and its edge is much sharper."

"It looks like half of it is missing," Katie added.

"Exactly. Something was blocking the liquid, so that all of it didn't reach the carpet." He picked up the novel from beside him and placed it next to the carpet stain. "But when we add the book, the whole picture becomes clear."

Katie gasped.

The patterns on the book and the carpet matched, creating one continuous stain.

"So what do you think happened?" she asked.

Jackson cupped his chin between his thumb and index finger for several seconds. "I'm not sure," he said. "But I think you're right about the mug, that Tiffany would never have thrown it away. That means someone else had to be here in her cabin last night after I left. When you add the book and the carpet stain into the mix, it looks even more suspicious." He paused and rubbed his chin. "I think Tiffany was headed to bed, carrying the paperback and the cup of tea, was startled by something, and dropped both of them." He motioned with his hand to the mug and book on the floor. "Then, whoever was in here with her cleaned everything up. He was in a hurry, too." Jackson picked up the novel and the coffee mug and began to walk back toward the kitchen, speaking over his shoulder as he went. "He didn't take the time to clean the stain. He just grabbed the book and mug off the floor, rushed to the kitchen, and tossed them both into the trashcan, where they landed on top of the used tea bag."

Jackson looked up at Katie, who had followed him from the bedroom. "I know it's a wild theory, and maybe

I'm completely wrong, but it's the best I can come up with at the moment," he said.

Katie sighed. "Well, it sounds plausible. All the pieces do fit together." She paused and put her hand to her forehead, brushing the errant bangs away from her face. "I know it sounds crazy, Jackson, but Paul McMillan has something to do with this. I know he does."

Jackson wasn't sure what to say. He knew that when a man was dead, he was dead. But something in his gut told him to believe what Katie was saying. And his gut rarely proved wrong. It had saved his ass more than once during his tenure as a park ranger. "I believe you," he said, watching as relief filled Katie's eyes. "I'm sorry, Katie. Really, I'm so sorry. I wish she had been honest with me at dinner last night. If I'd had any clue that she was in danger, I would never have left her here alone. Please believe that." He felt guilty. It was his fault Tiffany was gone. He should've done more to protect her.

"Stop it, Jackson. It's not your fault. Blaming yourself is not going to help at all. We just have to do everything we can to find her before—" She stopped mid-sentence.

Jackson looked at Katie. He could tell by the look on her face what she had intended to say, but couldn't force herself to. "I know," he said.

Katie reached out and placed her hand on his shoulder.

Jackson still couldn't shake the feeling that somehow this whole thing was his fault. If anything happened to Tiffany, he would never forgive himself.

Why hadn't he walked her inside the cabin?

He hoped he wouldn't be asking himself that same question for the rest of his life.

"So what do we do now? Call the police and tell them what we've found?" Katie asked.

"Yeah, I'll call back, but I doubt it'll do any good. An odd-shaped stain on the carpet and a cherished mug in the trash isn't exactly going to bring out the cavalry to help. I'm afraid we're going to have to do this on our own, at least until we can find something more definitive as to her whereabouts."

Jackson stepped across the kitchen and rested his hands on the edge of the stainless steel sink. He peered out the window and watched a few more leaves fall to the ground. The wind was blowing even harder now, the sky heavy and thick with gray clouds. The realization that Tiffany had indeed been taken against her will hit him like a freight train, and he felt the ache in the pit of his stomach intensify.

He wished he knew what to do, which direction to head, at least a starting point—anything—instead, he felt like a flimsy lifeboat tossed on an angry sea.

The woman he loved was in danger, and he had to do something. He sure as hell wasn't going to sit on his hands while she was out there, whether the local authorities were willing to help or not. Thoughts of what she could be going through at the hands of her captor flashed through his mind. He felt the anger he had struggled to hold back begin to burn white-hot inside him.

If the son of a bitch who had taken Tiffany harmed her, he would kill him.

He was just about to turn from the window when he heard Katie speak. "Jackson," she said, "I think I know someone who might be able to help us."

20

Nathan Lansing knelt down and picked the last ripe tomato from his garden. The weatherman was predicting an unusually early frost in a few days, behind an approaching autumn storm system, and he wanted to salvage everything he could from the small garden in his backyard before Mother Nature took the rest.

He raised the barely ripe tomato to his face and examined it. It was a pitiful example of what a tomato should be, much smaller than the prime ones of the summer months that had long ago vanished. Its mottled, light red skin put a frown on his face. He sighed and gently lowered it into the plastic bag on the ground next to him. He always hated seeing the tomato plants produce their last fruits of the season. In his opinion, there was nothing finer than a thick-sliced garden tomato sandwiched between two slices of white bread, generously coated with mayonnaise.

He grabbed the plastic bag with his right hand and stood. He wiped the excess dirt on his left hand onto the bib of his denim overalls. His house sat on a small hill, offering a panoramic view of the countryside that was rare in this mostly-flat part of Georgia. He scanned the landscape that stretched beyond his small plot of land. It was forested with large tracts of pine trees, but was dotted with the occasional pasture or small farm. He saw several cows feeding near the Cables' barn.

He loved living in the country.

He drew a deep breath into his nostrils, the musky smell of the dirt awakening his senses. He always enjoyed spending time outside. Whether it was working in his garden or taking care of the two additional acres that surrounded his modest home in rural Hayward County, something about getting his hands dirty made him feel alive. After he was finished in the garden, he planned to spend the afternoon riding his John Deere mower, cutting the grass before the forecast rain moved in overnight.

While many people he knew dreaded doing outside chores, he relished them, and there was nothing else he would rather be doing on a Saturday. It was time away from the office, away from all the stress.

He had been sheriff of Hayward County for thirty years, but in the last few, the job had begun to weigh on him. He had just turned sixty the month before, and his wife, June, was pushing him to think about retiring. He wasn't so fired up on the idea just yet, but he had to admit to himself that he could feel his body slowing and wondered how many more years he would be able to handle the demands of his job. He had two years left in his current term, and he intended to serve it. He owed it to the voters who had elected him over and over during the past three decades.

Being the sheriff of a county in rural Georgia had its quirks, for sure. His job wasn't the pressure cooker most of his peers experienced, the ones who had larger metropolitan areas inside their counties, but he stayed plenty busy. One day he might be hauling in a drunk who had gotten mad at his girlfriend and decided to rough her up, and the next, he would be helping Mrs. Walbury recover her cat—for the hundredth time—that had gotten stuck in the large pine tree in her front yard.

It seemed he was out at the Widow Walbury's house three or four times a week, checking on something for her. If she heard a strange noise in the middle of the night, she wouldn't hesitate to call him and have him check it out—no matter how late it was. He didn't mind helping the old lady out, but the time he spent with her did eat into his other duties. But when you were the sheriff in a small town, everyone knew you by your first name, and they expected you to come running when they called, no matter how trivial the matter.

He walked down the row of tomato plants, passing green leaves that would be hit by frost and start to turn brown within a few days. When he reached the opposite end of the garden, he knelt down and checked on the spinach he had planted several weeks ago, when the weather had first begun to cool. They were maturing now and would provide fresh salad greens in a few more days. He touched his finger to one of the tender green leaves, lifting it slightly to examine it. He had always admired the spinach plant because it was hardy. It wasn't like the tomato that wilted at the first sign of frost. No, a spinach plant could hang on well into winter, until it was hit with a crippling cold snap, which sometimes never came in Central Georgia.

He hoped he was like the spinach plant and would be able to keep producing something useful well into the winter of his life.

"Nathan! Nathan!" he heard his wife call from the back deck of their home.

"Dammit," he whispered under his breath. He didn't want to raise his head in response because he knew his wife would bother him for only one thing while he was working in the garden. He had asked that she tell anyone who called looking for the sheriff that he was out of town today, but he had known she wouldn't listen, even as the words left his lips. It was just wishful thinking on his part, he guessed. He loved his wife dearly, but he thought she needed to learn to say no every now and then. It seemed she could never bring herself to deny a resident of Hayward County the opportunity to speak to the sheriff.

He kept his head down, still kneeling and inspecting the row of spinach plants. After several seconds of thoughtful delay, in which he found no satisfactory excuse not to answer his wife, he yelled back, "What?"

"Someone's on the phone for you!"

He sighed. "I told you to tell them I'm out of town today, June!"

"I know you did, Nathan, but this sounds important! Now, get your butt up here and answer the phone!" she persisted.

At last, he looked up from the spinach plants, toward June. He could see his wife standing on the deck, holding the cordless phone in her hand. She had the palm of her opposite hand covering the receiver so the caller couldn't hear her yelling at her ornery husband. She looked agitated, but he always thought she was most beautiful when she was just a little pissed off. She was wearing a knee-length blue and white dress, her graying brown hair flowing over her shoulders. He had been in love with her ever since they first met in the fifth grade and, even though she sometimes got on his last nerve, she still got his blood pumping every time.

He smiled and pushed his hands against the well-worn knees of his overalls. "Who is it?" he yelled, standing. He raised his voice enough to be heard by June, but not enough to convey anger.

"I'm not sure," she replied, still cupping the receiver with her palm. "Said he was a park ranger in North Carolina. Said you helped a friend of his out several years ago and that she's in trouble now."

"What?"

"Said you helped a friend of his out several years ago," she repeated.

"I heard that part, June! What's his friend's name?"

He watched as his wife put the phone back to her ear, spoke a few words, then placed her hand back over the receiver and shouted, "Tiffany Colson!"

Nathan hadn't heard that name in years, but he remembered it very clearly. He wondered why someone would be calling about her now, but knew instantly that this wasn't the run-of-the-mill cat emergency from Mrs. Walbury that he had been expecting. He rubbed his hand across his whiskered face. He never shaved on Saturdays, and he could feel the roughness of his chin against his palm. "Okay, just a minute! I'm coming," he yelled back to his wife.

He picked up the bag of less-than-stellar tomatoes from the ground and walked toward the house. With every step he took, he wondered what he would hear on the other end of the line. The last he had heard from Tiffany, she was working somewhere near Atlanta in a dentist's office, but that had to have been six, eight years ago at least. He couldn't remember for sure.

His memory of Tiffany Colson was that of a bright, attractive young girl who had gotten mixed up with the wrong man. But he had always thought she was a good person, and he was having a difficult time imagining what type of trouble she could be in now.

He reached the steps that led from the backyard up to the deck and climbed them quicker than he had intended to, leaving him somewhat winded by the time he reached the top.

"Be careful on those steps, Nathan," his wife admonished. "You're no spring chicken anymore."

"Yeah, yeah, I hear you." He smiled. "There may be snow on the roof, baby, but there's still a fire in the furnace." He winked at his wife as she handed him the phone. He saw the sheepish grin he loved come across her face. As she turned to go back inside the house, he reached out and swatted her on the butt. She giggled and looked back over her shoulder, giving him that flirtatious look he had come to know so well.

Maybe, if he played his cards right, he would get lucky tonight.

He set the bag of tomatoes on the circular, wrought iron table that stood in the center of the deck, then stretched out on a nearby lounge chair, letting his sore legs rest in front of him. He removed his straw hat and placed it on top of his thighs, then ran a hand through his sweaty salt-and-pepper hair before putting the phone to his ear. "This is Sheriff Lansing," he said, still slightly out of breath from his quick climb up the stairs.

"Hello, Sheriff Lansing. Thank you for taking my call. My name is Jackson Hart, and I'm a ranger with the U.S. Park Service. I was hoping you could help me out."

Nathan took a breath before speaking. "Well, I'll certainly try. What can I do for you, Ranger Hart?"

"Please, call me Jackson," the voice on the other end of the line said.

"Okay, Jackson. How can I help you?" Nathan asked again.

"I think you helped a friend of mine several years ago. Her name is Tiffany Colson, and she used to live in your county, I believe. Do you remember her?"

"Yes, I remember her very well," Nathan replied. "Nice young lady. Quite the looker, too, if I recall."

"Yes, she is that," Jackson replied. "Anyway, I'm up in Western North Carolina with Tiffany's best friend, Katie McAlister. I've got you on speaker phone so we can both talk with you."

"Hi, Sheriff," Nathan heard a young woman say in the background. He thought she sounded worried.

"Sheriff, we're calling because Tiffany has vanished from her home here in North Carolina, and we think it may have something to do with the case you were involved with several years ago," Jackson said.

"You mean when she killed that McMillan boy?" Nathan asked.

"Yes, that's the one. Can you tell me anything about it?"

Nathan sighed and wiped his brow clean of the drops of sweat that had gathered there. "Well, I'm not sure exactly what you're looking for, but I remember the details of the case fairly well." Nathan paused. "That was almost ten years ago, I believe. Why would that have anything to do with her disappearing?" he asked. "And you say she lives in North Carolina now? That seems like a bit of a stretch, if you ask me, Jackson."

"Yeah, I know it's a stretch, but it's all we have to go on right now. We were hoping you might be able to give us some information that would help us locate her."

Nathan could hear the tension rising in the ranger's voice. "Well, it was a pretty straightforward case as far as I was concerned. Paul McMillan was a troublemaker. Always had been. I had arrested him several times when he was a teenager for breaking and entering and a few times for drug possession. His family's money always got him off, though."

"Sheriff, can you tell us specifically about the night Tiffany killed him?" Katie asked.

"Well, when I arrived at the scene, ma'am, your friend was lying on the floor of the McMillan mansion with two cuts across her abdomen, and Paul was right beside her, with a large knife in his chest. I did a thorough investigation and concluded that it was self-defense. Seems the sick bastard had tried to set Tiffany on fire in the bathtub, but she somehow managed to escape. He then tried to kill her downstairs, near the front door, but she got the best of him." Nathan hesitated, then said, "I'm sorry for the bad language, ma'am, but that's exactly what he was and, to tell you the truth, I was glad to see him go." He cleared his throat, then added, "One thing's for sure. Once he was dead, his family's money and power couldn't help him . . . and I was just fine with that."

"So what happened after that?" Jackson asked.

"Well, the McMillan family pressured the DA to press charges against Tiffany, but I told him that if he pursued an indictment, he would have to contend with me as a witness for the defense. Everything Tiffany said checked out, and I wasn't about to let the McMillan name bulldoze me again. So, despite their threats, the case was closed. It was ruled justifiable homicide, and the McMillan clan tucked their tails and stayed low for a while." Nathan laughed softly. "It was a great day."

"So that was it? After the investigation, everything just died?" Jackson asked.

"Yeah, pretty much. They tried to kick up a stink about it every so often for a few years, but there wasn't much even they could do about it once the DA refused to press charges."

"Sheriff, before Tiffany disappeared, she told me she had been experiencing really bad nightmares about Paul and that she thought someone had been snooping around her cabin. Do you think any of the McMillans could be trying to seek revenge all these years later?" Katie asked.

"Hmm, it's possible, but I doubt it. I haven't heard much from them in the last year or two."

"You're sure they wouldn't, I don't know, try to get vengeance or something?" Katie persisted.

"Well, no, I'm not sure. Like I said, it is possible." Nathan took a breath and rubbed his face with his hand before continuing. "But I'll tell you one thing, ma'am, the McMillans are very powerful people in this state. I beat them at their own game once, but they are not people who are accustomed to losing, if you know what I mean." He paused and sat up in the lounge chair, letting his legs swing off to the sides and planting his boots on the wooden deck. "Dealing with people like the McMillans can be dangerous, that's for sure. If I were you, I would be very careful if you plan to go up against them."

There was silence on the line for several seconds, then Jackson began to speak again. "Sheriff, I'm going to ask you a crazy question. To be honest, I'm kinda shocked I'm even asking it myself." He paused.

"Okay. Go on, son," Nathan prodded. He could hear Jackson take a deep breath on the other end of the line.

"Before Tiffany disappeared, she told Katie that she wasn't sure that Paul had actually died that night when he attacked her. She had this idea that he had survived somehow and had come back to kill her. You know, make her pay for what she had done to him." Jackson paused again. "Is there any way that is even remotely possible?"

Nathan laughed softly into the phone. "No way in hell. That boy was graveyard dead."

"And you're sure about that?" Jackson asked again.

"Look, son, I may be a small town sheriff, but I've been around enough to know when someone's gone to meet their Maker. Trust me . . . he was dead."

"Sorry, Sheriff, I didn't mean to offend you. We just needed to know for certain that Paul was really dead," Jackson said, "that way we can move on to another theory."

"No, it's okay. Sorry if I snapped at you." Nathan got up from the chair, opened the sliding glass door, and walked inside the house. He went to the corner of the living room where his computer desk sat and pulled a pad of paper and a pen from one of the drawers. "Tell you what, give me your phone number, and I'll do some checking down here, see if I can find anything that might help you out," he said as he pulled the chair away from the desk and sat down.

"Thank you, Sheriff, we really appreciate it," Jackson said.

"No problem." Nathan wrote the phone number Jackson gave him on the paper, then added, "I hope you find Tiffany."

"Thanks, we're going to try our best."

"I'll see what I can dig up and be in touch." Nathan hung up, then set the phone down on the desk. He jiggled the computer mouse, and the monitor came to life.

He decided that mowing the lawn could wait until tomorrow.

21

Tiffany couldn't breathe. She watched in horror as the brass doorknob turned counterclockwise. Her heart was racing, and she could feel every pounding pulse of blood ricocheting in her head.

The door opened just a crack, letting in a thin stream of daylight. Every sound was intensified, her senses on overload as panic raced through her.

This couldn't be happening.

It wasn't real.

Just another bad dream.

She gasped, no longer able to hold her breath. The door moved another few inches, then swung wide.

And then she saw him.

Standing in the doorway was a tall man, backlit against the gray sky, his face obscured by the casting shadow of the door. He was an evil monster, a coal-black figure surrounded by a halo of autumn light.

But Tiffany didn't need to see his face.

She couldn't stand to look any longer. She snapped her head back down to the floor, the lifeless, acrylic eyes of the bearskin rug staring back at her. She silently wished the dead beast would resurrect itself and save her. A chill ran through her body, and she trembled. She forced the shaking to stop, not wanting Paul to see her fear.

She knew what awaited her.

She should've cut his head off. At least he would've been dead for sure. Now, she was going to pay the price for her carelessness.

She heard him step through the doorway, his heavy boots striking the floor and echoing off the log walls of the home. Then the sound of the door closing behind him and the thunder of the deadbolt sliding home.

"Good afternoon, Tiffany," he said in the same cutting southern drawl that had haunted her so many times in her dreams.

She didn't speak, but remained focused on the acrylic eyes in front of her, still wishing the bear would magically rise and finish the job she had failed to. She heard him moving again, and when she caught a glimpse of his hiking boots in the periphery of her vision, she closed her eyes, not willing to see even a part of the demon who had her in his grasp once again. She heard the unmistakable sound of car keys landing on the granite countertop of the kitchen island, then those heavy boots approaching her. She winced and squeezed her eyelids tight. He was just inches away now.

"Hello, Tiffany," he whispered into her right ear.

She felt his stale breath flow over her face. It smelled of beer and cigarettes. Her nostrils flared and she gagged. Goose bumps engulfed her flesh, as she felt a rush of lightheadedness overcome her. She wished she would pass out. Anything to escape what she knew Paul planned for her. If she could simply wish herself dead, she would do it.

He grabbed her chin and squeezed it tightly in his hand, then yanked her head to the right. "Open your eyes!"

She refused.

He released his grip on her chin and backhanded her across the cheek. An involuntary cry escaped, and her weakness shamed her. She wanted to be strong, to show him she wasn't afraid any longer—even if the reality was exactly the opposite.

She bit her lip, trying to keep from crying, but couldn't. She felt tears begin to stream down her face. He grasped her chin again and, for a second time, turned her face to meet his. "Open your eyes and look at me!" he screamed. When she hesitated, he dug his fingernails into her flesh. "NOW!"

She finally complied and cracked open her eyelids the slightest bit. Now, through watery eyes, she could see the face that had haunted her for ten years. His thick brown hair, his mustache, his gray eyes. One corner of his mouth turned up in the same evil grin she remembered. "Hello, Tiffany," he said again in a low, guttural growl.

She gritted her teeth, still trying to project confidence, despite the fact that she was falling apart inside. She breathed deeply, struggling in vain to calm her trembling body and runaway heartbeat. "Hello . . . Paul," she finally whispered.

"Long time no see, Tiffany."

"I'm . . . I'm sorry, Paul. Really, I am. I'm sorry I hurt you," she said in a halting cadence, interrupted by the gasps of her own rapid breathing.

Still squeezing her chin in his palm, he bent down and whispered in her ear, "Apology not accepted."

An involuntary sob escaped her body.

Tiffany knew that she wasn't hiding anything from Paul—her soul was laid bare in front of him. In an instant, she realized that what she had tried to deny, what she had most feared, had been true all along.

She was his.

22

You find anything?" Jackson asked Katie, the cell-phone pressed tight to his ear. He pushed the gas pedal and headed up the steep hill, away from the Mountain View Resort Marina. He glanced in his rearview mirror and saw Fontana Lake growing smaller behind him, the abundant hardwoods bathing the shoreline in hues of gold, crimson, and violet. When he reached the top of the hill, he accelerated as he pointed his pickup back toward the main resort area and Tiffany's cabin.

"No," Katie replied. "I drove by every building, checked every parking lot, and I saw no sign of her. I thought maybe we had missed something the first time, but I guess not. How 'bout you?"

"Nothing. I checked out by the dam and the marina. I'm headed back now."

"Did you call the police again?" Katie asked.

"Yeah. They said they'd send someone out first thing in the morning to file a missing person report if she doesn't show up tonight."

"Did you tell them about what we found in her cabin?"

"No, Katie, I didn't. Somehow, I figured that telling them about me playing CSI on the floor of her bedroom with a paperback novel and a coffee mug wouldn't really help the situation," Jackson replied. He tried to keep the sarcasm out of his voice, but couldn't help himself.

"I guess that's true."

Jackson thought he heard Katie stifle a chuckle, which was a good sign. They both needed to stay positive if they were going to find Tiffany.

"Besides," he continued, "if what we think happened to Tiffany really did, then waiting around for the local cops to decide to do something isn't going to cut it."

"So what do we do now?"

Jackson heard the frustration creeping back into her voice. "Now, we wait for Sheriff Lansing to call back and hope he has some information that will help us. We'll try to get into her computer, see what websites she visited, who she contacted . . . maybe we'll get lucky there. And we'll check with the hospitals and the state patrol again, just to make sure there wasn't an accident or something."

"If there had been an accident, they would've known about it when I called earlier."

"Most likely, but it won't hurt to double-check. Things do fall through the cracks occasionally."

"So that's it?" she asked.

"Yeah, Katie, that's it. I'm sorry, but right now, at least until we hear back from Sheriff Lansing, there's not much more we can do. If we don't find her by tomorrow, we'll contact local media and try to get them to run the story, even if the police won't start a search." Jackson paused and gave Katie an opportunity to comment, but she was silent. "I'll see you back at her cabin in a few minutes," he said, then hung up. He tossed the cellphone into the passenger seat of his pickup and rolled his window down.

The air was cool, and it had that sharpness to it that only autumn could produce—a subtle warning of the cold winter months that lay ahead. Jackson ran a hand through his thick black hair, letting the wind smack him directly in the face.

He was trying so hard to exhibit confidence for Katie, but the truth was, he was worried. The knot in the pit of his stomach showed no signs of easing but instead, had grown exponentially over the past couple of hours.

Several minutes later, he arrived back at Tiffany's cabin. He walked briskly onto the porch, then stepped through the already open front door. Katie was sitting in the recliner with Tiffany's laptop resting on her thighs. He closed the door behind him. "You probably shouldn't be here by yourself with the door standing wide open," Jackson said, then paused. "You know . . . considering everything that's happened."

"Sorry. I really needed some fresh air," Katie replied, never looking up, her eyes glued to the computer screen in front of her.

Jackson sighed at her indifference, but decided not to say anything else about her lapse in security. "Find anything on her laptop?"

"Not yet. I just hacked her password as you pulled up."

"How'd you manage to do that?" Jackson asked as he took a seat on the sofa across from Katie.

"I typed in Tiffany and Jackson," she said, still looking down at the screen and moving her index finger feverishly over the built-in touch pad, clicking the adjacent buttons every few seconds. "All one word, by the way." Katie finally looked up at Jackson and offered an I-told-you-so smile.

Jackson didn't know what to say. Actually, he was afraid to try to speak, afraid that his voice might crack. Instead, he just returned Katie's smile with a sheepish one of his own. She went back to the keyboard immediately and continued searching the laptop. Just that simple show of affection, something as seemingly insignificant as a computer password, one that he was probably never supposed to know about, made Jackson more determined than ever to find Tiffany. Part of him felt like an idiot, like a fifth-grader who had just gotten a love note from the cute girl in the back of the class. But he didn't care.

He had to find her.

He had spent countless hours helping other people find their missing loved ones, people who had walked off a hiking trail or wandered away from a campsite, during his career as a park ranger, but he never thought he would have to use his skills to find someone *he* loved. But Tiffany was the only woman he could imagine spending the rest of his life with, and, whatever the cost, he would find her. "Still nothing?" he asked Katie, who continued to type on the computer keyboard.

"Nope. I checked her Internet search history but didn't find anything suspicious, just some shopping and news websites. I'm going through her recently accessed files now, but, so far, I haven't seen anything that jumps out at me. It's probably a dead end," Katie said.

"Well, keep trying. We need to rule out everything we can." Jackson was just about to get up from the couch and go into the kitchen to grab a glass of water when the sound of his cellphone ringing startled him. He reached out and plucked it from the sofa cushion beside him and looked at the screen.

It was Sheriff Lansing calling.

23

Tiffany rubbed the cotton rope against the back of the chair. She had found an area where the wood was splintered along the left edge, and she had spent the last thirty minutes slowly abrading the rope against it. Her wrists were sore from the methodical up-and-down motion and the strain of the rope against her flesh, but her persistence was paying off, and she could now feel the outside layer of the cotton beginning to fray. That small bit of progress gave her the strength to keep going. She worked slowly, careful to be as quiet as possible.

She stared at Paul. He was asleep on the leather sofa in front of the fireplace, having passed out almost an hour ago after downing the last three beers of a six-pack. She suspected he had begun drinking long before she woke up from her own drug-induced stupor. She could see his feet hanging over the end of the couch, the top of his chest, and just part of one of his arms, the back of the sofa blocking most of her view.

Without warning, he let out a loud snore, causing Tiffany to jump in the chair. She froze, feeling her heart thumping against her eardrums again. She held her breath for several seconds, watching as he rolled over, drew his arms into his chest, then began to snore again. She prayed he wouldn't rouse.

He didn't.

She let out a silent sigh of relief and continued working on the rope. The visceral fear that had consumed her the moment he had first appeared in the doorway had been replaced with a fierce determination to survive.

She had to figure a way out of this.

Stay calm and think, Tiffany.

She had faced death just hours ago on the floor of her own cabin and had somehow survived. She wasn't going to waste the second chance she had been given by remaining strapped to the chair, just waiting for the inevitable.

No. She would fight.

But she wasn't sure what she intended to do if she actually did manage to free herself of the restraints. Run for the front door and hope for the best? She had no idea where she was. From the little she could see through the windows, she would be running barefoot into the wilderness, and she didn't like her chances if it came down to that. Sure, she spent a lot of time in the forest leading tourists on nature hikes, but she had no *real* outdoor skills to speak of. She sure as hell couldn't start a fire by rubbing two sticks together, so her chances of surviving with nothing but a pair of pink pajamas were slim. She would succumb to hypothermia in a few days. But she knew it would never come to that. The reality was, as soon as she made a run for it, Paul would catch her in a matter of seconds, and then it would be a thousand times worse for her.

But she had to do something. Had to give herself a goal to work toward. So she kept rubbing the rope against the back of the chair.

She decided she would need to incapacitate him somehow. As she continued to work on the rope, she glanced around the room, searching for something she could use as a weapon. She still wasn't sure she could even get free of the chair, but wanted to be ready in case the opportunity arose. After several seconds of searching, she spotted a set of kitchen knives protruding from a wooden block next to the refrigerator. She could tell from the length of the handles that at least two of the knives were large. She had stabbed Paul with a knife years ago, and she had no doubt she could and would do it again if it meant saving her life.

But this time—she would make sure he was dead.

24

Tiffany's arms and hands were tingling. They had been in an awkward position for too long, and the intense sensation was transitioning from annoying to painful. She tried to wiggle her fingers to keep the blood flowing, but it didn't help.

She strained against the last bit of rope that bound her wrists, but she still couldn't break it. The skin on her wrists was raw, and pain shot up her arm with each movement as the rope dug into her flesh. She had to be close, though. She had been working for what felt like an eternity and could feel the bindings weakening.

She gritted her teeth and rubbed the cotton rope against the cracked wood several more times with a quick up-and-down motion.

She held her breath and strained against the binding, trying to force her wrists apart once more. She pushed and pulled with every ounce of strength that remained in her forearms. At last, she heard the muted sound of cotton fibers rending behind her back. She exhaled in relief, careful not to make any noise that might wake Paul.

After watching him for several seconds and seeing no sign of movement from the couch, she allowed her numb arms to swing to her sides. As the blood flow quickly returned to her limbs, the tingling sensation of a thousand pricking needles almost made her gasp, but she bit her lip again to keep from making a sound. She removed the rope from both her wrists and then shook her arms out, opening and closing her hands slowly. She waited silently, impatiently, in the chair, allowing the feeling to return to her extremities while, at the same time, keeping an eye on Paul. She was ready to move her hands behind her back at any second, hoping that if he just glanced at her, he wouldn't be able to see she had freed her arms and would then simply roll over and go back to sleep.

Once her arms and hands began to feel better, she turned her attention to the rope tied around her thighs. She ran her hand along the length of it, searching for the knot. She found it just under the seat on her right side. She was working blind again, just as she had been forced to do to free her wrists, tugging and pulling at the edges of the knot with her fingers, gradually loosening it.

She managed to untie the knot in just over a minute. She was thankful Paul wasn't an expert at tying knots. She pulled the section of rope free from under the chair and placed it on the wooden floor, next to the ones she had removed from her wrists.

She paused her escape attempt and stared at Paul. He was still breathing heavily and seemed to have drifted into a deep, alcohol-induced sleep. She waited another minute, just to be sure, because once she started working on the rope that went around her chest, there would be no pretending if he awoke. He would see what she was doing immediately.

But she really had no choice. She had to get away from him, and every second was crucial.

Confident he was sound asleep, Tiffany raised her arms to her chest and began to loosen the rope that ran just under her breasts. She was elated to find that the rope wasn't as tight as the first two, and she actually managed to work both of her hands between the rope and her chest.

She pulled hard to her left and felt the rope begin to move. Her next pull caught the knot on the corner of the chair's back. *Dammit,* she thought. She considered pulling again, but was afraid the sudden movement of trying to dislodge the knot would make too much noise.

Instead, she turned her palms outward and pushed against the rope. She glanced down and could see that a gap, about an inch or so wide, now existed between her body and the rope. Using her hands, she began to slide the rope upward, over her breasts, twisting her body slightly as she went. In just a few seconds, she had the loosened rope near her neck. She thrust it quickly over her head and added it to the growing pile on the floor.

Once again, a loud snore shattered the silence of the room, reverberating off the log walls.

She turned her head slightly to the left and stared at Paul. She was terrified he would suddenly rise from the sofa. She waited a few more seconds, not moving a muscle. She could hear her heart pounding against her chest and was sure Paul could hear it, too.

But she had come too far to stop.

She had to act now.

She moved her hands to her feet and worked as fast and as silently as she could. She untied the knots that secured her ankles to the wooden legs with surprising speed, letting the cotton rope fall to the floor.

She knew she had to get out of the chair and make it to the block of knives on the kitchen counter, but she also knew this was the most dangerous part of her escape. One squeaking floor board, one jostle of the chair, would be fatal.

She steeled herself for what she had to do. She took a deep breath, then braced the chair with her hands. She stood slowly, keeping her eyes on the sleeping monster as she moved. If he woke, she would make a mad dash for the front door and forget about the knife. That would be her best chance for survival. She would run into the forest and try to lose Paul in the trees. Even if her bare feet were punctured by the forest litter, she would push the pain out of her mind and run. Run like hell.

She took her first step, gingerly placing her right foot in front of her left and letting it return to the floor as softly as she could. Now, she was thankful that she wasn't wearing shoes; their absence made it much easier to walk quietly.

She eased herself around the island that separated the living room from the kitchen, then took several more steps toward the wooden knife block. She reached for the one with the largest handle and pulled. An enormous, shiny blade slid from the block.

Just having the knife in her hand made her pulse quicken. She lowered it to her side and turned around. Paul was still asleep on the sofa. She hadn't heard a peep out of him in several minutes, and she took that as a positive sign.

She eased her way back into the living room, gliding around the chair that had previously held her captive, and stopped directly behind the sofa. Paul's face was buried in the back of the leather cushion, facing her. His arms were drawn into his chest, reminding Tiffany of an innocent, sleeping baby.

But she knew better. She knew what he really was inside.

She raised the knife.

The side of his neck was exposed, giving her a perfect target, and she watched as his veins pulsed with every beat of his evil heart. She could feel the hatred running through her, like a roaring river overflowing its banks.

She took a deep breath and held it.

She started to swing downward and then stopped the knife in midair.

She raised the knife again. Watched the veins throbbing.

She couldn't do it.

She lowered the knife to her side. When she had stabbed Paul the first time, it had been an act of pure self-defense. But this was different. He posed no threat to her asleep on the sofa. She could just turn and walk out the front door. If she killed him here, while he was sleeping, it would be cold-blooded murder.

She didn't want to become what he already was.

She was not a murderer.

She sighed quietly, convinced she was making the right decision, then turned and began walking toward the door. As she drew closer, she thought she spotted the back of her Corolla out the window. With any luck Paul had left the keys in it and she could just drive to safety. She took another couple of steps and then heard a loud pop as she stepped on a loose plank of the hardwood floor.

She froze.

Terror surged through her body in waves that threatened to paralyze her.

Should she run now?

She glanced back at the sofa, ready to dart out the door and run for her life at the first sign of movement from Paul.

He was still asleep.

Relief replaced the terror. She took a deep, cleansing breath and turned back toward the door. She was almost home, just a few more steps.

One . . . two . . . three. She reached out and grabbed the knob for the deadbolt. She turned it so slowly that she wondered if it would ever open, but she didn't want to risk another loud noise. A small smile spread across her face when, at last, she saw the steel shaft withdraw into the door. She placed her hand on the doorknob and began to turn it just as carefully as she had the deadbolt. She prayed the hinges had been oiled recently and that they wouldn't scream a warning to Paul.

She heard the sound of a pistol being racked.

Her body went numb, and the knife slipped from her hand.

"Don't move," she heard Paul say from the sofa.

25

Jackson slid his thumb across the screen of the cellphone and quickly put it to his ear. "Hello?" he said as he stood from the couch and walked into the kitchen. He saw Katie following him from the corner of his eye.

"Jackson, this is Sheriff Lansing—"

"Hi, Sheriff. I hope you have some good news for me," Jackson interrupted, anxious to see if the sheriff had managed to gather any information that would help him find Tiffany.

"I just wanted to call and let you know that I've been trying to find out what the McMillans have been up to lately. I've made a lot of phone calls, but I'm sorry to say that I haven't had much luck. As I told you before, they're powerful people, and when you start snooping around in their business, well, most people around here would rather just stay out of it. In other words, they're not all fired up to help you out. Some folks are just plain scared to death of them. They're afraid to say anything negative about them at all."

"What's he saying?" Katie asked, her eyes widening as she drew closer to Jackson.

"Hold on," Jackson mouthed to her, while at the same time holding up his index finger, hoping that would make her back off for a minute or two. She started to ask another question, her lips opening to speak, but instead, she quickly closed them.

"Yes, I understand that, Sheriff, but surely you were able to find *something*," Jackson said.

"Well . . . maybe."

"Maybe? What do you mean?"

"To tell you the truth, I don't know if it's significant or not. It could be nothing, but I did find out one interesting fact." The sheriff paused.

"Go on, Sheriff. What did you learn?" Jackson pressed.

"Well, I contacted a local businessman I've known since high school. We were on the football team together. Guy had a hell of an arm, I tell you. Anyway, he's had some dealings with the McMillan family through the years. He's not a big fan of them, if you catch my drift. Seems they screwed him over several years ago on a real estate deal."

"Sheriff, can you just please tell me what you found out. We need to find Tiffany as soon as possible," Jackson interrupted. The sheriff went silent for several seconds, and Jackson was afraid he had offended the only person who might be able to help them. "I'm sorry, Sheriff, I didn't mean to—" Jackson was relieved when he heard the sheriff laugh softly on the other end of the line.

"No, no, I'm sorry, Jackson. I get carried away telling my stories sometimes. My apologies."

Jackson heard the sheriff take a deep breath, and he desperately hoped that the older man would get straight to the point.

"So, I asked my buddy if he knew of any connection the McMillans might have to Western North Carolina. That's where you said you are, right?"

"Yes, that's correct." Jackson turned his head to look at Katie again. Her hands were tucked into the back pockets of her blue jeans, and the anxious look on her face made him feel guilty that he had rebuffed her inquiry earlier. She was just as worried about Tiffany as he was, and he shouldn't have been so dismissive. He smiled at her, hoping the gesture would convey his remorse, then turned his attention back to the phone call. "So what did your friend say, Sheriff?" he persisted.

"He said that Fredrick McMillan, that's Paul's dad, had a brother who owned a cabin up in the Smokies somewhere. Well, at least he owned it the last my friend heard. He could've sold it by now, but that's the best info he had. Oh, and he said he thought the brother's name was Adam or something like that, but he wasn't sure."

"So did your friend know where this cabin is located?" Jackson tore a piece of paper from the magnetic notepad hanging on the refrigerator door and wrote Adam McMillan on it, underlining it three times. He handed the paper to Katie and motioned toward the laptop that was sitting in the living room recliner.

"Not really. He said Fredrick and his wife, Heather, had taken him up to the cabin once or twice. Sort of wined and dined him to seal the real estate deal he was involved in. As soon as the papers were signed, they drove the knife right in his back. That's the way he described it, anyway." The sheriff chuckled. "This friend of mine can be a little gullible from time to time. He's made some money over the years, but he's lost a hell of a lot, too, if you know what I mean."

"So he had *no* idea where the cabin was located?" Jackson asked again, praying he wouldn't be delayed by another one of the sheriff's stories.

"Well, he said it was a log home and that there was a lake nearby and lots of mountains. He remembered that much. Said the roads were real curvy getting up to the house. Like I said, this Adam fellow might not even own the house anymore. My friend said it was over ten years ago since he was there."

Jackson sighed. Ten years was a long time. The chances that this lead was anything significant were slim to none. "Okay, Sheriff. Thanks again for your help," he said, disappointed not to have more to go on. He glanced into the living room and saw Katie sitting in the recliner, already typing furiously on the laptop.

"Yeah, no problem. Sorry I wasn't more help to you. I'll keep digging, though, and if I find anything else, I'll give you a holler."

"Thanks, Sheriff. I'd appreciate that," Jackson said, then hung up the phone. He walked into the living room and slumped onto the sofa.

"What'd he say?" Katie asked, never moving her eyes from the computer screen.

Jackson sighed and tossed the phone onto the adjacent sofa cushion. He was frustrated. He had hoped for more solid information. He summed up his conversation with the sheriff, then added, "The cabin is probably a dead end, anyway."

"That's it?" Katie asked, disappointment in her voice. She kept working on the keyboard.

"Yeah, pretty much. I mean, from his description of the place, it could be around here: mountains, a lake, curvy roads." He sighed again and ran his hand up his face, then through his hair. "But that describes this entire part of the state." He tilted his head back and rested it on the top of the sofa cushion. He let his eyelids drift shut. The mental stress of Tiffany's disappearance had left him completely drained. Finally, after several seconds of silence, he asked, "You find anything?"

"Not yet," Katie replied, "but I'm still working on it. There's no listing for a McMillan in the local phone book."

"Try the county tax records," Jackson said. "A lot of people just have cellphones nowadays." When she didn't say anything, he lifted his head. "Did you hear me, Katie?"

She finally looked up from the laptop and gave him a sly grin. "I was already checking them before you said anything."

"Sorry." He smiled back, then let his head collapse into the cushion again. The cabin was silent, with the exception of the methodical clicking of the keyboard as Katie's fingers continued to work. He wanted to curl up on the sofa and take a nap, hoping that when he awoke, this whole mess would have disappeared, just a terrible dream. He hadn't slept much last night, worrying about what had happened at dinner, and his eyelids felt heavy. Despite his best efforts to stay focused, he was about to doze off when Katie sighed, pulling him back from the persistent fatigue washing over his body. "There's nothing for an Adam McMillan," she said.

"Dammit," Jackson whispered, but he didn't raise his head or even open his eyes this time. He once again let the sound of Katie's fingers tapping the keyboard fill his ears. He tried to pull some morsel from his memory that would help them. He tried to remember if he had ever seen any houses that fit the vague description Sheriff Lansing had provided.

He had.

The problem wasn't that he hadn't seen any log home like the one the sheriff described; it was that he had seen *too* many houses in the area that matched the description—three dozen, at least. Then he tried to re-call whether Tiffany had ever mentioned anything to him about a house in the area, but if she had, he had no recollection of it.

After several minutes of combing his memory for a clue, he decided it was pointless. He wished he could remember something—anything—that would help. But if there was some snippet of information buried in the recesses of his mind that held the key to finding Tiffany, he couldn't extract it.

"Got something," Katie said.

"What?" Jackson raised his head from the back of the sofa and rubbed his eyes with his palms, attempting to banish the drowsiness.

"I said, I've got something," Katie repeated.

Jackson leapt from the sofa and covered the short distance to the recliner in a split second. He knelt beside Katie and looked at the computer screen. "What'd you find?"

"Well, I found only one McMillan listed in the whole county. His name's Andrew McMillan. Do you think that could be the same guy the sheriff was talking about?"

"Yeah, it's got to be him," Jackson replied. "The sheriff wasn't sure of the first name anyway. Adam and Andrew are pretty damn close. It's likely the sheriff's friend just got the names mixed up. That's got to be him," he repeated.

"The property appraisal was updated last year, so he probably still owns the house," Katie said. She tapped the touchpad a few more times, and Andrew McMillan's address popped up on the screen.

"Wait just a second," Jackson said over her shoulder. He took large strides toward the kitchen, grabbed another piece of paper and the pen from the notepad on the refrigerator, then hurried back to the living room, the sound of his heavy boots striking the floor and echoing through the old house. He wrote the address down on the paper, at the same time trying to recall if he had ever seen it before. He decided he had not. When he was finished, he said to Katie, "Okay, I got it. Now, map it."

Jackson read the address back to her. "111 Mockingbird Lane, Fontana Dam, North Carolina," he said, then waited for the map to appear in the browser. "Does the address ring a bell with you?" he asked Katie.

"No."

"Tiffany never mentioned it?"

Katie was tapping her fingers on the side of the computer while the little blue icon continued to spin at the top of the browser. "Not that I recall."

At last, the map appeared, followed a few seconds later by the satellite overlay. A single red dot in the middle of the screen marked the address. "Zoom in," he said.

Jackson watched the screen blur, then gradually clear as the satellite resolution readjusted. There, in the center of the map, was the top of what appeared to be a log home. A large peak thrust skyward at the center of the house, creating what he imagined would be one heck of a great room. Two wings, one on the left and one on the right, jutted out from the center section. He spotted a small outbuilding twenty or thirty yards from the house, and while he couldn't see the sides of the main house, they were visible on the outbuilding. It was definitely a log structure. A small gravel driveway, void of any vehicles, led from the front of the house into the forest. "Okay, Katie, now zoom out slowly."

Jackson kept his eyes on the computer screen, straining to pick up every detail. He watched as the map expanded, slowly revealing the surrounding area. He saw a paved road running through the middle of the expansive forest. Then the lake. "A little more," he said. He involuntarily squeezed Katie's shoulder with his left hand as she zoomed the computer screen out farther, the tension increasing as the pixels readjusted and once again formed a clear image.

Jackson couldn't believe what he was seeing.

"Son of a bitch," he whispered.

Katie turned her head toward Jackson. "What is it?" she asked.

"I know where that is. It's just east of here on Highway 28, probably not more than five or six miles."

"Really? Are you sure?" she asked, excited.

"Yeah, really."

"Wouldn't that be pretty stupid? I mean, to take Tiffany only a few miles away?"

"Not necessarily. Sometimes hiding in plain sight, so to speak, is the best option. Don't get your hopes up yet, though." Jackson walked back to the sofa and picked up his cellphone. "It's probably nothing, but it's the best we've got to go on right now," he added.

Katie rose from the recliner and put Tiffany's laptop on the coffee table. "Okay, you want to take my 4Runner or your truck?" she asked.

"What? You're not coming with me," Jackson said as he shoved the phone into his pocket.

"Oh, yes, I am!" Katie drew closer to Jackson, just inches from his face. "Tiffany's my best friend, and I'm *not* going to sit on the sidelines while she is still missing. No way!"

Jackson sighed. He could see the anger in her eyes. "Katie, please don't do this. Like I said, it's probably nothing, but if it does turn out to be something, it could be dangerous, and the last thing I need is another woman to have to look out for."

"Don't you worry about me, Jackson Hart! I can take care of myself," she snapped back.

"Sorry. Look, I didn't mean to offend you. I'm just trying to think about what's best all the way around." Jackson noticed that her face was reddening, her crystal blue eyes now on fire. He motioned with his hand toward the laptop. "Besides, I need you to stay here and keep searching the computer. Maybe you'll come across something important. I *promise*, I'll just go take a quick look, and if I find anything, I'll come right back and tell you." He hoped his attempt to thaw the icy chill forming between them had worked.

"I don't believe you," she replied.

It hadn't.

"You're just trying to get rid of me! I'm not stupid, Jackson," she added.

He sighed again and stared at the determination on her face. He should have known better. Tiffany and Katie were both hardheaded women, and he knew he wouldn't be able to talk her out of coming with him. "Okay, fine. You can go, but hurry; we need to get out there as soon as we can. If it turns out to be a dead end, we can rule it out and move on to something else."

Katie smiled. "Just give me a minute. I need to run to the restroom."

"Okay." Jackson watched as Katie rushed away and disappeared around the corner. As soon as he heard the bathroom door close, he opened the front door, quietly walked off the porch, then jogged to his pickup truck. He was pulling onto the paved road that ran through the resort less than thirty seconds later.

At the bottom of the hill, he took a left, then followed the road to the resort's small gas station, which sat at the intersection of Highway 28. He barely slowed for the stop sign, his pickup leaning sharply as he made the right turn onto the highway.

As he accelerated down the curvy two-lane road, he felt a little guilty for leaving Katie behind, and he knew he would get an earful about it later. As harsh as what he had told her sounded, it was the truth—the last thing he needed was to worry about protecting her as well. Right now, all he wanted to do was find Tiffany.

But part of him couldn't help wondering if he was already too late.

By the time he passed the turnoff for the marina, he was doing sixty on the twisting mountain road. Fontana Lake appeared below him on the left side of the highway, its waters rippling in the late autumn afternoon. A thick blanket of grayish-blue clouds hung in the sky, and the wind blew ruby and gold leaves across the pavement in front of him. It would be dark in a couple more hours.

He had to find her soon.

A flash in his rearview mirror caught his attention, and he glanced up.

It was Katie's blue 4Runner. And, by the looks of things, she was gaining on him.

26

That was a stupid thing to do, Tiffany," he said as he wrapped the length of telephone cord around her. "I could've just killed you, you know," he added flatly. He finished restraining her by wrapping the cord around her wrists several more times, then pulling down forcefully and securing the line to the brace that ran between the back legs of the chair.

Tiffany winced and let out an involuntary whimper as the thin cord cut into her skin.

"Shut up!" he barked.

Unlike before, when she actually had a little slack in the rope, this time, he had made the bindings twice as restrictive. Her body was so tightly attached to the wooden chair that she couldn't move at all. In fact, it was difficult to breathe normally. The cord traveled up from her ankles, across her thighs and abdomen several times, then behind her back, where he had bound her arms and hands. No way was she going to be able to cut through the cord. Besides, she doubted Paul would be stupid enough to nap again and give her another opportunity to try.

She was helpless.

Paul stepped around the side of the chair and towered over her. "Are we going to have any more problems?" he asked, his voice booming and authoritative.

Tiffany shook her head and then dropped her eyes to the floor, defeated.

Humiliated.

She silently cursed herself for not driving the butcher knife straight into Paul's neck when she had the chance.

How could she have been so stupid, so naïve? This was the real world, where good morals and *doing the right thing*, don't always come out on top. Her reluctance to act would be her death sentence. And the worst part was . . . she had put the noose around her own neck by being too weak to kill him.

Stupid.

Paul turned and walked into the kitchen. Tiffany watched his legs move across the room in the periphery of her vision. She kept her gaze fixed on the wooden floor in front of her, so ashamed of her weakness that she couldn't even raise her head to him.

He opened the refrigerator and pulled out what Tiffany assumed was another beer. He walked back across the room, stepping on the bearskin rug as he passed in front of her, and plopped down on the sofa. This time, he sat up instead of stretching out on his back, and turned the TV on. Tiffany recognized the audio; it was a rerun of an old *Seinfeld* episode. She could hear Elaine and George arguing about George's toupee. Tiffany had laughed when she originally saw the episode, when Elaine ripped the hairpiece off George's head and threw it out the window of Jerry's apartment.

But not now. Not this time. She just kept staring at the floor. Numb.

Part of her wanted to give up hope and just accept she was about to die. But another part, the part that had always pulled her through in the past, the part that really mattered, still had fight in it.

Paul laughed at the TV. Tiffany caught a glimpse of him out the corner of her eye and saw him throw his head back, chugging the can of beer. Then he laughed again.

Something wasn't right.

Her mind raced. *What is it? What isn't right?* Her thoughts were muddled from the adrenaline rush and subsequent letdown of the failed escape attempt. She concentrated, desperately searching for the answer to her own questions. After what seemed like an eternity, it finally came to her.

His laugh.

There was something different about it. She couldn't identify it exactly, but something had definitely changed. She hadn't heard Paul's laugh in ten years, but she remembered it clearly. It was always cold and insincere. Even when he was trying to be funny or was laughing at a joke, it had an unusual, counterfeit quality to it. And when he was angry, his laugh was pure, bone-chilling evil.

But this laugh, the one she had just heard bounce off the log walls surrounding her, sounded genuine.

Real.

She wondered what it meant. Why had such a fundamental part of Paul's personality changed? It didn't make sense. Then, still staring blankly at the floor, another thought hit her—this one much more profound than even the transformed laugh.

Why was she still alive?

By all rights, she should have been cold by now, resting under a blanket of loose dirt somewhere deep in the forest.

So why wasn't she?

Why hadn't Paul killed her right away?

She raised her head and turned it to the left, staring at the back of Paul's head. Her mind whirled, trying to come up with a reason, even one, that she was still breathing. But she couldn't. If Paul had come back to take his revenge on her—and she had been so certain of that earlier—then why hadn't he just gotten it over with? Why hadn't he just shot her dead when she tried to escape? Or at least maimed her to ensure she wouldn't run out the door?

They were alone, and he obviously wasn't worried about someone hearing them because he still hadn't gagged her, even after the escape attempt. Add to that the fact that she had seen no signs of civilization outside the windows, and it was obvious they were somewhere deep in the wilderness.

He'd had ample opportunity to do whatever he wanted with her but, so far at least, he hadn't.

It made no sense.

What was he waiting for?

The only explanation—and she hesitated to even call it an explanation—she could come up with was that the man on the couch wasn't really Paul. But that made no sense, either. Everything that had happened to her—the nightmares; the mysterious mug in the sink; the flower on her pillow—she hadn't just imagined all those things. They had actually happened. No one else but Paul would know the fear a misplaced mug or a rose on her pillow would send through her.

No one.

So what the hell was going on?

He laughed again. That same genuine, *unfamiliar* laugh.

Could it be possible that the man on the couch was an imposter? If so, who was he? And how did he know things only Paul would know?

But he looked like Paul. Sure, he was a little heavier than she remembered, but it wasn't unusual for adults to put on a few extra pounds as they aged. He had the same hair, the same mustache . . . the same eyes.

But something in her gut told her that everything was not as it seemed with the man sitting on the sofa just feet from her. Then she remembered the strong odor of cigarette smoke on his breath when he first leaned in and spoke to her. She had never seen Paul smoke. Of course, he could've started at some point during the past ten years, so that didn't really prove anything.

There was one way to tell for sure. Tiffany remembered that Paul had a small, circular birthmark on his right, lower eyelid, next to the bridge of his nose. She had been so sure that the man who stepped through the doorway of the cabin a couple of hours ago had been Paul that she hadn't noticed if he had a birthmark.

She struggled to find a way to check without making Paul—or whoever he was—suspicious. Finally, she decided to just take a chance and go for it. "Can I please have a glass of water?" she asked.

"No," the man on the sofa said, his eyes fixed on the television set.

She waited almost a minute, pondering whether or not she should push the issue. But she had to know. If he wasn't Paul, maybe she still had a chance to get out of this alive. "Please, I'm really thirsty. I feel like I'm going to be sick," she persisted.

After several seconds, the man let out an exasperated sigh. "Fine," he said, obviously irritated by her request. He got up from the sofa and walked into the kitchen. He downed the last of his beer and threw the empty can into the trash. Tiffany watched as he pulled a glass from the hickory cabinet above the sink, then filled it with tap water. Her heart raced as he turned and began to approach her.

She had to get a good look at him without raising his suspicions.

He stood by her right side and bent over slightly, bringing the edge of the glass to her lips. "Here, drink up," he said.

Tiffany took a long drink, keeping her eyes pointed straight ahead, waiting for the perfect chance to steal a look at his face. The cool water felt good on her dry throat and, although the request for water had been just a ruse to bring him closer to her, she was thankful for the drink. She took several more sips, then whispered, "Thank you, Paul." Just as the words escaped her lips, she shot her eyes up to meet his, glancing at his right eye.

There was no birthmark.

She quickly averted her eyes, looking again at the hardwood floor, careful not to stare at his face too long. He withdrew the glass from her mouth and walked back into the kitchen. Tiffany stared at his back as he peered out the window above the sink. She couldn't tell if he was looking for anything in particular or just enjoying the mountain scenery.

The fact that the man had no birthmark stunned her. She had been so sure that he was Paul. But then she began to doubt her own conclusion. What if the birthmark had faded with age and was no longer as noticeable as it had once been? That was certainly possible. Plus, she had gotten only a brief glance at his face, one or two seconds at most; hardly a conclusive identification. The fact was, he could be Paul, and she found herself disappointed that she still had no definitive answer, despite her efforts.

She decided to try something risky, something that could backfire on her, but she had to know for sure if the man was really Paul or not. She took a deep breath, then released it slowly, trying to calm herself before she spoke. She needed to sound normal, like she was having a conversation with an old friend. When, at last, she felt her heart rate slow, she began to speak. "Paul, do you remember the time you took me to the Virgin Islands, and we spent all day cuddled together on the beach?" she asked, still watching the man's back.

He was silent for several seconds. Tiffany began to wonder if he simply hadn't heard her question or if he was stalling. Finally, he answered, "Yes . . . yes, I do remember that. You were so beautiful walking on the beach. What was the name of the place we stayed?" he asked, still staring out the kitchen window, never turning his head to look at Tiffany.

"The Sand Dollar, I think."

"Right, The Sand Dollar. That was a great time, wasn't it, Tiffany?"

"Yes, it was. It was a great time."

Tiffany felt beads of sweat pop on her forehead, her mind reeling with the truth she had just exposed. Paul had never taken her to the Virgin Islands, and The Sand Dollar was a restaurant where she had worked as a teenager. Thankfully, the name of her first employer had sprung into her mind as soon as the stranger asked the question, because she hadn't anticipated him turning her own trick against her.

But it had been worth the risk.

Because now, she knew for certain the man standing in the kitchen wasn't who he pretended to be.

He turned from the sink. Tiffany shot her eyes back to the floor. She wasn't sure what to do. He stopped in front of her and stared. "You need anything else while I'm up?" he asked.

In an instant, Tiffany's mind cleared, and she knew what she had to do. Without hesitation, she looked up from the floor and stared straight into his gray eyes. "Yes," she said, pausing as she swallowed hard, her pulse racing. "Who are you?"

27

Tiffany continued to stare into the cold eyes of the man she had been so sure was Paul McMillan, waiting for a response. When none came, she asked again. "Who are you?"

A thin smile came across his face. "What gave me away?" he asked.

Tiffany sighed and dropped her head. Part of her was relieved that Paul actually was dead, that she really had killed him all those years ago, but the other part was rife with confusion. She had no idea what was going on—but she knew she'd better figure it out fast.

"Was it the Virgin Islands?" the man asked as he went to the refrigerator and retrieved another beer. "I knew you were trying to trip me up," he turned and pointed his finger at Tiffany, smiling, "but I figured it was a fifty-fifty shot, either way." He didn't look angry, but somewhat amused instead.

Tiffany studied the stranger's face again. It really was amazing how much he resembled Paul. It was no wonder she had been fooled. She took a deep breath and then said softly, "It wasn't just the trip to the beach. It was a few things, actually."

"Oh well, what does it matter now anyway? I knew you'd figure it out eventually," he said as he set his beer down and propped one elbow on the edge of the island countertop. He looked more relaxed now.

"Who are you?" Tiffany persisted. She could feel her eyes beginning to well up, the combination of anxiety, confusion, and frustration bringing her almost to her breaking point.

"My name's William. Well, that's my real name, but I haven't answered to it for the past five years."

"What's that supposed to mean?"

He chuckled. "I'm sorry. I take it you're not familiar with the way things run in prison? Everyone goes by nicknames. Mine was Cheater."

"No, I—" Tiffany began to say.

"But why would *you* know how it is in prison?" he interrupted, his tone rising noticeably. "I mean, hell, all I did was borrow a little money, and they put me away for thirty years." He pushed against the countertop with his elbow and began to amble back toward Tiffany, the almost jovial expression he had worn after she had first discovered his secret gone. Now, he was all business.

"Yep, I had my own little enterprise going. I was pulling in some serious cash, too. Had all the money I could spend, and then some. I was doing real well for myself, until I got caught. And let me tell you, they threw the book at me. Sent me straight to the state pen. But I guess you wouldn't know anything about that."

William was now standing directly in front of Tiffany, rubbing his hands together like a mad scientist ready to start his long-awaited experiment on the patient.

Stay calm, Tiffany. You can get through this.

She tried to remember what a person was supposed to do in a circumstance such as this, but couldn't think of anything specific. She had seen a TV show a couple of months back about surviving dangerous situations. She remembered one about being trapped in a blizzard, and another about escaping a burning building, but she couldn't remember anything about what she was supposed to do if kidnapped by a maniac.

She knew one thing for sure. She didn't want him to see how terrified she was.

She looked straight at him as he started to speak again, still rubbing his hands together slowly. "But not you! Oh no, there was no prison time for you, was there, dear little Tiffany?" he yelled.

She didn't respond. She didn't know what to say, afraid that whatever feeling she tried to communicate would only infuriate him more. She could hear the hatred in his words, see it on his furrowed brow. His nostrils flared, and his upper lip began to quiver slightly, creating an ominous mask where there had been a smile just a moment ago.

"Answer me!" Spittle flew from his mouth.

"I . . . I don't know what you want me to say," Tiffany said, struggling to keep her composure under the barrage of anger that was spewing out of the still unknown man in front of her.

A shallow laugh escaped him, and he shook his head slightly. "You just don't get it, do you?"

"Get what? I don't know what you're talking about."

"Don't lie to me, Tiffany! Do you think I'm stupid?" he yelled, as he took a few steps forward and placed his hands on the arms of the chair. His face was only inches from Tiffany's now, the stale stench of cigarettes and beer once again drifting up her nose.

She coughed and dropped her head, searching in vain for a breath of fresh air. "I'm not lying," she responded softly. "Why are you doing this to me?" She was struggling to keep herself together; she couldn't just roll over and give up.

"Why am I doing this to you?" he said in a low, growling voice.

Silence.

"Because you killed my brother!" he screamed. Flecks of spittle hit Tiffany on the forehead. She jumped in the chair, the restraints protesting even the slightest movement of her body. The fragile dam that had been holding her emotions in check finally broke, and she began to sob.

She couldn't recall ever knowing that Paul even had a brother. Maybe Paul had mentioned him in passing to her, but if he had, she had long ago forgotten. He must have concealed his personal life from her, much as he had kept his inner demons secret from the rest of the world. But she knew the man now standing in front of her was telling the truth. Because no one, aside from someone intimately close to Paul, could have known about such things as errant coffee mugs and roses on her pillow.

"You killed my brother!" William repeated, then shook the chair violently with his hands, pushing then pulling it across the floor. The banging of the chair legs against the hardwood, coupled with his screams, amplified Tiffany's terror. "You killed my brother!" he screamed for the third time.

Tiffany tried to stifle her sobs, her chin resting against her chest. She was weak, ashamed that another

McMillan had brought her to the point of tears. She raised her head slightly and saw Paul's brother turned away from her, his hand to his forehead, staring at the closed front door. Then, in an instant, her fear transformed to fury, and she couldn't hold back any longer. "He tried to burn me alive in that bathtub, you son of a bitch!" she screamed, her fierceness surprising even herself. It felt good to fight back, and she didn't stop. "If you want me to apologize, it's not going to happen! Because I'm not sorry! Paul got what he deserved," she said flatly.

"You're a liar," he said, his back still to Tiffany, "and you always have been. You destroyed my family. Mom and Dad were never the same after Paul died." He paused for several seconds. "Paul was a good guy . . . a good brother . . . and he told me all about you."

"Then you didn't know him like I did. He was . . . . different around me. You have to believe me, and as much as you don't want to believe it . . . he was an evil person," Tiffany said, her voice stronger now. Poised. Confident. Unwilling to show any remorse for Paul's death.

"I don't believe you," William said, his voice almost inaudible.

"It's true. I swear it is," Tiffany said. She paused, not sure what to say next, praying that somehow she would be able to get through to him, make him see the truth. "He used to beat me, William, just for the fun of it."

"Shut up!" William spun around, his eyes wide and laser-focused on Tiffany. "I don't want to hear any more of your—"

"Just because you don't want to hear it doesn't mean it's not true!" she interrupted. She was determined not to let him dominate her. She might be strapped to a wooden chair and completely at his mercy, but she refused to allow him to intimidate her any longer. Maybe she was signing her own death warrant, but she was through running from her past. She watched as the surprise washed over his face, and she knew exactly why he was shocked; he never expected her to stand up to him. But she wasn't going to roll over and let another McMillan crush her spirit. Not again. She was different now.

Stronger.

"The night your brother tried to kill me, I had to fight for my life. He had been abusing me for months, but that night was different," she explained, her voice calmer now. She paused again to let her words sink in. "He was going to kill me, William. There was no doubt about that." She watched his expression carefully, trying to read his thoughts.

His eyes narrowed, cutting through her newfound confidence. He pulled to within inches of her face once more, his hands grasping the chair arms. Tiffany felt the fear rising again, but she pushed it down. Refused to let it gain a foothold again. "You didn't have to stick a knife in his chest," he said in a low, measured voice.

She shook her head. "You're wrong, William. You weren't there. I was." She took a deep breath, trying to regain control of the situation. "And believe me, I had no choice. I wish it hadn't come to that, but it did, and I'm not sorry for defending myself."

"Just . . . just stop talking," he said, sighing. "I've heard enough of your lies." He pushed himself off the chair, finally giving Tiffany some breathing room, and walked toward the large kitchen island. He put his forearms on the granite and lowered his head, his back facing her.

She turned her head so she could see him. His muscles were tensed. He looked tired—and stressed. She started to say something but then changed her mind. She thought it best to give him some time to consider what she had already said. Plus, her head was still pounding, so the silence was nice.

Neither of them spoke for a while.

Tiffany shifted her gaze from William back to the floor in front of her. Her head dipped. Her whole body ached, and the telephone cord was cutting into her flesh, causing a painful, stinging sensation. She was so tired. All she wanted to do was sleep.

"Can you tell me one thing?" William asked, his voice shattering the uneasy calm that had descended over the room. Tiffany jerked in her seat, startled by the noise. "Why was there never a trial? How did you get away with killing my brother without getting even a slap on the wrist?" He paused, his voice calmer, more measured now. "I mean, you got away scot-free . . . that's the part I never could accept."

Tiffany looked toward William again. He was still leaning on the countertop, but he had shifted his head to the right, glaring over his shoulder and waiting for her response. She stalled for a few seconds, thinking; she needed to choose her words carefully. At last, she took a deep breath and began to speak with as much confidence as she could muster. "William," she said, hoping that he would be able to sense her genuineness, hoping that she would be able to make some sort of personal connection with the man who held her life in his hands, "there was nothing to get away with. I didn't have a choice . . . it was him or me. I didn't do anything wrong," she finished.

"Yeah, right. You expect me to believe that?"

"That's up to you, William. But there's one thing about the truth . . . it doesn't care if you believe it or not; it stays the same, either way."

He sighed and stared straight ahead once more. Tiffany was still looking at his back, wondering why he didn't seem to want to face her anymore. "Trust me, William, there was a thorough investigation. If there had been any evidence that I was guilty—*any* evidence at all—I would be locked up right now." She stopped speaking and waited for his response. He didn't say anything.

Tiffany wondered what must be going through his mind. She hoped he was realizing she wasn't the monster his family had undoubtedly painted her as. "You know I'm telling the truth, William. You *know* I am," she said, almost in a whisper.

Silence.

"Paul was different from you. I can see you're not a bad person." She was still trying to form a genuine connection with him, hoping he would see who she truly was. It was very likely her only chance of survival. "Sure, you've made some mistakes," she continued, "just like everyone else in this world. I know I've made more than my fair share, but making mistakes doesn't make you a bad person." She paused and took a calming breath. "But your brother wasn't just someone who made mistakes, William. He was pure evil. He had two sides. There was the smiling, successful, perfect-son mask he wore when everyone was looking. But he also had a dark side . . . the jealous, violent side." Another pause. "You're different, though, William. I can see that. Surely, you can see it, too. Because if you really wanted to kill me, you'd have already done it. Deep down, you're a good man, aren't you?"

She swallowed hard, praying that he wouldn't turn and kill her, proving her observations of him horribly wrong. Then she saw a tremor run through his back, and heard what sounded like a stifled sob.

Thank God. She was finally getting through to him.

Then she heard a sound pierce the air—a chime of some sort, but it sounded muted, distant. William pushed away from the kitchen island and began walking toward the front door. He didn't look down at her as he passed by; instead, he just pulled a cellphone from his front pocket and opened the door. Tiffany watched as he put the phone to his ear and stepped onto the porch, slamming the door behind him.

William remained hidden for several seconds. But then she saw him through the tall window just to the right of the large oak door. He turned and disappeared again, then reemerged on the left side. He was pacing on the front deck and gesturing with his hands as he walked, the cellphone held between his cheek and shoulder.

A deep sigh of relief escaped her. She was sure she had gotten through to him. She didn't know where she had gotten the strength to speak so freely and truthfully, but she was grateful for it, nonetheless. She knew her only chance of getting out alive was for William to see the truth. It couldn't have been an easy thing for him, to admit to himself that the brother he had grown up with, the brother he had loved, had, in reality, been cruel and evil.

But somehow, she had *made* William see the truth.

A cold shiver ran through her body as the adrenaline that had sustained her began to evaporate. The exhaustion returned, and she fought to keep her eyes open. Maybe when William returned from the porch, she could convince him to let her lie down on a bed and sleep for a little while. That would be nice. She closed her eyes and, at the same moment, allowed the tension that had permeated her muscles since she had been taken from her cabin to leave her body. Her head slumped forward, and she started to doze.

She was startled a few seconds later when she heard the front door swing open. She jumped in the chair, and her eyes snapped open.

William was standing in the doorway, holding a hypodermic needle in his right hand. There were no tears in his eyes, only determination. He began walking toward her.

"William, stop. Please! What are you doing?" she asked, the fear once again trying to steal in.

He didn't speak.

"Please, William, don't do this!" she pleaded again.

But he ignored her. He grabbed the top of her head and tilted it to the side, then jabbed the needle into her neck. Tiffany felt a stinging sensation as William depressed the plunger. She fought to remain conscious, struggled not to give in to the drug, but it was no use.

Her world went black.

28

Jackson whipped into the parking lot of a roadside motel, the deteriorating building testament to glory days long past. Several shingles were missing off the roof of the long, narrow structure, and the lime green paint was peeling off the exterior in large chunks. The room doors looked well-worn, and more than a few of the white window shutters were missing. A single car was parked at the end of the row of windows, under a flashing neon sign that read, *OFFICE.*

He pulled into one of the empty parking spots, the white lines on the pavement all but gone after years of neglect, and quickly turned around, throwing his pickup into reverse. He accelerated out of the parking lot and headed back west on Highway 28. He glanced up to his rearview mirror and saw Katie still following him close behind, the dilapidated motel vanishing behind him.

He was frustrated, and he let out an exasperated sigh. He had left his GPS in his work truck, and his cellphone wasn't able to get a good signal, which meant he was searching the old-fashioned way. He had driven almost ten miles looking for the small gravel driveway that led to the log home owned by Andrew McMillan. Somehow, he had missed the turnoff for the house he had seen on the satellite image, and he knew he was wasting valuable time. A few sprinkles of rain fell onto his windshield from the darkening sky.

He slowed to 25 mph, taking his time to study the left side of the two-lane road, searching for any break in the tree line that would indicate a road entrance. The decrease in speed allowed Katie to draw even closer to him, but, at this point, he didn't care anymore. He wasn't going to convince her to go back to the resort, and he knew any attempt to try would result in a severe verbal beat down from her.

He had driven the highway numerous times since he had been stationed at Twentymile Creek, as it was the main thoroughfare out of the remote resort to larger cities, like Asheville. And he knew he had seen the entrance to the house at some point in the past, he just couldn't remember when, or exactly where.

The rainfall increased, creating a steady mist on his windshield. He turned his wipers on and again glanced in the rearview mirror. Katie was so close to his vehicle now that he could see her face, and her scowl told him she was in no mood to hear anything he had to say.

He drove on, ignoring the tailgating 4Runner behind him. He kept staring at the unending swath of trees flying past his window. Suddenly, he heard a car horn blare, jolting him from his search and interrupting the methodical swiping of the windshield wipers. He looked up to see a set of headlights coming straight for him. He quickly swerved back to the right side of the road, narrowly avoiding a collision.

His heart raced from the adrenaline jolt, and he glanced back to check on Katie. Her eyes were wide, and he could see her lips moving furiously, but she was okay. Jackson couldn't make out what she was saying, but knew it was a verbal tirade aimed directly at him.

He turned his eyes back to the windshield and focused once again on finding the house. If this lead turned out to be a dead end, as he expected it might, they would be back to square one, with no idea where Tiffany was. But they had to rule it out, and to do that, he had to find the driveway.

He drove for two or three more miles with no luck, and his frustration was a fireball of anxiety in the pit of his stomach. The rain was coming down at a steady, more intense pace now and was making it difficult to see. A thin fog formed on the inside of the windshield, further complicating his search. "Dammit," he muttered, then reached up and feverishly wiped at the moisture with his right hand, at the same time concentrating on keeping his truck on the right side of the road. One near-death experience per day was enough for him.

Then he saw it.

A small gravel drive appeared between two large oak trees, just ahead of him. It turned uphill, running parallel to Highway 28, and was immediately surrounded by forest. It was tucked into a notch in the mountainside, which made it almost impossible to see when driving the opposite direction. He would have seen it during his previous search only if he had been looking in his rear-view mirror at the exact second he passed by.

He flipped his left turn signal, then tapped the brakes, hoping Katie wouldn't rear-end his truck. As he drove off the highway and onto the gravel drive, the terrain turned sharply uphill, and he felt his rear tires start to spin. He punched the four-wheel drive button on the dash and kept going.

Jackson could see a clearing at the top of the hill, where the trees had been cut for a building lot. He slowed before he reached the top, keeping his truck below the apex and out of sight of anyone who might be in the house. He parked, turned off the headlights, and killed the engine. It was silent now, with the exception of the rhythmic, hypnotic tapping of the rain on the truck's sheet metal body. He reached into the backseat and grabbed the green rain jacket he always kept in his pickup, then unbuckled his seatbelt and slid it on.

He checked his rearview mirror and saw Katie right behind him, her headlights now off. He wondered how he was going to handle this. He didn't want her coming with him into the house, especially since he had no idea what he would be walking into. He didn't know for sure what he was going to say. He guessed he'd just have to wing it.

He opened the door and stepped outside. The air was heavy with the sweet smell of the new rain, and the biting wind against his face made him shiver. He reached back and lifted the hood of the rain jacket over the ball cap he was wearing. His breath fogged in front of him as he turned and walked back toward Katie's vehicle. When he reached the driver's side, he bent over and motioned for her to roll down her window.

The window shot down a few inches, and Jackson could tell by the look on Katie's face that she was about to let him have it, her eyes narrowed and her mouth agape, ready to speak. He held his hand up and spoke before she could. "I know, I know, I shouldn't have left without you, Katie. I'm sorry. I should've known you would follow me anyway."

"Yeah, you should've!"

"Shhh! Be quiet. And kill your engine. We don't want whoever's in that house to know we're here."

Katie reached down and turned the ignition switch off. "Sorry."

"It's okay. Listen, I'm going to walk up to the house and see if I can spot anyone."

"Okay, I'll go with you," Katie replied.

Jackson sighed and hung his head. He wondered if he should even waste his breath trying to convince her to stay. He looked at her and shook his head. "No, Katie. We don't know what's waiting for us up there. There's no way you're going. Besides, I need someone to be able to get help if anything goes wrong."

She looked like she wanted to rip his throat out.

"So how am I supposed to know to go get help if I'm all the way down here?" she asked. "I can't even see the house."

"Trust me, if something goes wrong, you'll know it." She didn't look convinced. "Okay, look, if I'm not back in twenty minutes, get out of here and call the police. Tell them where I am. The cell coverage is spotty around here, so if you can't get a signal, just drive back to the motel where we turned around and ask to use their phone."

"But I—" Katie protested.

Jackson cut her off before she could get a complete sentence out of her mouth. "Katie, I'm sorry, but I'm putting my foot down on this one. You have to stay here."

She rolled her eyes. "Fine."

"Okay. Thank you." Jackson looked down at his wristwatch. Raindrops splattered on the glass face, and he wiped them away with his thumb. "It's 5:30 right now. If I'm not back by 5:50, go get help."

"Yeah . . . okay," she said as she rolled the window back up.

Jackson could tell she was still pissed off, but he wasn't going to waste any more time worrying about it. He turned from the car and proceeded up the hill, passing between his pickup on the right and the thick stand of hardwoods on the left. As he neared the top of the driveway, he crouched behind a large poplar. Wind-driven rain pelted his face, and he wiped his hand across his forehead and cheeks, studying the imposing log home in front of him.

Large pine logs formed the exterior, and the green metal roof looked slick in the rain. The peak at the center section of the house sloped gently downward toward the two wings, one on the east and the other on the west side, of the structure. Several large windows were positioned at regular intervals across the front wall and overlooked a wide deck that spanned the entire front of the house. Log railings ran the length of the deck, and a spacious, manicured lawn spread out in every direction, filling the space between the residence and the surrounding forest with a carpet of grass that was obviously headed toward its winter slumber. The gravel driveway extended to the front of the house, terminating at the corner closest to Jackson, just in front of a small set of stairs that led onto the deck.

Jackson scanned the area around the house, searching for anything out of the ordinary. There were no vehicles parked out front, and he saw no lights on inside. He couldn't be sure it was unoccupied, but it sure looked that way to him. He was disappointed. He had hoped to find Tiffany here, but so far, it seemed this trip would turn out just as he had feared it might—another dead end.

He moved from behind the giant hardwood and crept along the eastern tree line, keeping the house in view at all times, still searching for some sign of life inside. But he didn't see anything other than rain-soaked pine logs and darkened windows, void of any warmth or signs of human activity. He continued down the edge of the lawn, ready to duck back into the woods at a second's notice, until he could see around the back of the house. Another deck, this one built in the shape of an octagon, extended toward the forest.

A distant rumble of thunder mingled with the symphony of raindrops smacking the ground. A plethora of leaves were falling onto the lawn, victims of the rain and wind, creating a splotchy, colorful mat in front of Jackson.

There was nothing behind the house either. No car or any other sign of habitation. He quickly crossed the lawn, the rain stinging his eyes, and pressed himself against the side of the house. He began to make his way toward the front deck, still keeping a low profile on the off chance there was someone peering outside. He took a risk and sneaked a look inside both of the windows that were along the exterior wall as he passed by, but saw nothing but two bedrooms and darkness.

As he approached the front deck, he paused at the bottom of the short staircase and gazed across the north side of the structure. He could see only halfway down the deck, the center section of the house jutting out and blocking his view of the opposite wing. As he placed his foot on the first step, he reached beneath his rain jacket and Carhartt shirt and placed his right hand on the butt of his Glock.

He ascended the three wide stairs, then put his back against the front wall of the house. He moved along the exterior, keeping his left hand on the pine logs and the other on the pistol. He checked each of the windows as he went, but still saw no indication the house was occupied.

When he reached the center of the house, he peeked into the large vertical window adjacent to the front door. He could see a spacious room and an adjoining, open kitchen. There were no lights on, and it looked spotless; no dishes in the sink, no newspaper on the countertops, nothing that would indicate anyone had recently been there. A large bearskin rug rested on the hardwood floor in the center of the great room.

Jackson moved his hand to the doorknob and tried to turn it. It was locked. He could stop and call the police, try to get them to pursue a search warrant, but he knew that would just be wasting time. No judge would sign off on a search warrant with the flimsy information he had. If Tiffany had been here, he needed to find out as soon as possible. A delay while waiting for the cops to do things by the book could be deadly.

And he wasn't willing to risk that.

The only option he had was to break a window. He swung the Glock back, ready to smash it into the glass but, at the last second, he stopped. He looked down and saw two large flower pots, the contents of which had wilted and died, sitting on either side of the front door. He bent down and tilted the one nearest him backward, exposing the deck below.

Nothing.

He walked to the one on the opposite side of the door and checked underneath it.

Bingo.

A single door key lay on the deck. He picked it up, slid it into the deadbolt, and turned. "Yes," he whispered when he felt the lock disengage. He inserted the same key into the lock on the doorknob, and it clicked open just as easily.

He turned the knob and leaned against the solid oak door. It swung open, and he stepped inside, easing the door shut behind him. He removed the hood of the rain jacket from his head in order to regain all of his peripheral vision. The room was dead silent, with the exception of the pitter-patter of the drops of water falling off his body and striking the hardwood floor below.

He pushed the Glock out in front of him, sweeping the room as he walked through it. The wet soles of his boots squeaked against the polished floor. He passed a leather sofa and fireplace on his right as he stepped around the bearskin rug. He checked behind the kitchen island, but found nothing. Then, just as he had done in Tiffany's cabin, he checked the trash can. As soon as he swung the lid open, the sickening aroma of cigarettes and warm beer hit him in the face. There were several crushed beer cans and a couple of crumpled packs of Marlboros in the bottom of the bag.

Someone had definitely been here recently, and that realization put Jackson's senses on alert.

He made his way to the back of the great room, where an opening led to the hallway that ran the length of the house. Carrying the Glock at the ready, he swung into the hallway, looking quickly to his left, then his right.

It was empty.

He began walking down the hall to his right, his pulse racing. He checked every room, cleared every closet.

Nothing.

When he was finished with the west wing of the house, he checked the opposite end in the same manner. All he found were more rooms decorated with expensive furniture; nothing else.

He returned to the great room and, satisfied the house was empty, holstered the Glock. He found a panel of light switches on the wall to his left and flipped all of them on. A fan hanging from the tall, vaulted ceiling glowed, as did recessed lights above the rock fireplace and several others in the kitchen area. He scanned the room more thoroughly this time, trying to find something he might have missed. He walked to the fireplace and placed his hands near the gas logs inside. They were warm. Whoever had been here, left recently.

Very recently.

He walked back to the kitchen and searched it again. A rectangular magnet on the refrigerator read *Great Smoky Mountains National Park* and held a photo of a smiling man, maybe in his mid-fifties, with his arm around a striking blonde. The picture appeared to have been taken from the front deck of the house, the surrounding mountains and Fontana Lake creating a picturesque backdrop. He pulled it from the refrigerator and shoved it into his jacket pocket.

He opened the refrigerator door and discovered a half-consumed six-pack of Bud Light on the middle shelf. There was also a bottle of ketchup and a container of yellow mustard, but that was all. He opened the freezer side and found it sparsely stocked as well, holding only a single frozen pepperoni pizza.

He closed the freezer door and walked back into the living room, lifting up the bearskin rug and checking underneath; all he saw was more hardwood flooring. He put the rug back down and sighed.

Then he saw something peculiar next to the rug. Several deep scratches in an otherwise flawless oak floor. They seemed strangely out of place, and he bent down and examined them, letting his index finger trace the channels.

The scratches were located in four separate areas; he wiped a hand down his face, still wet from the cold rain, as he studied the pattern. He drew a line on the floor with his fingertip, connecting the sets of scrapes to one another, forming an almost perfect square. The only thing he could think of that would have made such a pattern was the legs of a chair, and the abrasions to the wood looked fresh, with no signs of dirt or dust in the deep grooves. He wondered if it was significant. Maybe, maybe not. There was just no way to be sure.

He heard the front door swing open behind him.

His senses pricked. In one swift movement, he pivoted on the balls of his feet while simultaneously ripping the Glock from its holster.

29

Jackson's hands were shaking, his finger on the trigger and ready to fire.

Katie was standing in the doorway, her eyes wide with fear and her soaking wet hair hanging off her shoulders.

"Dammit, Katie!" Jackson screamed as he lowered the firearm, his hands still quaking from the adrenaline rush. "You scared the shit out of me!" He wiped his sweating palms on his already wet pant legs. Angry, he looked up at her and added, "I thought I told you to stay put!"

"You did. I . . . I'm . . . sorry, I just thought—"

"Yeah, well, you weren't thinking, Katie," he interrupted. "That's the problem. You're lucky you didn't get yourself shot!" Jackson holstered the pistol and drew in a deep breath, trying to calm himself.

"I'm sorry. I just wanted to help," Katie said as she stepped into the house and closed the door behind her, the pale color of her skin evidence of the terror that had washed through her when she had found herself looking down the barrel of a loaded .45.

Jackson wanted to read her the riot act, tell her how important it was to follow directions in a situation like this, but decided it wouldn't accomplish anything. Besides, the experience of almost shooting a friend had left him drained of energy, and he was too tired to argue with her any longer.

"Did you find anything?" Katie asked as she stepped around the rug and stood next to him.

"No . . . well, maybe. I'm not sure." He motioned toward the grooves in the floor. "I found these right before you burst in and almost caused me to send you straight to the pearly gates."

"At least I'd have been headed in the right direction," Katie said, then stifled a giggle.

Jackson was still fuming about the incident, his hands continuing to tremble, but he couldn't help cracking a half-hearted smile at the joke. He took another calming breath before continuing. "It looks like maybe a chair was in the center of the room, and its legs scratched the floor."

"Seems like a strange place for a single chair to be," Katie said, staring at the odd abrasions on the floor.

"Yeah, I was thinking the same thing. I searched the house, and it's empty, but there are cigarette packs and beer cans in the trash. The fireplace felt warm, too. I'm sure we didn't miss whoever was here by much." Jackson bent over at the waist and studied the scratches again.

"But where did the chair go?" Katie asked.

"Who knows? Maybe it's here in the house somewhere or maybe whoever was using it took it with them."

"You think Tiffany was here?"

"Impossible to say. Maybe, but there's nothing concrete that points to it. Not yet, anyway." Jackson stood back up and looked at Katie. "I'm afraid we still don't have a lot to go on." He paused and scanned the room. His vision was blurry after staring at the scratches so intently. He rubbed his eyelids with his fingers, then allowed time for his eyes to refocus on the distant wall. "Help me look around again; maybe I missed something."

"Okay, where do you want me to start?" she asked.

"You look in here; I'll go check the other rooms again."

Jackson watched as Katie walked into the kitchen and began searching the cabinets, her drenched blonde hair swinging halfway down her back. He turned and walked down the right hallway, all the way to the end, where the master suite was located.

He stepped into the large room and studied the king-size bed that sat against the wall. It didn't look as though it had been slept in recently, the thick comforter on top clear of any wrinkles or depressions in the fabric. The headboard and footboard were crafted of logs, similar to the ones used in the construction of the walls, only smaller in diameter. Matching wooden nightstands flanked the bed, and Jackson noticed several pictures hanging on the wall, all featuring the same man and woman he had seen earlier, in the photo on the refrigerator door.

He checked the walk-in closet and found several pairs of blue jeans, some T-shirts, blouses, and a few dresses, but nothing more significant than that. The large master bath yielded no clues, either.

He walked back to the head of the bed and pulled the top drawer from the left nightstand. It was full of folded letters and other documents. He dumped the entire contents on top of the comforter, then spread everything on top of the bed.

He began looking through them, but was disappointed when he found nothing of any particular interest. There were several bills addressed to Andrew and Terri McMillan, whom he assumed was the couple in the photographs dotting the room. He also found a few birthday and Valentine's cards they had given to each other, but nothing else. He picked the drawer off the floor and replaced the contents before sliding it back into position. He was just about to make his way over to the matching nightstand when he heard Katie yell, "I think I've found something!"

Jackson hurried out of the bedroom and down the hallway. When he turned the corner and looked into the great room, he saw Katie bending over the bearskin rug, pointing at something with her index finger. "Look at this," she said.

Jackson drew closer and knelt down in front of the rug. He didn't see anything. "What?" he asked, confused.

"Bet you wouldn't have found this," Katie said as she pulled a long auburn strand from the mass of black animal hair. "See, Jackson, you do need me," she said, a self-satisfied look on her face.

Jackson rolled his eyes slightly and gave her a half smile. "Fair enough," he replied.

"You think it's Tiffany's?" Katie asked, holding the hair between her thumb and index finger.

"Could be. It's certainly the best clue we've found. The woman who lives here is blonde, so it definitely didn't come from her."

"How do you know that?"

Jackson pulled the picture he had taken from the refrigerator out of his pocket and handed it to Katie. "From the pictures."

She studied the photo, then handed it back to Jackson. "That makes sense. So what do we do with this?" she asked, still holding the single red hair between her fingers.

"Wait just a second," Jackson said as he stood up and walked into the kitchen. He quickly searched several of the cabinets before he found what he was looking for. He pulled a single Ziploc bag from the box he found on the shelf above the coffeemaker. He took it to Katie and said, "Here, put it in this. It could be evidence." He pulled apart the top of the bag and held it open. Once Katie dropped the hair inside, he resealed the bag and tucked it into the pocket of his rain jacket.

"Did you find anything else?" he asked.

"Nope, that was it."

"Well, let's keep looking." Jackson stood and turned from Katie, trying to process the new information: a chair in the center of the room that had been moved so violently it gouged deep scratches in the floor and a single hair that looked very much like Tiffany's, both found in a house owned by a McMillan family member. He could draw only one conclusion. His cellphone rang and disrupted his train of thought. He quickly pulled it from his pocket. "Hello?"

"Jackson, this is Sheriff Lansing again. I've got some more information for you."

The sheriff sounded emotionless, and Jackson felt his heart begin to pound deep inside his chest, desperately hoping whatever he was about to hear wasn't bad news. "Okay, Sheriff. What is it?" he asked with more than a little trepidation.

"I've been making phone calls all afternoon, trying to find out anything I didn't already know about the McMillans. Just a few minutes ago, I finally got in touch with the warden down at Central State Prison in Macon. You're not going to believe this, but Paul's brother, William, escaped last Tuesday."

"What?" Jackson asked, stunned.

"Yeah, it's true. I'm sorry I didn't know about it when we talked earlier. The state police sent out an alert about the escape soon after it happened, but I guess that dumb-ass new deputy of mine somehow let it fall through the cracks."

"Do you know why he was in prison?"

"Hell, I didn't even know he had been sent to the pen. Guess the McMillans kept it hush-hush around here. From what the warden told me, William got caught with his hand in the cookie jar. He was convicted of embezzling close to a million dollars from an investment firm he worked for up in Atlanta. If I know the McMillans, and I do, they would've done anything to keep that story hidden. Seems like they did a pretty good job of it, too."

"So he hasn't been found yet?"

"No, not yet, but I've got all my deputies looking for him. I don't think he's headed home, though," the sheriff replied matter-of-factly.

"Why do you say that, Sheriff?" Jackson asked, the urgency in his voice becoming apparent, even to himself. Katie must've noticed it, too, because she was standing in front of him with a concerned look on her face.

"Well, because they think he might've been spotted at a gas station north of Atlanta. If it was him, he was moving in the wrong direction to have been headed home."

"But the right direction if he was headed up this way," Jackson said.

The sheriff remained silent for a few seconds, then added, "Yeah, that's what I was thinking, too. That's why I called right away. I thought you'd better know about it as soon as possible."

"So do you know William, Sheriff? Is there anything else you can tell me about him?"

"Yes, I knew him when he was growing up. Paul was always the meaner of the two. William didn't get into as much trouble. I used to think that Paul was just a bad influence on his brother and that William, deep down, was an okay kid. But it seems like I might've been wrong about that."

"Yeah, I guess so," Jackson said. Katie was staring at him, her eyes telling him she wanted to know what the sheriff was saying.

"Jackson, there's something else."

"What's that?"

"They think William sneaked out of the prison in the back of a delivery truck. They found the truck just a few miles down the road. The driver had been shot in the head." The sheriff paused again, clearing his throat. "This isn't a guy to underestimate."

"I understand, Sheriff. Thank you for the information."

"Did you have any luck finding the house?"

"Yeah, we found it, and we think that Tiffany, and now I'm guessing William, too, may've been here. But it looks like we just missed them. The place is empty now. We'll keep looking, though."

"Wait, Jackson, there's one more thing. I almost forgot about it. They were able to pull a partial tag number off the car William was driving at the gas station. Well, like I said, they aren't sure it was him, the video quality was real poor, but they're confident enough that they're running the partial through the state system to see if they can trace it back to anyone."

Jackson ran to the other side of the kitchen island and began pulling drawers open, searching for something to write with. "Hold on, Sheriff," he said. He finally managed to find a pen and a pad of paper. "Okay, go ahead with the number."

"They were able to get just the first three letters: GHZ. And it appeared to be a Georgia plate, but they couldn't say for sure. The car was a gray or tan sedan, maybe a Ford."

Jackson quickly scribbled down the partial tag number and the description of the vehicle, then tore off the piece of paper and shoved it into his pants pocket. "Okay, I've got it. Thank you again, Sheriff Lansing. I really appreciate it."

"No problem, Jackson. I'll keep digging on my end, and if I find anything more, I'll let you know as soon as I can. And Jackson . . ."

"Yes?"

"Be careful."

"I always am, Sheriff." Jackson disconnected, and as he shoved the phone back into his pocket, Katie was already asking for information. He had decided as soon as he had learned of the dead delivery driver that he would withhold that piece of information from her. It would serve no purpose other than to increase her anxiety about Tiffany.

"What did he say?" Katie asked.

Jackson filled her in, as much as he was willing to, at least.

"That's it?" Katie asked.

"Yep, that's it." Jackson could see the distrust in her eyes, but he still had no intention of telling her about the dead driver.

"You think William could be the one behind all of this?" she asked.

Jackson sighed. "It's certainly looking that way. I'm sorry I doubted you about the McMillans being involved in the beginning. You were right, and I should've listened to you."

"That's okay. At least we have something to go on now."

Jackson could see the stress on his friend's face and figured she probably saw the same on his.

"So now what?" she asked.

Jackson copied the information the sheriff had given him onto a separate sheet of paper, then handed it to Katie. "Here's the car we're looking for. Sorry the description isn't better, but that's the best they had."

Katie looked at the paper, confused. "But Tiffany's car is missing, too. What happened to it?"

"I don't know, Katie. Maybe he hid it somewhere, or maybe he stashed his car and took hers when he abducted her. Who knows? But we have to check it out."

"Okay."

"I'll call the local police and give them this information, tell them to be on the lookout for the vehicle. The fact that it was involved in a prison escape should get their attention."

"But what are *we* going to do? We can't just sit around and do nothing. It's not like the local cops have been jumping at the bit to help us. What makes you think they'll be of any use to us now?" Katie asked, the agitation and tension spilling out in her voice.

Jackson was frustrated, too. Much more than he wanted to admit. They should have found Tiffany by now, but he had to stay focused on the task at hand.

Getting angry at the situation would only lead to mistakes and, right now, that's the last thing he needed.

He put his hands on Katie's shoulders and gave her the best comforting smile he could manage, hoping to convey to her that he knew exactly what she was going through because he was going through the same thing. "Katie, have you ever known me to just sit around on my butt and do nothing?"

She smiled softly, and Jackson could see that she got the message. "No . . . no, I haven't. I'm sorry, I shouldn't have said that. I guess I'm just letting the stress get to me."

"It's all right. No apology necessary. Let's head back to the resort and split up, try to find this car. Maybe there's something inside that can help us."

"Okay," she replied.

Jackson noticed for the first time that Katie wasn't wearing a rain jacket, and her jeans and blouse were soaked almost through. "Here," he said, "take this." He removed his jacket and helped her put it on over her wet clothing.

"Thank you," she said as she began following him toward the front door. "Jackson?" she whispered.

"Yeah?"

"I feel like we're just going in circles."

Jackson opened the front door. Daylight was fading fast, the mountaintops enveloped in a thick blanket of clouds. He paused and looked back over his shoulder. "You and me both, Katie. You and me both."

Then he stepped into the cold, driving rain.

30

William sat in the darkened room, head in hands and his elbows resting on the wooden table.

He didn't know what to do.

Mom and Dad had been right about him all along—he was nothing more than an incompetent loser. He had never been able to live up to Paul's example, and he doubted he ever would. What had seemed like an opportunity to prove his family wrong about him had turned into one hell of a nightmare, and he had managed to screw this up just like the job his father had gotten for him at the investment firm.

What would they say about him now?

He wasn't sure he even cared what they thought anymore.

Part of him wished he had never accepted the offer to escape from prison. But, dear God, how he had hated the monotony of the place. He had been forced to work in the sewing room, where the prisoners made garments for the Georgia Department of Corrections. It was the same thing, over and over again, day in and day out. His fingers had stopped bleeding after the calluses formed, but had still ached every day from the tedious work. He couldn't imagine himself continuing like that for another twenty-five years. Just the thought of it drove him to the brink of madness. He had wanted out of there so badly, he had been willing to do anything.

But the price he had been forced to pay was higher than he ever imagined.

Now, every time he closed his eyes, William was tortured by the look on the delivery driver's face right before he had put the gun to his forehead and pulled the trigger. Since the escape, sleep was counted in minutes rather than hours, and he often woke up with the man's bloody face pressed against his mind's eye. The driver had been just a pawn in the whole scheme, a middle-aged man who took a bribe to help pay his daughter's college tuition. William sighed heavily. The weight of his misery was like an anvil constantly sitting on his chest. And now, because of what he had done, the man's poor daughter had lost her father.

He wished he could go back, just say no to the whole idea from the very beginning.

And, more than anything, he wished he had just let Tiffany run out the door and into the forest earlier.

At one time, he had hated her. He thought he would be able to kill her without a moment's hesitation, with no feeling at all. She had, after all, taken Paul away from him. Despite his faults, Paul had been a great brother. He was the only other person in the world who knew what it was like to be the son of Fredrick McMillan—an overbearing narcissist and cruel taskmaster. That bond alone had seen them through many dark times as they grew up together.

But he had found that he wasn't very good at playing the role of the bad guy, and he didn't know how much longer he could continue. Deep down, he knew Tiffany was telling the truth about Paul—he'd had a dark side. William had seen it himself more than a couple of times, though never anything to the extent of the abuse—no, the torture—Tiffany described.

But he had seen enough to make him believe her story.

And now, he was trapped.

He didn't know what to do.

31

Darkness.
A penetrating chill.

Tiffany felt twinges of consciousness moving through her drug-clouded mind. She was aware of her own existence but not much else, her slow pulse and shallow respiration the only confirmation she was still alive. Her whole body was spinning, reminding her of being on a carnival tilt-a-whirl she rode as a teenager at the county fair. She was so weak, her muscles felt like giant rubber bands.

From somewhere in the darkness, she could hear an odd, methodical booming in her ears, the drumming ricocheting inside her head and making her sick to her stomach. She wished it would stop.

The smell of brewing coffee wafted under her nose.

Boom. Boom. Boom.

She wondered where the sound was coming from and again wished it would cease. She tried to raise her slumped head, but it felt like a bowling ball, too heavy for her to right on her own shoulders.

She wondered where she was and why it was so dark. Then she realized that the answer was a simple one—her eyes were closed. She tried to open them, but managed only a brief glance before they slipped shut again, clothing her small world in shadows, only the occasional shaft of amber light penetrating her eyelids.

She remained still for several minutes. She forced herself to take deep breaths. As she rested, the spinning sensation slowed, the tilt-a-whirl came to a stop, and the nausea subsided.

Boom. Boom. Boom.

She struggled to remember where she was, what had happened to her, but couldn't.

She tried to open her eyes again. She willed her brain to make her eyelids separate, struggling against the fierce desire to just sleep. This time she managed to keep them ajar for several seconds before they involuntarily closed again, her urine-stained pink pajamas staring back at her and slowly pulling the cobwebs from her mind.

She tried to move her hands to her face to wipe away the beads of sweat that had popped up on her forehead, but they wouldn't move. Something was holding them behind her back.

She remembered.

The pink pajamas she was wearing before someone took her.

The booming sound of a man walking on a hardwood floor.

The fear.

"You're awake," she heard a deep voice say. Then the footfalls coming closer. Someone lifting her chin. "Here, drink this. It will help with the effects of the sedative."

Part of her didn't want to see what lay on the other side of the blackness, didn't want to awaken to the reality that faced her, but she opened her eyes slowly, afraid of what the man might do if she refused. The room was dark save for a single lamp on a small table to her left, its dim light doing little to illuminate her surroundings.

The same brown-haired man who looked so much like Paul was bent over her, holding a cup of coffee to her lips. Only she knew he wasn't Paul; she remembered that. *What is his name?* She couldn't recall.

She took a sip, the hot liquid burning her parched throat. "Thank you," she whispered.

"I'm surprised you're coming around so soon." The man glanced down at his wristwatch. "You were out less than two hours this time."

"What did you give me?"

"Just a little something to help you sleep. I didn't want you waking up while we moved."

"Moved where?" she asked, her addled brain still trying to recall the details of what had happened to her.

The man didn't answer. Instead, he lifted the coffee mug to her lips again. "Here, drink some more," he said.

Tiffany took another drink, this time managing to gulp down more than she had the first time. "Where did you take me?" she persisted. No answer. He disappeared into the shadows, and she heard him put the coffee mug down.

"Will . . . William, please tell me what's going on." Tiffany didn't know how she recalled the man's name; it just slipped off the tip of her tongue, a memory pulled from her subconscious.

He began to pace again, the light from the single lamp casting soft, dancing shadows on his face as he walked back and forth in front of her.

Still, he didn't speak.

Tiffany recognized the telephone cord as the same one that had bound her at the cabin, but the chair was different. It was a high-backed, cushioned chair instead of the small wooden one she had sat in earlier. She pulled against the cord, but her arms wouldn't budge. She wondered if she would ever get out of this alive. Wondered if she would ever see Jackson or Katie or Cody or little Missy again. She thought about Missy's brilliant toddler smile. Jackson's loving embrace. Shopping trips with Katie. The thought of never seeing them again brought her almost to the breaking point.

Almost.

She wasn't going to give up hope. Not yet, anyway.

She couldn't stop trying to survive.

She lifted her head and stared at the man pacing in front of her. Beyond him was a small kitchen, the window shades drawn, blocking any available outside light. She had no clue where she was. Maybe he had lied and she had been unconscious for much longer than he'd told her. If that was the case, she could be anywhere, hundreds of miles from any source of help. She hoped Jackson was looking for her. Hoped he hadn't given up on her yet, because if anyone could find her, it was Jackson. But then she remembered the dinner they had shared the night she was taken. Her heart sank. What if he thought she had just run away? What if he thought she didn't love him anymore? Would he look for her at all?

A single tear ran down her cheek.

She took a deep breath, pushing down the emotions that were struggling to boil over inside of her. "Are you going to kill me, William?" she asked point-blank, her soft voice breaking up the monotonous sound of his boots hammering against the floor.

He remained silent, still pacing, his head down.

Tiffany sighed and hung her head. She had hoped her question would make William stop and consider what he was doing.

"I . . . I don't know," he finally replied.

Tiffany raised her head. He had stopped walking, but now his back was to her, and he was staring into the dark kitchen.

"Why would you want to kill me, William?"

"For Paul."

William's voice sounded hollow, and she wasn't sure what to make of it. "William, do you remember our conversation earlier?" she asked. "You know I didn't have a choice."

Silence.

He sighed deeply. "I believe you."

Tiffany let the breath she had been holding in flow out of her body in one continuous, cleansing stream. She felt relief, but knew she was still far from safe.

"The thing is, I thought I wanted to kill you more than anything in the world. Make you pay. And I thought I could do it with no problem, no feeling . . . but now, I'm not sure I can."

As she listened to William, Tiffany didn't know what to do. Should she press him further? Or should she just be quiet and let him work it out for himself?

She stayed quiet, watching him from the large chair. William stood like a stone statue in front of her, her only beacon of hope. And he was just gazing into empty space. She wondered what he was thinking.

After what seemed an eternity of silence, William finally spoke. "As much as I don't want to believe what you're saying about Paul, I know you're telling the truth. Sometimes brotherly love blinds a man to a certain extent, I guess." He paused, taking a deep, ragged breath. "Paul always was a mean son of a bitch."

"I know," Tiffany whispered into the blackness. She paused and then added, "You could just let me go, William." The minute the words left her mouth, she regretted them. She shouldn't have pushed him so far. Not yet. He was coming around, but pushing too hard could undo all the progress she had made in an instant.

"I'm afraid that's not an option, either," he replied.

"Okay," she said, trying to take a more gentle approach. "Can you tell me why?"

"I can't go back to prison."

Tiffany didn't respond right away. She took a moment to gather the right words. "William, there are worse things than prison."

He turned his head and looked over his shoulder toward her. "Yeah? How would you know? You've never been, remember?"

Dammit, Tiffany. That was exactly the wrong thing to say.

She scrambled, trying to find the words to recover before he blew up again. "That's true, I haven't. But if you kill me, you'll live the rest of your life knowing you murdered an innocent person."

He turned his head forward again, leaving Tiffany staring at his back once more. She wished she could see his face, his emotions, what thoughts were running through his mind, but, instead, her view provided nothing useful.

"A little too late for that," he said.

Tiffany was confused. "What do you mean, it's too late? You haven't hurt me yet. You can still do the right thing, Will—"

"I wasn't talking about you!" he roared, interrupting her.

Her heart sank. This man had killed before. Her hope that she could get through to him, that he was different from his brother, was lost with his admission. He wasn't going to let her go, not after what he had just confessed.

He finally moved from his stoic position of the last several minutes, walking a few steps to his right and sitting down at a small dining table. Tiffany could see the profile of his left side, but the low light in the small room kept his facial features hidden.

She just sat in the chair, not knowing what to do, what more to say. What *could* she say, really? She couldn't think of anything positive, so finally, she simply asked, "Do you want to tell me what happened?"

"Not really."

"Okay." She watched as he put his head in his hands, resting his elbows on the table. He sat motionless for several minutes. She remained quiet, afraid she might say the wrong thing again. When his voice shattered the silence unexpectedly, it surprised her.

"I had an opportunity to escape from prison and take my revenge on you at the same time. Somehow, at least in my mind, it seemed perfect . . . quite logical, actually." He paused and inhaled deeply. "I thought I could be the tough guy for once in my life, you know?" He gestured with his hands as he spoke, still not looking toward Tiffany but, instead, into the dark shadows of the kitchen. "But I was wrong about that, too."

"We've all done things we regret, William. But it doesn't make sense to keep going down the same path once you realize you took a wrong turn somewhere along the way."

He laughed sarcastically. "I'm afraid I've done a little more than just take a *wrong turn*, Tiffany," he said, making air quotes.

Silence.

"Look," she said, "I'm not going to lie; I really don't know what to say to you, except that I don't want to die. My life is finally back on track after spending the last ten years believing I could never be normal again. Now, I've met a man I want to spend the rest of my life with, have kids, all of it. And I'm just asking you to please not take that away from me." She paused, her voice beginning to crack. She felt her eyes well up. "I'm sorry your brother had to die, but he didn't give me a choice. He was going to kill me . . . and I chose to live."

Tiffany waited for William's reaction. He sat motionless in the chair as he began to speak again.

"You know, all I see when I close my eyes now is the look on the guy's face right before I pulled the trigger. His eyes were wide open. Then his lips started to shake, like he was about to beg for his life, but I never gave him a chance." He paused. "I haven't gotten a good night's sleep since it happened."

"William," Tiffany said, "while it's true I've never been in the same situation you are right now, I have made my share of mistakes, and the one thing I've learned is that running from them will only make them worse. I can see that, deep down, you aren't like Paul. Just the fact that you regret what happened proves that. At your core, you're not an evil person."

"I've gone too far to turn around," he said, his voice trembling. He leaned back in his chair and stared at the ceiling.

"It's never too late, William, to—"

Something outside banged against the side of the house, interrupting Tiffany. William jumped from his seat at the table and hurried into the kitchen. He threw open the blinds above the sink and peered outside, looking left and right. The wind howled against the rain-splattered window.

Tiffany squinted as the gray light sifted through the house, illuminating the kitchen where William was standing. After a few seconds, her eyes adjusted, and she opened them fully.

She gasped.

Why hadn't she recognized the house before? She guessed it was a combination of the sedative in her system and the dim lighting.

But now she did.

And what she saw scared the hell out of her.

32

Jackson rubbed his eyes, then pounded his palm against the steering wheel. He had been looking for a gray or tan sedan with Georgia plates for the last forty-five minutes, staring out rain-spattered windows. Now his eyes were scratchy and his vision was shot. He fought against the lulling effect of the constant drumming of the raindrops.

He had searched through the entire resort two times already and had found nothing. Katie was also searching, but the last time he had talked to her by phone, she hadn't had any luck, either.

He felt like giving up.

But he knew he couldn't.

He continued up the hill, checking every cabin, every parking lot, but didn't see anything that resembled the sedan Sheriff Lansing had described. He slowed as he passed Tiffany's cabin for the third time, and he almost pulled into the driveway, ready to abandon the fruitless search and try to think of something else.

But he didn't stop. Right now, this mystery sedan was his only solid lead, and he had to find it.

He drove to the top of the hill, stopped his pickup truck, and looked out the driver's window. The water was running down the glass in sheets, making it impossible to see anything outside clearly. Everything looked like he was viewing it from the inside of a giant aquarium.

Next to the road was a small parking lot. He scanned it and the surrounding tree line.

Nothing.

The lot was empty, just as it had been during his previous two searches. He wouldn't have expected anything different on a day like this. The parking area was used by guests while they hiked the mountain trail that ran above the resort, and no one in their right mind would be out on a day hike in weather like this.

He whipped the steering wheel to the left and pulled his truck off the road and into the parking lot. He would turn around and keep searching—it was the only thing he could do.

He gazed out the windows, looking skyward. The clouds were even lower than before, some even starting to touch the treetops now. Daylight was almost gone, and the rain showed no signs of letting up anytime soon. Wind whipped the branches of the oaks and poplars in front of his truck, scattering leaves on his hood.

He sighed.

He felt defeated. He began to doubt he would be able to find Tiffany before it was too late. He wasn't used to this type of search. He typically had to worry about someone who was lost in the wilderness running out of food or water, or becoming hypothermic. Things that could be planned for, even managed. But this was different. Tiffany had been taken by a madman, and Jackson had no clue what William might do next.

Jackson had tried so hard, but now he was at a loss. He had no idea what else to do. It felt so unfair that after the countless searches during his Park Service career, the one that meant the most to him might end up being his greatest failure. If that happened, he would never be able to forgive himself.

He looked to his left as he put the truck in reverse and started backing out of the parking lot. Then, out the driver's side window, something caught his eye. It happened so fast he almost missed it.

In the last parking spot to his left sat a gray sedan.

At first, he wondered how he had missed the car during his previous trips past the parking area. But it was tucked into the corner of the lot, where the concrete met the forest floor, blending into the surrounding trees, and out of sight of passersby on the road. It was understandable that he had missed it because this was the first time he had actually pulled into the lot, but it was no excuse, and he was mad at himself. He should've done a more thorough search.

He exited his pickup and stepped out into the driving rain. He approached the car cautiously, scanning the area for anything out of the ordinary, his hand instinctively moving to the Glock strapped onto his right hip. As he drew closer, he bent down to peer in the windows. The interior was dark, and the torrential rain pouring down the vehicle made getting a clear view difficult. He pressed his face to the glass.

Nothing.

The Ford was clean, except for a half-empty bottle of soda between the two front bucket seats. Satisfied no one was hiding inside, Jackson moved to the rear of the car and stared.

Georgia plates.

His eyes moved instantly to the first three letters—GHZ.

It was a match.

He didn't even need to pull the scrap of paper from his pocket to check. The three letters had been imprinted on his brain as he searched the resort for the vehicle.

He walked back to the driver's side door and lifted the handle. It was locked.

Without hesitation this time, he drew his gun and slammed the steel slide of the pistol into the tempered glass window, shattering it into thousands of tiny, irregular pieces. He reached inside and unlocked the door, then pulled the trunk release. He hurried back to the rear of the car and threw open the trunk lid.

It was empty.

He breathed a sigh of relief, thankful he hadn't found Tiffany dead inside. He slammed the lid closed, holstered his pistol, then walked back to the front of the car and sat down in the driver's seat. He glanced around the interior, but discovered nothing odd.

He opened the glove compartment and found a car rental contract. He quickly unfolded the document and searched for the name of the renter. Flying raindrops peppered the folds of paper through the destroyed window. Jackson was becoming soaked as well, now that he had given Katie his rain jacket. He coughed and tried to ignore the chill as he shivered.

The name on the contract was Samuel Hirsch. Jackson had never heard of him and assumed it was probably an alias for William McMillan or one of his friends. There was also an Atlanta address listed for Mr. Hirsch, but Jackson figured it was probably fake as well.

The fact was, nothing in the vehicle had gotten him closer to finding Tiffany. Locating the car just a stone's throw from her cabin had confirmed that William Mc-Millan was almost certainly behind her disappearance, but Jackson had already known that after his last conversation with Sheriff Lansing. But he still had no idea where William had taken Tiffany after leaving the log home on Highway 28. He felt like he had been playing catch-up all day, always two or three steps behind.

He sighed and kept searching.

A few seconds later, he looked up when he heard a vehicle whip into the parking lot, the tires screeching as the driver slammed on the brakes.

It was Katie.

She got out of her 4Runner and walked toward him, her stringy, half-dry hair quickly becoming soaked again. She pulled the hood of his rain jacket over her head. "Is this the car?" she asked.

"Yeah!" Jackson yelled over the pounding rainfall.

As Katie drew closer, he motioned for her to go around to the passenger side. She opened the door and plopped down in the seat next to him. "Find anything that will help us?" she asked.

Jackson lifted the rental agreement from the dash and showed it to her. "Just this. I didn't recognize the name on it, but I'm sure it's an alias anyway, so I guess it doesn't really matter."

Katie studied the document, flipping quickly through the numerous pages. "No, I don't recognize the name, either." She paused and set the contract back on the dash. "Have you heard anything from the local cops? Has anyone spotted William?"

"No, I called in the info Sheriff Lansing gave me about William's escape. They said they would start looking for him, but they still didn't sound convinced that his escape has anything to do with Tiffany's disappearance.

I was just about to call back and tell them we found his car when you pulled up. Maybe that will help change their minds."

"That's ridiculous. Of course they're related."

"Yeah, you and I know they're related, but you have to look at it from their point of view. There was nothing solid connecting the two events until now. Let's just hope that finding William's car right up the hill from Tiffany's cabin will get their attention."

"I sure hope so," Katie said, sighing.

"Well, if not, we'll just keep searching."

Katie looked at him with a soft smile. "Thank you, Jackson. I mean, for not giving up."

He could see the strain on her face. "I would never consider giving up. We'll find her, Katie. She's a strong woman. I really believe she'll be okay."

"I think so, too," she replied, but the tone of her voice led Jackson to doubt she really believed it.

He wondered if *he* really believed it.

Or was he just saying something he wanted so desperately to be true, not only for Katie's sake, but for his own? He couldn't deal with even the thought of losing Tiffany forever.

"Help me search the car again before we call it in," he said to Katie, who was still staring at him, her damp blonde bangs pressed against her forehead. Jackson turned around and looked once again in the backseat. He ran his hand between the cushions and scoured the floorboard as well, but still came up empty-handed. He turned back around and checked the driver's door compartment, then above the sun visor. Katie was searching her side of the car at the same time, but neither of them found anything.

Then Jackson shoved his right hand between the seat and the center console. His fingertips brushed against what felt like folded paper. He forced his hand farther down and pinched the paper between his index and middle fingers. He slowly pulled until the top of it cleared the cushion, then he grasped it with his other hand and pulled it free.

It was a folded North Carolina roadmap.

He spread it out on his lap as Katie looked over his shoulder. He found the resort, then traced Highway 28 with his finger to Andrew McMillan's house. It had been circled with a black marker. He scanned the rest of the map, looking for other markings or notes.

His heart sank when he saw another location circled.

He opened the door, stepped out, and ran for his truck.

"What is it, Jackson? What did you find?" Katie yelled after him. She was out of the car and running toward his pickup by the time he opened his door and jumped behind the wheel. "What's going on?" she persisted.

"Call the police," he yelled. "Tell them we found the car and have them meet me—"

"What are you talking about? Meet you where?" Katie interrupted.

The truck's engine roared to life, and Jackson threw the transmission into reverse. "My house," he yelled, then slammed his door shut, stomped on the gas pedal, and pulled out of the parking lot.

33

Betrayal.
Fear.

Confusion.

Tiffany's head spun.

Staring back at her was the green granite countertop she had helped Jackson pick out for his kitchen remodel.

She turned her head over her shoulder. Behind her was the stone fireplace where she had first realized Jackson was attracted to her. It was the night that she and Katie had arrived to help search for Cody. The two of them had met Jackson at the marina, and he had offered to let them stay the night at his house. She had just gotten out of the shower, and she approached him as he was getting a fire started. She noticed his eyes lingering on her breasts when he looked up at her, her thin cotton T-shirt leaving little to the imagination. She had been embarrassed and, at first, thought he was a total jerk. But through the search for Cody and the following months, she had grown to love him.

Maybe her first instincts about him had been right all along.

Now, here she was in front of the same fireplace, but under ominous circumstances.

How? Why was Jackson involved in this?

She had trusted him completely. He was the first man she had allowed to get close to her since Paul. It had been no easy task, but slowly, he gained her trust.

Her heart.

Now, her heart was shattered. She felt her eyes well up and the tears begin to stream down her cheeks. They weren't tears of fear this time, but of sadness.

She had loved him.

And now he had betrayed her.

How could she have been so foolish? She cursed herself for being so trusting, for letting someone get so close to her again. He had been playing her all along.

She was an idiot.

William closed the kitchen blinds, again plunging Jackson's house into darkness. Only the lamp to her left still offered its meager light. "It was just the wind," he mumbled. "Must've knocked a tree limb against the house."

William returned to his seat at the wooden table where she had shared a meal with Jackson and Katie that first night. William's body was quartering away from her, and she couldn't see his face. Then a strange thought occurred to her.

Maybe the reason for the darkness was not to keep her from trying to escape again, as she had assumed. Perhaps, it was meant to keep her from knowing where she was. The house where she was being held was full of so many good memories for her, but now they were all tarnished.

Tiffany was thankful that William hadn't looked in her direction when he turned from the window. If he had, he surely would've seen the look of surprise and shock on her face, even in the dim lighting.

She wondered if she should say something else to him.

Wondered why Jackson had used and betrayed her.

She remained silent.

Except for her soft weeping . . .

34

Katie ran to her vehicle, flung open the door, and jumped inside. Now behind the steering wheel, she pulled her cellphone from the front pocket of her jeans. She wiped the rain from her face, pulling her soaked hair away from her eyes, then swiped her thumb across the phone's screen.

But nothing happened. The screen was blank.

She hit the power button again.

Nothing.

No! This can't be happening!

Her phone was dead. How had that happened? She thought it had been fully charged when she left her house earlier in the day. Then she realized she had not called Cody back as she had promised. He would be worried sick by now. "Dammit," she whispered as she tossed the phone in the passenger seat and pulled onto the road.

Tiffany had no landline, so Katie drove past her house and down the hill to the resort's general store. She pulled into the parking lot, jumped from her seat, and ran to the door.

It was locked.

She pounded on the window, yelling for someone's attention, but no one came. And the lights inside were turned off.

Frustrated, she ran back to her car, turned around, and headed out of the parking lot and toward Jackson's house at Twentymile Creek. She knew he probably didn't want to see her following him again, but she couldn't just wait around while Tiffany was in danger. They could call the cops from Jackson's house once they made sure Tiffany was all right.

Besides, Jackson was better than any cop she had ever met. If there was one person in the world who would make sure Tiffany was safe, it was him.

She sped down the hill and through the resort, the fading twilight, coupled with the heavy rain, making it nearly impossible to see the road. She turned her headlights on and her wipers on high.

She didn't slow at the Highway 28 intersection, the back end of her 4Runner fishtailing on the wet asphalt as she took the corner too fast. She took a deep breath and told herself to slow down—but her right foot didn't get the message. She accelerated down the curvy mountain road toward the Twentymile Ranger Station six miles away.

She wondered why Paul's brother—she was convinced he was the one who had taken Tiffany—was now at Jackson's house. It made no sense. Maybe she had misunderstood Jackson as he left the parking lot, but she didn't think so. He wouldn't have left in such a hurry if he had thought it was just another clue. He had to know that Tiffany was there.

She picked her phone up off the seat, hit the power button again, hoping in vain the phone would come to life. It didn't. She tossed it back down.

When she looked up, she saw headlights rapidly approaching in her rearview mirror, the bright beams almost blinding her as the pickup truck closed in. She waited for the driver to dim his lights, but it never happened. She was reaching up to reposition her mirror, hoping to avert the intense reflection, when the truck slammed into her rear bumper, throwing her forward.

"What the—"

She felt the seatbelt press into her chest as it held her body back. Her head snapped forward, then whipped back in a split second. The 4Runner began to slide on the wet pavement as she approached the next curve. To her left was a solid, rocky mountainside, to her right, a deep ravine. Neither option was good.

Katie struggled with the steering wheel, turning it left, then right, trying desperately to stop the out-of-control vehicle. Her tires squealed as they skidded through the sharp curve to the left. She knew she was about to go over the side of the mountain. But she kept fighting and, at the last second, managed to straighten the wheel and keep the 4Runner on the road.

She gasped, sucking in a lungful of air.

But there was no time to relax.

She heard the roar of the truck's engine behind her, then the interior of the 4Runner was once again flooded with blinding white light. She glanced in her mirror to see the pickup on her tail again. This time, it was weaving left and right, grinding its front bumper against the back of her vehicle.

Katie's heart pounded against her ribcage. She jumped when the driver behind her blasted his horn.

He's trying to kill me!

She fought again with the steering wheel. Every time the truck behind her swerved, it sent her careening in the opposite direction, the 4Runner weaving back and forth over the double yellow lines. She could barely see the road now. The windshield wipers weren't keeping up with the heavy rain, and she was so blinded by her pursuer's reflected headlights, it was damn near impossible to stay on the road, much less on the right side.

She pressed hard on the accelerator, trying to escape, and she felt the 4Runner buck beneath her as it lunged forward. Maybe she could outrun him. She took another sharp curve to the left, again barely managing to maintain control. She looked down at the speedometer: 45 mph . . . 50 mph . . . 60mph. She looked in the rearview mirror once more; the headlights were shrinking behind her. The curves were coming faster now, and she was having difficulty holding the 4Runner steady, but at least she had put some distance between herself and the maniac behind her. She tried to ignore her pursuer and simply concentrate on keeping her speed up and negotiating the narrow road.

Then came the familiar, terrifying sound of the truck's engine racing up behind her, the two glowing orbs once more growing larger in her rearview mirror. "No," she moaned. She couldn't die, not now. Cody and Missy needed her.

She slammed forward again as the truck crashed violently into the back of the 4Runner, momentarily losing her grip on the steering wheel. She heard the scraping and bending of sheet metal, then the explosive sound of the rear window being shattered.

The *whoosh* of tires beginning to hydroplane.

She grabbed the wheel, spinning it left, then right.

Dazed, she could barely see the sharp left turn coming up, her world a mixture of rain-streaked glass and rays of artificial light reflecting off her mirror, the surrounding hardwoods a blur of darkened figures.

The curve was coming quickly. Too quickly. She had to get away.

Now, sliding out of control and headed for the curve, she slammed her foot down, pinning the gas pedal to the floor. It was a last-ditch effort to regain control and escape, but instead of a burst of speed, all she heard was the roar of the engine and the sound of tires spinning on wet asphalt.

The rear of the 4Runner came around. She looked out the passenger window and saw the curve approaching. She spun the wheel hard right, until it wouldn't turn anymore, but her tires couldn't find traction, and she continued her slide toward the ravine.

Now, she slammed on the brakes in a futile attempt to stop her sideways slide.

The truck rammed into her door, almost knocking her unconscious. She felt the side airbag deploy. Dazed, she heard the driver accelerate, pushing her closer to the curve. She turned her head toward the pickup, trying to see who was behind the wheel. But all she could see were the blinding lights, now just inches away.

She glanced toward the oncoming curve. She realized she was going to go over the embankment. There was nothing she could do to stop it.

She asked God to watch over Cody and Missy.

She gritted her teeth, all her muscles tense.

As the 4Runner left the road, she felt like she was floating. The sound of her tires scrubbing the pavement ceased, the engine nothing more than a muted purr.

She heard the whistle of the wind blowing past her.

If it weren't for the fear of the impending crash racing through her, it would have been almost peaceful.

35

William was pacing again.

Tiffany strained against the telephone cord around her wrists until it felt like she had no skin left, like the cord was rubbing against naked muscle, but she couldn't get even an inch of slack.

Unfortunately, William had learned his lesson from her first escape attempt.

Her mind raced. She tried to formulate a plan that would get her out of Jackson's house alive.

William continued pacing, his head down.

Her tears had dried now, and she was refocused on what had to be done. However Jackson was involved— whatever he truly was—was no longer her primary concern. She hoped she was wrong about him, but she just wasn't sure anymore.

And if she wasn't sure, then she couldn't trust him.

She swallowed hard. Pain shot through the back of her dry, scratchy throat as the small amount of saliva she was able to produce slid down her esophagus. The coffee had done little to quench her thirst.

William stopped pacing and walked back to the window above the kitchen sink. He drew back the shade, but this time, no late-evening sunlight pierced the darkness. Night had fallen. She could still hear the sound of rain pounding on the shingles and against the windows.

He released the plastic shade, letting it fall back over the window, and returned to the dining table. The soft glow from the living room lamp just reached his face, revealing the anxiety Tiffany had already known was present.

She thought about trying to speak to him again, to try just one more time to convince him to do the right thing, but found herself at a loss for words, not knowing where to even begin.

He just didn't seem like a cold-blooded murderer. But he had already confessed to one homicide, and that fact alone meant she couldn't trust him, either.

Worse than that, he seemed to grow more on edge with every passing second.

If she were to have any say in her own fate, she would have to act. There was no one else to turn to—no one else to count on.

She was alone.

She gritted her teeth and pulled harder against the telephone cord.

36

It was dark by the time Jackson reached the sharp left turn on Highway 28 that told him he had arrived at Twentymile Creek. He crossed the short bridge that spanned the creek, then slowed at the apex of the turn and pointed the front of his pickup to the right, off the highway and onto the narrow gravel road that led to his house.

When he had traveled far enough to be out of sight of anyone on the highway, he pulled to the shoulder, turned off his headlights, and killed the engine. His house was another hundred yards up the road, but he didn't want to pull right up to the front door and announce his arrival. He turned the interior light switch off so it wouldn't illuminate when he opened the door.

He had found during his career with the Park Service that in situations like this, surprise was his greatest asset. Whether he was sneaking up on illegal poachers or just doing regular campsite patrols, he felt it was always best to remain undetected until the last possible moment. He never knew what he was walking into, and going in unannounced gave him the upper hand.

He stepped out of the pickup and quietly closed the driver's door. He began walking along the edge of the road, the outline of his body blending in with the tree line of the small patch of woods between the road and Twentymile Creek. He stayed low, ready to dart behind one of the large pines if another person or vehicle approached.

After traveling halfway up the road to his house, he paused to catch his breath. He knelt down and tried to make out the distant outline of the roof but couldn't, the thick cloud cover blotting out any moonlight. Jackson felt as if he were surrounded by a black veil, unable to see even ten feet in front of him. His clothing was now completely soaked, and a steady stream of water ran off the bill of his baseball cap. Tendrils of gray mist moved along the ground, the surrounding air saturated by the falling rain.

When he finally reached the spot where the corner of his front yard and the tree line met, he knelt again, concealing himself behind a large maple. He stared at the front of the house. He could now make out the outline of the roof and the covered front porch, but that was all.

The house was dark, with the exception of a faint glow, the weak rays barely making it to the kitchen window. Jackson remained still and simply observed for a few moments. He saw no one enter or leave the house. The waiting was killing him—he *had* to know if Tiffany really was inside.

A stream of rainwater flowed from the back of his head, underneath his shirt, and down his spine. He felt himself start to shiver, but quickly shook it off. He didn't have time to surrender to discomfort.

He tried to recall if he had left a light on inside the house. He couldn't remember. He had been so focused on getting to Tiffany's cabin to check on her, he had left his own home in a hurry, so it was unlikely he would've noticed a single light bulb left on.

Maybe William wasn't here after all.

Maybe it had all been a ruse.

Had he been too predictable?

Too easy to lead down a rabbit trail?

He didn't know, but the best clue he had found was the map in William's car with both the McMillan log house and his own home circled.

He wiped the water from his forehead and eyes to clear his vision as he began to move again, snaking along the tree line as it made a ninety-degree turn, and continuing along the west side of his front yard. Jackson had begun to doubt whether there was anyone in the house at all, but in case there was, he wanted to stay hidden.

The house was on his left, and once he drew even with the edge of the front porch, he quickly crossed the small yard. He stopped at the center of the porch and pressed his back against the wooden lattice that ran around the bottom. He listened, trying to pick up any sound from inside.

Only silence.

Was he wasting time here?

Was Tiffany already hundreds of miles away?

When he began to move again, his feet slipped on a patch of slimy mud, and he dropped to his knees, the water splashing up around him and causing him to let out an involuntary grunt. He quickly retreated back to the lattice and waited to see if anyone would come to investigate the noise. When no one came after a couple of minutes, he continued along the front porch, crouching low to the ground. He passed the small set of wooden steps on the opposite end, then went around the northeast corner of the house.

He stopped and stood up, then pressed his back to the white clapboard siding. There were two windows on this side of the house, one in the dining area and the other in the living room.

He moved slowly, pausing just shy of the first window. He felt his hand instinctively return to the Glock. He inched closer to the edge of the glass and peeked inside.

He saw the dining table just a few feet away, then the silhouette of a man highlighted by the soft glow of the living room lamp. He was sitting at the table, his body turned at a forty-five-degree angle, blocking his face from Jackson's view.

It had to be William.

Jackson looked through the window for only a second, then retreated back into the shadows. He was shocked that William was actually here. He had all but convinced himself that he was on a wild-goose chase. But he had been wrong.

And if William was here, Tiffany would almost certainly be as well.

Jackson's heart raced, and even in the chilling rain, he could feel beads of sweat forming on his forehead and palms.

So far, he hadn't seen any sign of Tiffany, but William's body blocked his view of most of the living room. It was also possible that she was being held in one of the bedrooms, or even the bathroom.

He knelt and slid under the window carefully so his body wasn't visible to the man inside. Once he had safely reached the opposite side, he stood again and quickly moved toward the next window. When he let his eyes move past the corner of the windowsill, he saw Tiffany sitting in a chair, bound with some type of cord.

She was alive.

And he could see that she was struggling to free her hands, which were tied behind her back. *That's my girl*, he thought. He had always known she was a strong woman—even when she hadn't believed it herself—and the fact that she was still fighting after all she had been through proved him one hundred percent right.

The feeling of relief that washed over him almost took his breath. His heart was pounding against the wall of his chest. All he wanted to do was crash through the window and rescue her, but he knew he couldn't do that, not yet.

He pulled away from the window quickly. He wanted to just keep looking at Tiffany, so thankful she was still alive, but he didn't want her to see him. Out of surprise or relief, she could unintentionally signal his presence to William.

He swiftly continued around the corner to the back of the house. Both bedroom windows were dark, with no sign of activity. Then, he spotted Tiffany's Toyota Corolla parked under a large oak tree at the edge of the backyard.

He approached cautiously, then peered inside, pressing his face against the right rear window. The backseat was empty. Next, he checked the front. Sitting in the passenger seat was Tiffany's backpack. Jackson could see the tip of what looked like a rose poking out the top. His anger burned. He knew exactly what the rose had been used for.

Twentymile Creek, swollen by the rain, roared above the drumming of the raindrops on the surrounding trees. His drenched clothes stuck to his frigid body, making it difficult for him to move about freely.

He left the car and walked back to the exterior wall of the house, then made his way to his bedroom window. He normally left it unlocked and cracked to allow the cool nighttime breezes to enter his room. He prayed he hadn't shut it prior to leaving earlier. He was relieved to see the window open, about three inches or so. That would be his way in.

He considered climbing inside immediately and confronting William in the dining room, but deemed that too risky. William likely had a gun, and if there were shots fired, Tiffany might be hit. He decided he needed to draw William out of the house, or at least distract him, so he could get into position to rescue Tiffany.

Jackson left his bedroom window and continued around the exterior of the house, returning to the front porch. He picked up a few small stones from the flowerbed that Tiffany had put in during the spring. He stood, aimed for the kitchen window, and tossed the rocks, one at a time. They each found their mark, striking the center of the glass a few seconds apart.

He hurried back around the side of the house and returned to his bedroom window. He didn't know how long his simple distraction would hold William's attention, so he wasted no time. He thrust the window upward, but the old wooden frame, swollen by the humidity, got stuck. Cursing silently, he persisted and finally managed to create an opening big enough to fit through.

He grabbed the bottom of the window jamb with his large hands and pulled himself into the opening, his upper body now hanging six inches above his worn-out mattress. He put his hands on the rumpled quilt that had been soaked by the driving rain and pulled his legs inside.

He moved slowly, quietly, as he stood from the bed.

Then he drew his .45 and started toward the living room.

37

Tiffany almost had her left hand free. The pain was so intense that she gnawed at her lower lip to keep from crying out as she wrestled her wrist through the last binding. She could feel blood running down her hand and dripping off her fingertips to the floor below.

William was still sitting at the dining table, staring off blankly into the darkness. He wasn't watching her; he seemed to be lost in a world that was real only to him.

She snapped her head up when she heard something strike the kitchen window.

William didn't move.

Then another crack against the glass.

Then another.

It wasn't rain. It sounded more like a rock or piece of wood being thrown at the window.

At last, William came out of his daze and stood. He moved quickly toward the window and looked outside. Then, after a momentary pause, he opened the front door and stepped onto the porch.

Tiffany didn't know what was going on. But whatever it was, it probably wasn't good news for her. She refocused on freeing herself as quickly as possible. The cords dug into her bleeding, raw flesh, and she wanted to just scream and give up.

But she had no intention of doing so.

She jumped when she heard someone speak her name. She turned her head to the left and saw Jackson standing in the darkened hallway; the washed-out light from the lamp highlighted his chiseled face and the pistol he held in his hand.

Her heart sank.

He put his index finger to his lips, instructing her to remain silent.

Could she trust him?

Should she remain quiet as he requested or scream for help? Maybe William would have a change of heart and help her.

Maybe not.

She didn't know what to do. She was sure Jackson could hear the machine gun in her chest from his position, several feet away.

She watched as he strode across the living room floor toward her. Every fiber of her being wanted to trust the man she had come to love, to rejoice that he had come to rescue her, but she couldn't let go of the lingering doubt bubbling up inside her as he bent down behind her back.

"Are you okay?" he whispered.

She heard him holster his weapon and then felt him begin cutting the cord that secured her to the chair. "Yes, I'm okay."

"He didn't hurt you?"

"No."

"Can you walk?"

"Yes, I think so."

Jackson leaned forward and kissed the side of her face. "I love you, Tiffany," he whispered, his warm breath blowing across her tear-stained cheek. "I just want you to know that."

Her heart melted.

Whatever doubts she had about Jackson vanished in that moment.

And she had no reason not to trust him. Unlike Paul, he had never done anything to make her fear him. And he had never harmed her.

Never.

She *had* been right about him.

She still had no idea why William had brought her to Jackson's house, but she now knew, deep in her soul, that Jackson hadn't had anything to do with it. He was here to help her.

"I love you, too," she replied. "But hurry. He's still outside."

"I'm going as fast as I can. Watch the front door for me while I untie your feet." He moved in front of her and began cutting more of the telephone cord.

She stared over his back and toward the door. It was ajar, and she heard William walking on the porch, investigating the sounds at the window. Surely, he would return at any moment.

"Tiffany, listen to me," Jackson said.

She looked down and found him staring into her eyes.

"As soon as you're free, go to my bedroom and climb out the window. It's already open. My truck is parked near the highway. Just go there and wait for me."

"I'm not leaving you, Jackson," she objected.

"It's not up for debate, Tiffany," he said flatly, then looked back down and slid the large knife blade under the two remaining cords that held her thighs to the chair. He cut through them in just a few seconds. He gave her lips a quick kiss and said, "Okay, go. Wait in the truck."

"Jackson, I'm not leaving you—"

The sound of the front door slamming shut stopped Tiffany in mid-sentence. The kitchen lights came on, instantly banishing the darkness.

"What the hell?" William muttered, a look of shock and confusion on his face. He sprinted toward the dining table where he had left his gun.

"Run, Tiffany!" Jackson yelled as he simultaneously turned to meet William.

Tiffany jumped from the chair, her legs like wet sponges after being idle for so many hours. She stumbled forward and almost fell to her knees, then managed to regain her balance at the last second.

When she looked up, she saw Jackson charging William. He slammed into William's midsection, just like a football player sacking the opposing quarterback. William's body folded on impact, sending the pistol he had just snatched from the table flying from his hand. It hit the kitchen floor and skidded toward Tiffany.

Jackson pushed William forward, pinning him against the front door. "Tiffany, grab the gun and RUN!"

She hesitated for a split second, then ran forward and picked up the pistol. She aimed it at William, but Jackson kept getting in her line of sight. She couldn't take the chance. She lowered the gun and saw Jackson hit William with a right hand to the jaw. William continued to fight, even after the direct blow. His face was ruby red and his eyes wide. He was now grasping at Jackson's neck.

"Tiffany, I left my cellphone in the truck. Go call for help! NOW!" Jackson screamed, then grabbed William in a bear hug and threw him to the floor.

She didn't hesitate this time.

She ran down the hallway and into Jackson's bedroom. She searched the dark room with her arms out in front of her, the right one still grasping William's semi-automatic handgun. When her knees hit the side of the bed, she fell forward, then crawled on the mattress until she could grasp the windowsill. She quickly swung her legs out the opening, then jumped to the ground below. The rain-soaked earth shifted beneath her feet, and she fell to her side. She regained her footing, then ran around the side of the house and toward the gravel road.

Dressed only in her pajamas, she was shivering from the cold wind and rain by the time she reached the road in front of the house. She turned left and headed toward Highway 28, searching for Jackson's truck. She was running blind, unable to see anything in front of her.

She kept running.

The sharp gravel cut at her feet, digging in and tearing the tender flesh. She cried out from the pain. Her weak body felt as though it would give out at any moment.

She didn't stop.

She kept going, ignoring the pain and the cold through sheer determination. She had to make it to the truck and call for help.

Just when she thought she couldn't go any farther, she saw the grill of Jackson's pickup truck in front of her. By the time it emerged from the darkness, it was less than five feet in front of her, and she almost slammed into it.

Out of breath, she stumbled to the driver's side and threw open the door, then slowly climbed inside. She set the gun down on the passenger seat and began searching blindly for the switch to the dome light. Her bloody, wet fingers felt across the dash until she found it just to the left of the steering wheel. She flipped it on, and the cab of the truck filled with bright, incandescent light, causing her to squint for several seconds.

She checked the glove compartment, then the center console, for the cellphone but couldn't find it. She stuck her hand between the seat cushions, but again came away with nothing. She checked the floor and the backseat, too.

Nothing.

The phone was not there.

38

Jackson had William pinned to the kitchen floor, his forearm against the man's neck. "Stop fighting! It's over," he yelled, but William ignored his command and kept struggling to free himself. Jackson was amazed at William's almost superhuman strength. He should've been able to subdue William with no problem, but the man just wouldn't give up. Jackson looked around to make sure Tiffany had left and was relieved when he saw that she had.

William screamed, "I can't go back to prison! I won't!"

Jackson turned his head back toward the man beneath him, then, in an instant, felt his nose explode as William got free of his hold and thrust his head upward.

Jackson flew backward, his eyes immediately filling with tears. The pain of his broken nose made him light-headed, and he felt William's legs slip from under him. He reached up and wiped his eyes, trying to clear his vision. The coppery taste of blood assaulted his tongue.

By the time Jackson could finally see again, William had gotten off the floor and was scrambling toward the hallway—the same direction Tiffany had gone.

Jackson jumped from the floor and lunged. He grabbed William's lower legs just as he was about to escape, sending him crashing back to the living room floor.

Jackson pushed himself up, narrowly missing a kick William threw toward his head, then pulled the Glock from his side and aimed it straight at the man's chest. "It's over, William," he repeated. "I don't want to kill you but, trust me, if you move again, I will pull this trigger without thinking twice." Jackson paused and took a deep breath. "Do we understand each other?"

Defeat swept William's pale face, and his head fell backward, smacking the hardwood floor. He began to sob.

"Do we understand each other, William?" Jackson asked again, this time shouting the question.

The man just nodded his head.

"Sit up," Jackson said, "and put your hands behind your back."

William obeyed. "I can't go back to prison," he whispered between sobs.

"Okay—"

A gunshot echoed off the walls of the old house, and William's head exploded like a ripe watermelon smashing against a brick wall.

39

Nathan Lansing sighed and tilted his head backward, resting it against the soft leather of his wingback chair. He rubbed his eyes and pushed away from the wooden desk. He had been working in his living room all afternoon doing Internet searches, reading articles, and making and taking phone calls, trying to gather more information about William McMillan and Tiffany Colson. He hadn't even stopped for dinner.

He was exhausted. All he wanted to do was take a hot shower and crawl into bed.

But something about the whole situation gnawed at him. He wasn't sure what it was, but the sick feeling in the pit of his stomach had been with him for the last several hours and showed no signs of abating.

He hadn't talked to the park ranger since earlier in the day, when he had relayed the information about the car William was believed to be driving. He had tried to contact Jackson and Katie again thirty minutes ago, but no one had answered. He hoped both were okay and that they would find Tiffany safe and sound.

He had always liked Tiffany, and had never regretted standing up to the McMillans on her behalf—even though it had almost cost him his career.

He closed his eyes, tired and burning after hours of staring at the bright screen, and enjoyed the darkness. He hated working on computers—always had—but found that if he wanted to function in modern society, he had no choice but to embrace them.

Sometimes, though, he wasn't sure if he wanted to function in modern society any longer.

Maybe it was time for him to retire, step away from police work, and just stay home with June and tend to his garden.

She seemed to think so, anyway. She had brought up taking a damn cruise again, too. She was all excited, talking about going to the Caribbean or maybe even Alaska. The thought of being on a big boat with a bunch of idiotic strangers who were stuffing themselves with endless buffets and engaging in the thrilling sport of ballroom dancing sounded like one street over from Hell to Nathan. He would rather keep working until they had to roll him into his office in a wheelchair and feed him through a straw.

He loved his job.

But he guessed he owed it to June to begin winding things down. He wasn't getting any younger, as she often reminded him, and she'd been awfully patient with him.

She had stuck by his side for the last forty-one years. He never had made a lot of money, and once he became sheriff, the opportunities for extended vacations were almost nonexistent. June had always wanted to travel and experience new things, something he had never been able to offer her—but she loved him anyway. And, the fact of the matter was, he figured she should get to live some of her dreams after he retired.

He would be going on a cruise soon.

Nathan heard his wife's soft footsteps approaching from behind, then her warm hands massaging his sore neck muscles.

"You ready for bed?" she asked.

"Uh-uh." He could feel the tension leaving his neck and shoulders as she continued to work her magic, her soft touch bringing instant relaxation. Normally, when she gave him a massage prior to bedtime, things ended well for him after the lights went out. "Yeah, I'm ready," he said quietly, the calming effect of the massage being replaced with the slow burn of passion.

He reached up and placed his hand on top of his wife's. He gave it a squeeze, and was beginning to stand from the chair when the phone on his desk rang. He picked it up and checked the caller ID. It was his friend with the state police. "Sorry, June, I have to take this," he said, looking into her disappointed eyes. "I'll be to bed in just a few minutes."

"Promise?" she asked as she walked across the living room floor. She looked over her shoulder and gave him the provocative gaze that she had perfected during their four decades of marriage.

Nathan smiled. "I promise." He watched her disappear down the hall before he answered the phone. "Hello?"

"I've got some more information for you, Nathan," Captain Smithfield said.

"Okay, shoot." Nathan grabbed a pen from his desk.

When he ended the call a few minutes later, he stared down at the name he had scrawled on the piece of paper. The captain had told him it was the person they suspected of orchestrating William's escape from prison. Nathan didn't know the name, but something about it seemed oddly familiar.

He struggled to remember where he had seen it before.

He was sure the name didn't belong to a local resident, otherwise he would've recognized it immediately. But he knew he had seen it somewhere.

Then it hit him.

He scooted his chair back up to the desk and pulled up a news article he had read earlier in the day on his computer screen. Then he looked back down at the name on the paper. His mind reeled, trying to connect the dots—but it didn't take him long to make the connection.

He picked up the phone and dialed Jackson's number, praying silently that someone would answer this time.

He had to warn him.

The ranger was walking straight into a trap.

40

"Hello, Jackson."

The hairs on the back of Jackson's neck pricked at the sound of the macabre greeting.

The voice behind him was low and shaking, but he recognized it immediately, despite the sharp ringing in his ears from the gunshot that had killed William.

"I have a .357 Magnum aimed straight at your back, and if you move a muscle, I'll cut you in two," the man added.

Jackson didn't move. He thought about swinging around and taking a shot, but the man had him square in his sights; it would be suicidal. He looked down at William's body, the back of his head blown out, blood and brain matter splattered on the back wall of the living room.

"Hello, Bobby," Jackson said, his voice deep, like hardened steel, with no hint of weakness or fear.

"Drop your gun and kick it back to me. Don't even think about turning around. Understand?"

"Yeah." Jackson let the Glock slide from his hand, the sound of the cold metal striking the hardwood floor reverberating throughout the house. He kicked it away as Bobby had ordered and, after a couple of seconds, he heard Bobby pick up the gun.

"Now, Jackson, turn around slowly . . . very slowly. You try anything, and I swear I'll split your skull wide open, just like ol' William's there."

Jackson started to turn slowly to his right.

"Easy, Jackson," Bobby warned. "Keep your hands where I can see 'em. I have a mighty itchy trigger finger tonight. It'd be a shame for me to kill you prematurely and ruin all the fun." He chuckled.

Jackson continued turning slowly, his hands at shoulder height. When at last he faced Bobby, his heart sank.

Tiffany was standing next to him.

41

Jackson stared at Tiffany. Her eyes were wide, and he could see her lips trembling. Her hands were dangling in front of her mud-stained pajamas, bound with a length of dirty cotton rope. Bobby held her tight, his bony fingers grasping her upper arm.

She was terrified.

Jackson gazed into her eyes, trying to silently convey that everything was going to be all right, but he wasn't sure she could believe that right now.

"Surprised to see her, Jackson? I bet you thought she'd escaped, didn't you?" Bobby cracked a thin, evil smile. "Probably didn't expect to see me either, did you?" He laughed again. "So what do you think of the big surprise, Jackson? Shocked?" he asked, his eyes wide like some freakish clown.

Jackson said nothing. He just stood there, stunned.

"And don't think there's any help coming, either. I followed your incompetent partner out of the resort. Katie is it?" When Jackson didn't answer, Bobby turned his head toward Tiffany. "Isn't that right, sweetheart?" he asked, squeezing her arm tightly.

She let out a muffled cry.

"Yep, it was a beautiful sight. Ran her right off the mountain. Headlights just disappeared into the ravine," Bobby added, smiling and waving his arm in a wide arc.

The man who stood before Jackson was almost unrecognizable. Bobby's physical appearance had changed so much in the two years since they had seen each other that if it weren't for his distinctive voice, Jackson wouldn't have known him.

When Bobby Donaldson had been Jackson's boss at the Park Service, he had weighed close to two hundred pounds, with a full, almost chubby face and dark brown hair. Now, he looked like someone who had just escaped the coroner's office right before the autopsy began. He was dressed in a dirty T-shirt and faded jeans. His face was ashen and gaunt, his hair was gray and thinning, and he must have lost seventy or eighty pounds. His eyes were hollow and wild, and they reminded Jackson of an animal caught in a steel trap. When he wasn't speaking, his thin lips twitched erratically.

Since the first time they met, Jackson and Bobby had never gotten along. The tension that had been building between the two men for years had finally came to a head when Bobby tried to thwart the search for Cody McAlister just to boost his ego and destroy Jackson's career. And it was all because of some twisted, personal vendetta that Bobby harbored and Jackson never understood. At the end of the search, Jackson had arrived at the evacuation scene to see Bobby hamming it up with local television reporters. Jackson had become enraged, then walked over and slugged Bobby square on the jaw.

Jackson saw his career with the Park Service ending as Bobby hit the ground.

But an investigation into Bobby's actions during the search revealed that he had acted inappropriately, needlessly delaying important resources needed to find Cody. Bobby had been given a choice of taking an early retirement from his position as head ranger for the Great Smoky Mountains National Park and slipping away quietly, or being fired.

He chose retirement.

Jackson's anger burned inside of him. He had always disliked Bobby, and they had certainly had their differences, but he would never have thought him capable of something as heinous as this. The sight of Tiffany standing helpless by his side fueled Jackson's rage. He wanted to kill Bobby. Now.

Jackson clenched his fists.

His jaw muscles tensed.

"Bobby, you son of a bitch," Jackson said through gritted teeth, then took two large strides toward him.

Bobby raised the .357 revolver and fired.

Tiffany screamed.

But Jackson couldn't hear her, deafened by the sound of the gunshot as it reverberated off the confining walls of the house. His ears were ringing, his head spinning. His vision blurred as Bobby and Tiffany moved out of focus in front of him.

He staggered back, then felt his right leg collapse beneath him. He tried to stay on his feet, waving his arms wildly in an attempt to regain his balance, but his legs would no longer support him. He crumpled to the floor, then slumped over onto his right side. He tried to prop himself back up on his forearm, but couldn't. He rolled onto his back, gasping for air.

The ringing in his ears diminished enough that he could hear Tiffany crying. Adrenaline surged through his body. His heart was pounding. He couldn't breathe. He raised his head to look at Bobby and Tiffany. He blinked his eyes slowly, hoping they would clear, but everything in front of him looked as if he were viewing it through the bottom of a Mason jar. He saw Bobby grab Tiffany by her forearm and thrust her forward, making her cry out in pain and sending her tumbling to the floor next to Jackson.

"You two get over there," Bobby said, motioning with the gun to the area in front of the fireplace.

Tiffany was trying to muffle her sobs as she drew close to Jackson and wrapped her arms around him. "Here, I'll help you," she whispered in his ear. "You've been shot." She lifted his head off the floor and cradled it in her hands. "The fireplace is right behind you, just scoot backward."

Jackson grunted from the pain, as he propped himself up on his elbows and used his forearms to pull himself toward the fireplace. Tiffany stayed by his side, encouraging him to keep moving. He inched backward on his butt until he felt his lower back contact the raised hearth. He rested against it, exhausted from the short trip across the floor.

He felt Tiffany cup his face in her bound hands and kiss him softly on the lips. "It's going to be okay. I'm here with you."

Jackson's vision began to clear, and he looked into her emerald eyes, knowing he had never loved anyone as much as he loved her in that moment. He would do whatever was necessary to make sure she survived this nightmare—even if it meant his life.

He let his gaze drift down to the source of the intense pain his brain was just now acknowledging. His right leg was bleeding heavily, a half-inch crimson hole in his jeans indicating the bullet's entry. It was just to the right of his femur. He didn't think the .357 slug had broken his leg, but he couldn't be sure. And although the bleeding was heavy, soaking his jeans in a large circular pattern around the wound, he could tell the bullet hadn't struck a major artery. If it had, he would likely be unconscious already.

"Why are you doing this, Bobby?" Jackson asked, his voice surprisingly strong for a man who had just been shot.

He watched as Bobby staggered forward, his sickly figure unsteady and frail. He smiled, and his thin lips parted, exposing his stained teeth. "Why did I do it?" he said, his voice low. "I'll tell you *exactly* why, Jackson." His voice rose with each word. He waved the gun in front of him, and the smile vanished from his face, replaced by a hate-filled sneer. "Because you ruined my life!" He took another step, spittle escaping his mouth and landing on his bony chin.

Jackson was afraid Bobby was about to murder both of them right then. He had to keep Tiffany safe—whatever the cost.

"You took everything from me, Jackson!" Bobby screamed, still gesturing wildly with the gun as he continued his venomous tirade. His face was red and burning with rage. "Look at me! I look like a damn skeleton! I hardly eat anymore, and every time I try to sleep, I think about what you stole from me. I was one hell of a ranger, Jackson . . . better than you'll ever be." He paused. "And now, you're going to pay for what you did to me." Bobby pointed the gun straight at Tiffany.

"NO!" Jackson screamed and lifted his left hand in front of Tiffany's chest. "She's innocent in this whole thing, Bobby. She had nothing to do with what went on between us." Jackson took a breath, trying to calm both his own voice and Bobby, as well. "Just let her go, and you can do whatever you want with me," he pleaded, although he knew that once Tiffany was safe, he would fight Bobby with everything he had.

Bobby chuckled, a dry rattle coursing through his emaciated body. The evil grin returned. He lowered the handgun and turned his gaze toward Jackson. "Always the hero, aren't you, Jackson? You made me look like a fool, and I lost everything. You want to know why she's here?" he asked.

Jackson didn't respond; he just stared into the eyes of a madman.

"She's here because she's what you treasure most in this world. More than anything, isn't that right?"

Jackson nodded slightly. The pain from the gunshot wound was so sharp it was hard to stay focused. He heard Tiffany sob.

"So, the way I see it," Bobby paused and breathed in deeply for dramatic effect, "you took away the thing I valued most . . . so I'm going to take away the thing that means the most to you." Bobby motioned with the gun toward Tiffany.

Jackson swallowed hard, his throat dry from stress. "Bobby, you don't want to do this."

Bobby ignored him and walked toward the dining table. He picked up the closest wooden chair and returned to the living room. He set it down in front of Jackson and took a seat. "Of course I want to do this, Jackson! Look at all the trouble I've gone to just to make this night possible." He gestured toward William's body lying on the floor to Jackson's right.

"You probably don't know this, but ever since I *retired* from the Park Service, I've spent my time learning everything I could about you and your pretty little girl-friend here. I guess you could say I became obsessed." Bobby laughed softly. "Hell, my wife even left me, said I'd gone off the deep end, but I didn't care, I never really liked her anyway.

"I followed your career. Every time a newspaper mentioned your name, I pored over the article." Bobby chuckled. "Listen to me; I *do* sound like I went off the deep end. Maybe the old hag was right after all." He slumped his shoulders, relaxing in the chair. "Oh well, some things are worth a little obsession, Jackson. Don't you agree?"

"I wouldn't know, Bobby."

The grin vanished from Bobby's face as he leaned forward. "Of course you wouldn't know, Jackson! You're Captain freakin' America, aren't you? Always doing the right thing," Bobby opened his arms wide and stared at the ceiling like a televangelist asking for donations, "and always the perfect example of what a *real* park ranger should be!" He stared back at Jackson. "Let me ask you something. Have they made you superintendent yet?" he asked in a sarcastic whisper. Then he laughed again.

Jackson didn't respond. He just kept staring into Bobby's empty eyes, unfazed. He felt Tiffany rub his upper left arm with her hand, trying to comfort him. He wasn't about to give in to Bobby, not for a second. Even if Bobby shot him dead right here in his own home, he wouldn't give his former boss the satisfaction of seeing him beg for his life like a little coward.

But he would beg for Tiffany's life.

"Please, Bobby, just let Tiffany go. She's done nothing to you," Jackson said.

"Bullshit!" Bobby yelled. "She's done plenty to me! She makes *you* happy . . . and, for that reason alone, she has to die." He tilted his head toward Tiffany and said, "Sorry," raising his eyebrows mockingly.

Bobby exhaled deeply. "You know, Jackson, I found out a very interesting fact about your lovely girlfriend." He paused. "She's a killer." Bobby undoubtedly expected a shocked reaction from Jackson, and when he didn't get it, he smiled and chuckled. "So you know already?" he asked, leaning forward and resting his forearms on his knees, the gun dangling between his legs.

Jackson felt Tiffany's grip on his bicep tighten.

Bobby straightened up and leaned back in the chair, letting his hands rest on his upper thighs, the gun loosely gripped in his right hand, the barrel aimed straight at Jackson. "Yep, she's a regular Jack the Ripper. Sliced some poor bastard up good, didn't you, sweetheart?" Bobby asked, staring at her.

Jackson didn't look at Tiffany. He kept his eyes on Bobby. He knew Tiffany was no murderer.

"Got off scot-free, too, didn't you?" Bobby asked.

"You're a liar," Tiffany said. "You don't know anything about me."

"Oh, I'm afraid that's not true at all. In fact, I know *everything* about you, Tiff." He leaned forward, licking his dry, thin lips. "I think that's what your friends call you, isn't it . . . Tiff? Since we've gotten to know each other, you don't mind if I call you Tiff, do you?"

"Actually, I do. We're not friends. Never will be."

Bobby let out another icy laugh. "I heard you had a bit of a temper, *Tiff*. Guess it's true what they say about redheads, huh, Jackson?" Bobby glanced back toward Jackson, then returned his cold eyes to Tiffany. He took a deep breath and sighed. "Yes, Ms. Colson, I know everything about you . . . and that's where he came in." He motioned toward William's body lying on the floor.

J. MICHAEL STEWART

"Once I found out about your ex, the one that you sliced and diced, I did a little research and, what do you know, I found his brother sitting in state prison for embezzlement." Bobby rubbed his bony chin, smiling. "It's amazing what a man will do for you when you offer him his freedom.

"I made a few phone calls, arranged for William's transportation and supplies, and paid off a delivery driver to let William hitch a ride out the prison's front gate in the back of his truck." He paused. "The whole thing was really too easy for a man of my skills.

"And he was more than willing to help me out, especially when he found out he could get payback for his brother's murder." Bobby cracked another smile. "Of course, I'm sure he would've had second thoughts if he'd known he would end up with a bullet in his head, but, as they say, hindsight is 20/20. I never intended for him to leave this house alive anyway. I couldn't leave a witness, Jackson. Even you must understand that."

Bobby looked down at the corpse just a few feet away. "I'll clean up the mess and dispose of the body later. Kind of a shame, really. I didn't need his help, of course, but I couldn't resist the temptation to make a little game out of all this. I wanted to toy with your girlfriend, scare her out of her mind." He chuckled. "I wanted to make *you* think she'd gone crazy." He paused and glared at Jackson. "But mainly, I just wanted to see if The Great Jackson Hart could figure out who was behind the whole thing. I knew you would probably connect the dots eventually, but I have to say, Jackson, I'm a little disappointed in you. I thought for sure you would've pieced everything together a lot sooner."

Bobby grinned, and Jackson could tell he was taking great pleasure in demeaning him in front of Tiffany.

But Jackson didn't respond, refusing to be goaded into doing something stupid. He just kept staring at the madman in front of him, meeting him with steel resolve.

"But I could tell by the shock on your face when I walked in, you had no clue," Bobby cackled. "Guess maybe you're not as good as everyone thinks you are. I told William to leave the map in his car, but I really was surprised it took that to clue you in. If you had just done a little digging around, you would've found out that I've been the caretaker for the McMillan house out on Highway 28 ever since the Park Service threw me out on my ass."

Bobby leaned forward, and leveled his face only inches from Jackson's. His lips were doing their involuntary twitching again. "I wanted to see you worry, see you afraid that you were losing the thing that meant the most to you in life . . . just like I did. And you know something, Jackson? It was worth every damn hoop I had to jump through to make it happen," he said, his words cold with what Jackson knew was years of pent-up hatred.

"You're a horrible person," Tiffany said, her voice strong and clear.

Bobby turned his head slowly toward Tiffany. "Is that so? Well, let me tell you something, little lady . . . you ain't seen nothin' yet."

42

Tiffany watched the man in front of her. She could feel the evil, could see it in his soulless eyes. She had heard Jackson talk about Bobby before, and was even there when Jackson had punched him out, but she had never met the man until earlier when he drove up and discovered her inside Jackson's truck.

She looked over at William on the floor. His face had gone pale now, his lips a sickly shade of gray. His eyes were open wide, staring at the ceiling. Part of her felt sorry for him.

She turned her stare back toward Bobby—for him, she had no empathy. Nor did she fear him. Instead, she was fiercely determined that she and Jackson *would* survive. She glanced down at the gunshot wound in Jackson's thigh. The pool of blood surrounding the injury had expanded. He needed to get to a hospital.

"So, this is how it's going to go down," Bobby said, pushing with the palms of his hands against his knees and standing up. He was towering over both of them now, his eyes callous, cold as he looked down. Bobby exhaled slowly, letting the air almost whistle across his thin lips. Then he smiled wide, exposing his caramel-colored teeth.

He looked like he was having the time of his life, pleased by what he had already accomplished and by what was to come.

So confident.

So calculating.

"There's going to be a murder-suicide at the Hart residence tonight," he said.

43

Jackson knew Bobby wasn't joking—he intended to kill both of them before the night was over.

He had to think of something quick. He looked to his left at Tiffany, who was still grasping his arm. He expected to see unvarnished fear, but saw strength instead.

Courage.

He wished he could figure out how to free her hands, at least give her a fighting chance to escape, but he knew Bobby would shoot them both if he even tried.

But if he could hold Bobby down long enough for her to run to the front door, she would be able to make it out, even with her hands tied. She could run away from the house and into the woods, where Bobby would never find her. He was a shell of his former self, and Jackson knew he wouldn't have the strength to pursue Tiffany through all the challenges the forest presented.

Jackson quietly determined that was the only viable option. It was what had to be done. He would jump Bobby when he wasn't expecting it and fight with him until either Bobby or he was dead. Tiffany would survive, and that was all that mattered.

"So, Jackson, when I was devising this brilliant plan, I tried to come up with a grand finale. Sure, I wanted to see you squirm and chase after your girlfriend, but then I thought of something even better. The perfect payback."

"Yeah, and what would that be, Bobby?" Jackson asked. He lifted his right leg slightly to test its strength. It felt in fairly decent shape, despite the .357 slug that had just passed through it a few minutes ago. His vision was clear, and the lightheadedness had vanished. When the time was right, he had to go for it.

Bobby ignored Jackson's question. Instead, fury flooded his face. "You destroyed me, Jackson! You took away my reputation! Everything I worked so hard for!" Bobby paused and took a deep breath, his frail body exhausted by the screaming. After a few seconds, his wild eyes refocused on Jackson once more. "My job . . . being a ranger . . . was all I had." Another pause. "It was everything to me, Jackson, and you tore it away. You made me look like a fool!"

"You did that all by yourself, Bobby," Jackson said bluntly.

Bobby's faced burned with rage. His eyes were bulging, his lips shaking. He lifted the large revolver in his trembling right hand and aimed it straight at Jackson. He pulled the hammer back, the clicking sound of the rotating cylinder resonating above the pounding rain outside.

Light from the kitchen reflected off the stainless steel gun and made it look even brighter than it was. Jackson wondered if that was the last sight he would ever see. He reached over and touched Tiffany's leg, squeezing it gently. He cursed himself for not making his move earlier, before the gun was cocked and pointed squarely at his chest, but he couldn't do anything about that now—all he could do was wait, and pray for another opportunity.

"No, Jackson, *you* did it to me. And now it's time for me to return the favor. You see, that's the best part of my plan . . . you're going to kill Tiffany here in a lover's spat, and then you're going to kill yourself." Bobby's hand was shaking even worse now, and Jackson was afraid he might accidentally pull the trigger.

He had to make his move soon.

Bobby grinned and, for the first time, Jackson saw a glint of delight in his eyes. "Well, you're not going to kill her . . . I am . . . and then I'll take care of you. But she goes first. I want you to experience the pain that I did. Eye for an eye, right, Jackson?"

"How are you going to explain the hole in my leg, dumb-ass?"

Bobby chuckled, causing the gun to wobble wildly in his unsteady hand. His thin legs were barely holding him up. "Jackson, you *so* underestimate me. Even that was part of the plan, you idiot. You two got into a lover's quarrel, one of you threatened the other with the gun, there was a struggle, and you got shot in the leg. Then you killed her, and finally, out of grief over what you'd done, you took your own life. And the *best* part is, you did it all right here, inside this house owned by the United States Park Service. I'm sure it will make quite the story on the six o'clock news. I can see the headline now: HERO U.S. PARK RANGER KILLS GIRLFRIEND, THEN SHOOTS HIMSELF! Film at eleven." Bobby threw his head back and laughed out loud. "It's going to be so much fun for me to watch your reputation being dragged through the gutter just like mine was. Oh, you have no idea how much I will enjoy seeing you destroyed, Jackson. Yes, The Great Jackson Hart will turn out to be nothing but a cold-blooded murderer."

Bobby coughed, the force of it rattling his feeble body. He shuffled over to the chair and sat down again, obviously exhausted by his own antics. He grinned and leaned back, spreading his arms open in a joyful expression of self-gratitude, the barrel of the gun aimed down the hallway. "I've thought of everything, Jackson."

It was now or never.

"Bet you didn't think of this!" Jackson tore his left arm free of Tiffany's grasp, and in one swift, painful motion, thrust himself off the floor and leaped into the center of Bobby's chest, sending the man toppling over and onto his back. Jackson followed Bobby over, the wooden chair breaking beneath their combined weight. The revolver fired, sending chunks of drywall falling down on the hallway floor. Jackson struck Bobby with a forearm across his face, stunning him. Then he grabbed Bobby's right hand, the one holding the gun, and pinned it to the floor.

Bobby let out a muffled cry.

Jackson hit him again with another right forearm, simultaneously struggling to hold the gun down with his left.

"Run, Tiffany. GO! NOW!" He turned his head back toward the fireplace where she was still sitting. "Tiffany, listen to me! RUN!" Jackson watched as she hesitated for a second, then got up and ran for the front door.

Tiffany's head was spinning from the adrenaline. She glanced down at Jackson and Bobby struggling on the floor. She considered staying.

She didn't want to leave Jackson.

But she had to.

She ran out of the house and into the cold October rain.

44

Jackson wrestled with Bobby on the floor of the living room. For a man who looked half-dead, he had a surprising amount of fight left in him. Jackson was still spread-eagle on top, struggling to hold down the wild-eyed, gray-haired devil beneath him. Bobby's face was reddened and strained as he struggled to escape.

"Give it up, Bobby," Jackson said. "It's over."

"Like hell it is," Bobby grunted.

Jackson felt Bobby's right wrist twisting inside his hand, and he sensed his own palm becoming slippery with sweat. He knew if Bobby managed to gain control of the gun again, he would use it—only, this time, he wouldn't aim for his leg.

Jackson held Bobby's wrist as best he could, then lifted it several inches off the floor before slamming it back down, trying to dislodge the revolver from Bobby's grip. The gun didn't come free. Jackson held his right forearm on top of Bobby's neck; he couldn't go for the gun with both hands at once, because he knew that would give Bobby too much mobility. Instead, he increased the pressure on the man's throat, pressing his forearm into the center of Bobby's esophagus.

Bobby's eyes began to bulge. Saliva was running out of the corners of his mouth. Still, he wouldn't release his grip on the gun, even as Jackson knew the man must be nearing unconsciousness. He was bearing down so hard that he was sure he would crush Bobby's throat at any second.

And Jackson knew it wasn't Bobby's will to live that kept him going. Instead, it was pure, unadulterated hatred of Jackson himself—his quest for revenge—that kept him from going to sleep.

Jackson turned his head and stared at the gun. Bobby's skeletal fingers were still wrapped tightly around the wooden handle, his knuckles white from the strain. Jackson lifted Bobby's arm again and slammed it back down to the floor.

Nothing.

Then, Jackson felt Bobby wrestle his right leg free. A split second later, Jackson felt the sickening sensation of a groin strike as Bobby drove his knee squarely into his testicles.

Jackson's eyes went wide, and he gasped deeply, momentarily losing his concentration . . . and his grip around Bobby's wrist.

Before Jackson could react, Bobby tore his hand free.

Another gunshot.

Jackson felt his left shoulder explode. He tried to stand but, a second later, he was tumbling backward toward the fireplace when Bobby kicked him in the stomach.

Jackson landed on his side, then grasped his injured shoulder, trying to slow the blood flow. The pain was unbearable, and he thought for a moment that he would pass out. He fought to remain conscious. He wasn't sure it even mattered at this point—he was probably a dead man anyway—but he sure as hell wasn't going to just roll over and let Bobby win without a fight.

Jackson watched through watery eyes as Bobby crawled to his knees, then managed to stand. His breathing was rapid and labored, and he was unsteady on his feet, swaying from side to side as he struggled to gain his balance.

Jackson felt himself weakening with each passing second. He glanced at his shoulder, his right palm pressed against the bullet hole; it was doing little to stop the bleeding. A steady stream of blood flowed from beneath his hand and onto the floor. His vision began to dim, and an overpowering need to drift off to sleep came over him. But he kept fighting against the urge to just let go.

Bobby took a teetering step forward and raised the shaking gun in his hand. "I hate you, Jackson," he said between ragged breaths. He looked like he was barely hanging on himself. Blood was streaming from his nose where Jackson's forearms had hit home. He massaged his throat, trying in vain to take a deep breath.

Even though Bobby was in bad shape, Jackson knew there was little more he could do to save himself. Bobby had the advantage, and as close as Jackson had come to defeating him, he had come up short. He was too weak to move another inch, and Bobby had the .357 Magnum pointed right at him. It was over.

At least Tiffany had gotten out alive.

And that alone made it possible for him to die in peace.

"I'm going to kill you, Jackson. Then, I'm going to hunt your girlfriend down like a dog and kill her, too." Bobby coughed and spit a huge stream of blood onto the floor. "I took the keys to your truck after I found her, so she won't make it far." Another cough. "I'll find her, I promise you that. And my plan will work out just as I envisioned," Bobby said, his eyes like those of a rabid dog, although Jackson could barely see them now.

Jackson knew Bobby was wrong about Tiffany. She was a strong woman, and she would make it. Bobby wouldn't be able to find her before she escaped. He was confident of that.

Bobby pulled the hammer back on the gun.

Jackson stared straight into his hollow eyes, unwilling to display any semblance of fear.

And he waited to die.

Three rapid gunshots rang out through the house.

Jackson didn't feel them, but he expected to drift off into darkness at any second.

Three red stains appeared on the front of Bobby's dirty T-shirt, then quickly ran together, forming one massive circle of crimson. A few seconds later, blood began to ooze from between Bobby's thin lips, traveling down his sharp chin, at first dripping, then steadily flowing to the floor below. The hatred still painted his face. His eyes went wide as the revolver slipped from his hand. He sank to his knees, then fell forward onto his face.

Tiffany stood behind him, holding a still-smoking gun.

45

Jackson looked up at Tiffany. She was standing in her soiled pink pajamas, holding a semiautomatic handgun—and she was the most beautiful sight he had ever seen.

She lowered the gun and rushed to his side. She started to cry as she embraced him, the sobs intermingled with kisses to his forehead. Wrapping her arms around his head, she whispered, "It's going to be okay."

"I told you to run," Jackson said between ragged breaths. The pain was radiating from his thigh and shoulder wounds throughout his entire body. His broken nose didn't feel great, either. It was a struggle to keep from crying out.

"I wasn't going to leave you," she said. "I ran back to your pickup and grabbed William's gun I had left there when I went to look for your cellphone. Bobby showed up and pulled me out of the truck before I had a chance to grab it."

"Sorry about that," Jackson said. "I had to think of something that would get you out of the house. The phone was in my pocket the whole time." He paused.

"And thank you for not leaving me." He looked into her beautiful eyes. "I'm glad you can be stubborn."

"I could never have left you. You didn't forget about me when I disappeared," she said as she wiped more tears away from her eyes.

Jackson smiled softly. "I could never forget about you," he whispered in response.

She smiled at him and kissed his forehead again. "Hold on."

Jackson watched as she vanished down the hallway and returned a few seconds later carrying a large towel and a pillow. She wrapped the towel around his shoulder and helped him position his hand to apply pressure to the wound. Then she put the pillow under his head. "Just stay still and take deep breaths. I'm going to call for help and then get you something to drink."

"Okay. Tell them to look for Katie's 4Runner off the road on Highway 28, just west of the resort," Jackson said. He heard Tiffany pick up the phone in the kitchen, then immediately hang it back up.

"Wait," she said, "they're already here."

The sound of sirens approaching his house cut through the night, then flashing red and blue strobe lights shone through the kitchen window and into the living room. Tiffany walked onto the porch and yelled for help. Jackson heard her talking to someone, but couldn't make out exactly what they were saying.

A moment later, two paramedics came rushing into the house and knelt down beside him. They took his vital signs and established an IV line in his right arm. Then they removed the towel from his shoulder, cut off his shirt and pants, and applied dressings to his wounds before walking back outside to the ambulance. One of them was talking on his radio.

Jackson looked to his left and saw Tiffany talking to two sheriff's deputies. Even after all she had been through, she looked strong.

Poised.

He loved her more than he ever had. She had saved his life, and he wasn't too proud to admit it. But he was worried about Katie, and he hoped the deputies had called in reinforcements to search for her.

The two paramedics returned, maneuvering a large stretcher through the front door. They returned to Jackson's side and lifted him onto it. Tiffany was standing next to him now, and Jackson felt her take his left hand into her own. "They found, Katie. She's got some cuts and bruises, but she's all right."

Jackson felt relief wash over him.

"Yes, sir," one of the deputies said as he walked to the side of the stretcher. He was a young guy with short brown hair. Jackson didn't recognize him. "We saw the headlights shining off the side of the road on the way down here. We left one of our units and the other ambulance there."

The paramedics strapped Jackson to the stretcher, then extended the scissor legs to raise it off the floor, the frame clicking as the wheels locked into position. "Who called you? How did you know we needed help?" Jackson asked the deputy.

"We got a call from a sheriff down in Georgia who said you guys were in big trouble." The deputy paused and grinned. "I don't recall his name, but he sure was a persistent fellow. He didn't ask—he *demanded* we check on you two."

Jackson laughed softly, but even that small movement sent waves of agony through his body. He grimaced and hoped the pain medication would kick in soon.

"Okay, let's get you to the hospital," one of the paramedics said over his shoulder. "Ma'am, you need to sit down and rest. We've already called another ambulance for you."

"I'm going with him," Tiffany said, nodding toward Jackson.

"But, ma'am, you need medical attention yourself. Another ambulance will be here in just a few minutes. You can see him at the hospital after a doctor checks you out."

"I'm going with him," Tiffany repeated, chin raised and the tone of her voice making it clear the subject was not open for debate.

Jackson glanced at the paramedic over his right shoulder. "Don't waste your breath arguing," he said, smiling the best he could manage. "She's a stubborn one."

"Okay, ma'am. You're riding with us," the paramedic said.

"Thank you," Tiffany responded courteously.

Jackson laughed softly, knowing the outcome of the argument had never really been in doubt. Tiffany was still holding his hand, taking slow steps as the paramedics began to roll him through the house toward the front door.

Jackson could feel the pain medication beginning to take effect, and he knew he would soon be drifting off to a deep and much-needed sleep. "Wait a second," he said. The stretcher stopped moving. "Give me my pants," he told the paramedic nearest his head. The man looked confused and didn't move. "Just hand them to me, please," Jackson persisted. The man placed a white plastic bag on Jackson's stomach.

Tiffany looked down at him, puzzled. Jackson slipped his right hand into the bag and found the pocket of his jeans.

His fingers wrapped around the velour ring box he had been carrying all day.

He looked into Tiffany's eyes and pulled it from the bag. He moved it toward her and opened it with his thumb, exposing the diamond engagement ring.

"I had a big speech planned for this moment, but I'm afraid I've forgotten it. So I'll just say it. Tiff, will you marry me?"

Jackson watched as the tears began to flow from her eyes again. She bent over and gave him a soft kiss on the lips.

"Yes," she whispered. "Yes, I will."

46

Six Months Later

Tiffany looked out the window of the camper and stared down at Cataloochee Creek. The water rippled and gurgled as it flowed over and around large, moss-covered rocks protruding from the streambed. The sun was shining, the trees bright green with new spring growth. Katie was behind her, attaching the veil to the top of her head. Tiffany's long hair flowed over her shoulders and onto the white wedding dress she wore. Katie had spent the last two hours helping her apply her makeup and put soft curls in her hair.

"You're beautiful," Katie said.

Tiffany smiled. "Thank you," she said, turning around to face her friend. "I hope Jackson will think so."

Katie grinned. "He will."

Tiffany leaned forward and wrapped her arms around Katie. "I love you," she said.

"I love you, too, Tiff." Katie hugged her friend tightly, then released her from the embrace. "I think we're finished. Are you ready?"

Tiffany took in a deep breath, trying to dispel the butterflies that were dancing in her stomach. "Yes, I'm ready," she said, exhaling deeply and smiling.

There was a knock on the door of the camper.

"Come in," Katie yelled.

The door swung open, and Nathan Lansing entered, followed by his wife, June, who was holding Missy's hand.

"Are we ready to get this show on the road?" Nathan asked, grinning. He stared at Tiffany. "Wow, you sure are a beautiful woman, Tiffany. I can see why Jackson fought so hard to find you." He was dressed in a black tuxedo, his salt-and-pepper hair combed perfectly across his forehead.

"Thank you, Nathan," Tiffany replied, nodding her head. "You look pretty darn good yourself."

"Well, I try," he said and laughed.

Tiffany stepped forward and gave him a hug around the neck. "Thank you for everything, Nathan. I really mean that. You helped make this day possible."

"Now, now," Nathan said, "don't be getting all mushy on me." He looked at his wife, who was standing at his side, then back at Tiffany. "See if you can talk June out of making me retire," he said with a chuckle. "I'm thinking of running for reelection."

"Well, I don't want to go against your wife, Nathan, but I'm sure there's not a better man in all of Hayward County."

"Thank you. That's awful nice of you to say," Nathan replied, looking slightly embarrassed by the praise.

June stepped forward. "I'm so happy for you, Tiffany." They embraced.

Missy walked toward Katie and wrapped her arms around her mother's legs. Tiffany looked down at her.

Missy wore a sapphire dress, an exquisite hair wreath, and carried a basket of rose petals. "Don't you look pretty, Missy!" Tiffany said. The little girl grinned, then buried her head in the folds of her mother's matching dress.

Nathan tapped the face of his wristwatch. "Well, we'd better get going."

Tiffany followed Nathan and June out of the camper and toward his pickup truck. He held the door open for her as she climbed into the backseat. Katie and Missy sat down next to her.

As they drove out of the campground, Tiffany gazed out the window of the truck. She watched as they passed families, some staying in tents and some in campers. A few were cooking lunch over a campfire.

Just minutes later, they passed through the lush, expansive fields of Cataloochee Valley. It was one of her and Jackson's favorite places in the park. It was dotted with old homesteads and other remnants of a bygone era. They often traveled here to enjoy a picnic lunch next to one of the many mountain streams meandering through the valley. She smiled at the memories.

Tiffany spotted a cow elk feeding in the field off the left side of the road. Trillium and showy orchis wildflowers painted the canvas of green grass with strokes of ivory and lavender. Signs of new life surrounded her, and she was happy to be alive.

"Okay, here we are," Nathan said from the driver's seat.

Tiffany saw the back of Palmer Chapel appear, sitting at the far end of a large green meadow. The front of the building faced Cataloochee Creek and wasn't visible from the gravel road. The old, white building's steeple rose gracefully to meet the clear blue April sky.

Long vertical windows adorned each side of the structure. It had stood there majestically for over a century, unmoved by the storms that battered it. White wooden chairs stood in rows near the church, their occupants all there to witness Tiffany and Jackson's vows.

Tiffany's heart beat faster, full of excitement.

Nathan stopped the truck. Cars lined the side of the narrow gravel road. He got out, then opened Tiffany's door, offering her his hand as she stepped down. A cool breeze brushed her face, causing strands of her auburn hair to dance in the sunlight. She took a deep breath and caught the sweet scent of wildflowers.

The group walked along the edge of the meadow, Nathan and June in the lead, with Katie and Missy on Tiffany's left side. Once they drew even with the last row of chairs, June left to take her seat. Katie gave Tiffany a kiss on the cheek, whispered, "I love you," then walked slowly down the aisle and took her place at the altar. Tiffany held tight to Missy's little hand, her palm sweating.

Nathan took his place on Tiffany's right side, looping his arm through hers. "You ready?" he asked.

Tiffany nodded slightly and let go of Missy's hand. She watched as the little girl walked to the center of the aisle, her awkward toddler steps causing her blonde curls to bounce in the spring breeze. Missy hesitated, unsure of herself for a few seconds, then slowly disappeared into the mass of guests.

Tiffany took a deep, calming breath, then felt Nathan step forward, his arm guiding her as she took her first step. At the center of the aisle, they turned and stopped, facing the altar. Missy was just completing her walk, a trail of red rose petals behind her.

Tiffany loved roses.

A violinist began playing Mendelssohn's Wedding March.

Tiffany looked up and saw Katie and Missy on the left side of the altar, Cody and Jackson on the right. She struggled to keep the tears from flowing. She knew it was a losing battle.

A single tear ran down her cheek as her eyes met Jackson's, his face beaming. Her heart raced as she took her first step down the aisle.

She had survived.

She was free.

And she wasn't afraid anymore.

Author's Note

It's hard for me to believe that the novel you just read had such a modest beginning. The genesis of this story came while I was doing the rewrite of my first novel. I really liked the character of Tiffany, but felt she needed something to make her a little more interesting and a way to explain why she was so cold and distant toward Jackson when they first met. That's when I came up with the idea of putting a couple of scars on her body and then being vague about how she got them. To tell you the truth, I didn't even know what had happened to her in the past. That part of the story didn't come along until much later.

When I first started writing *Smoke on the Mountain* several years ago, the characters of Jackson and Tiffany didn't figure into my plans at all. I just started with an idea about a guy surviving a fly fishing trip that went horribly wrong. But I'm very happy that both Jackson and Tiffany came into existence. I think their presence made *Smoke on the Mountain* a much better story, and I have enjoyed watching them develop over the course of this book as I spent countless hours in front of my computer screen.

Writing a novel is a lot of hard work, and I have to first thank my wife, Janice, and daughter, Grace, for giving me the extra time to follow my dream. I love you both very much.

I want to say a special thank you to my two editors, Sharon Jeffers and Melissa Gray. Their input and corrections keep me headed in the right direction, and if you found any errors while reading this book, rest assured, they are completely of my making.

Thank you to my parents, Mike and Jeannie, who have helped me spread the word about my writing and encouraged me to keep at it.

Thanks also to Travis at probookcovers.com for the awesome covers he creates for me. To my book designer, Amy Siders, and her team at 52 Novels, thanks for all your help and the great work you do!

I also want to tell everyone who has offered me words of encouragement, whether written or spoken, just how much I truly appreciate it. You all know who you are, and I thank each of you so much.

Finally, thanks to you, the reader, for taking the time to read my work. I hope you enjoyed it.

J. Michael Stewart

About the Author

FIRE ON THE WATER is J. Michael Stewart's second novel. He is also the author of *SMOKE ON THE MOUNTAIN: A Story of Survival*, the short story *A WINNING TICKET*, and the novella *DOSE OF VENGEANCE*. He is currently working on his next novel, along with several other projects.  An avid fly fisherman, he loves to go to the mountains and spend time on a trout stream whenever possible. He currently lives in Nebraska with his wife and daughter.

To contact him, or for more information about J. Michael Stewart, please visit www.authorjmichaelstewart.com.

Also by J. Michael Stewart

SMOKE ON THE MOUNTAIN:
A Story of Survival
(Ranger Jackson Hart Book 1)

Cody McAlister, a 32-year-old Atlanta attorney, had everything: his dream job, a healthy bank account, and a beautiful wife. But two years after a bitter divorce and a bout of heavy drinking, Cody is still struggling to put the pieces of his once-idyllic life back together. In an effort to regain his sanity, he embarks on a five-day backcountry fly fishing trip to revitalize and reassess his life. When the unthinkable happens, Cody finds himself in a fight for his life. It's a battle that no courtroom drama can match—a test that will challenge his own basic beliefs about success, happiness, and what it means to truly live. With the help of a widowed fly shop owner and U.S. Park Ranger Jackson Hart, Cody must dig deep within himself to survive.

A WINNING TICKET

Twin brothers Benjamin and Harrison Zimmerman are struggling just to keep their heads above water. Low crop prices and a recent drought have driven them to the brink of bankruptcy. The family farm is on the verge of foreclosure, and the mounting debt seems overwhelming. In the midst of a Nebraska blizzard, their luck suddenly changes when they hit it big by winning the lottery. In an instant they become multi-millionaires. Now richer than they ever dreamed possible, all their problems seem to be solved. But before the night is over, the brothers' true feelings about the farm and each other will be revealed and their relationship changed forever.

DOSE OF VENGEANCE

Everyone has secrets.

When the rich and powerful in Big Creek, Montana, are in danger of having their most private and embarrassing secrets exposed, they call Sean Foster. He gets paid to make other people's problems go away. And he's good at it—very good.

But when a simple morning jog goes horribly wrong, Sean is the one who needs a fixer. In the struggle to survive and return to his wife, he forgets the most important lesson he has learned in his business.

Everyone has secrets.

And sometimes, they will kill to keep them hidden . . .

Made in the USA
Coppell, TX
05 May 2021